MURDER AT THE MOVIES

They'd only gone a short distance when she spotted someone sitting in a lawn chair about ten feet into the trees. If she hadn't happened to shine her light in just the right direction, she might not have noticed him at all. The man was slumped down in the chair with a hat pulled low over his eyes, making it seem likely he'd dozed off during the movie. The empty beer cans scattered at his feet might've had something to do with that.

Her mom moved up beside her. "Oh my. Should we leave him to sleep it off or try to wake him up?"

Abby considered their options. "The park ordinarily closes at sundown. The city council made an official exception just for the movie-in-the-park program this summer. I'd hate to have him get in trouble just because he dozed off."

They continued to study the sleeping man, still maintaining a safe distance from him. "Do you know who he is?"

"I don't think so, but it's hard to tell, with his hat covering half his face like that."

Abby was picking up some bad vibes about the situation, but that was probably just her own nerves talking. After stumbling over three dead bodies since she'd moved to Snowberry Creek, she'd developed an unfortunate tendency to imagine the worst . . .

Books by Alexis Morgan

DEATH BY COMMITTEE

DEATH BY JACK-O-LANTERN

DEATH BY AUCTION

DEATH BY INTERMISSION

Published by Kensington Publishing Corporation

DEATH BY INTERMISSION

An Abby McCree Mystery

Alexis Morgan

KENSINGTON
PUBLISHING CORP.

www.kensingtonbooks.com

KENSINGTON BOOKS are published by

Kensington Publishing Corp.
119 West 40th Street
New York, NY 10018

All Kensington titles, imprints, and distributed lines are available at special quantity discounts for bulk purchases for sales promotion, premiums, fund-raising, educational, or institutional use.

Special book excerpts or customized printings can also be created to fit specific needs. For details, write or phone the office of the Kensington Sales Manager: Attn.: Sales Department. Kensington Publishing Corp., 119 West 40th Street, New York, NY 10018. Phone: 1-800-221-2647.

Kensington and the K logo Reg. U.S. Pat. & TM Off.

First Printing: February 2021
ISBN-13: 978-1-4967-3125-8
ISBN-10: 1-4967-3125-5

ISBN-13: 978-1-4967-3126-5 (ebook)
ISBN-10: 1-4967-3126-3 (ebook)

10 9 8 7 6 5 4 3 2 1

Printed in the United States of America

CHAPTER 1

Enough was enough. Actually, it was way too much. Abby McCree nudged her companion in the ribs with her elbow and whispered, "Switch sides with me."

Her friend and tenant, Tripp Blackston, had just gotten back from a refreshment run and looked a bit put out by her demand. Finally deciding she was dead serious, he grumbled and handed Abby his drink along with the huge tub of buttered popcorn she'd asked him to get. Ignoring the good-natured calls of "down in front" from the people seated on the ground behind them, Tripp shifted his big body around to the other side of their blanket while she scooted over to where he'd been sitting.

After they had everything rearranged to their satisfaction—or at least Abby's—Tripp leaned in close to ask her why the move had been necessary. She cringed, knowing he'd find her answer silly at best.

"Because it creeps me out, and I can't stand to watch."

Tripp looked truly perplexed. "Do I need to point out tonight's movie is animated and rated PG?"

"Yes, I know." Abby bit back a big sigh before adding, "But it's not the movie I object to."

That much was true. After all, she'd convinced the committee in charge of the town's Summer Nights in the Park program to show that particular film because it was one of her personal favorites. The real problem was sitting on another blanket about twenty feet off to their left.

Abby reached for a handful of popcorn to avoid any further explanations, but Tripp instantly thwarted her plan by holding the tub out of her reach. Surrendering to the inevitable, she whispered, "I don't like watching my mother canoodling with that man."

There'd been a brief respite when Owen Quinn had disappeared for a short time, probably to check on his food truck. But now that he was back, the couple had picked up right where they'd left off. Meanwhile, Tripp's deep laughter rang out over the hillside, drawing way too much unwanted attention in their direction. She elbowed him again, this time with a great deal more oomph. "Hush, you idiot."

After a quick glance back over his shoulder toward the pair in question, Tripp turned his attention back to her, his grin still firmly in place. "Come on, Abby. Canoodling? Were you born in the 1850s?"

"Call it whatever you want, but how would you like it if that was your mother and some guy sitting over there all snuggled up like they're back in high school?"

That mental image had him wincing a bit. "Okay, I get that. However, they're both adults, and your mom has been single for a long time."

Abby was in no mood for logical arguments. "That may be true, but she also hasn't acted like this with anyone she's dated since she and my father divorced. I don't want to see her get hurt."

Resisting the urge to take another peek at her maternal parent, Abby continued, "Not to mention Mom barely knows that man. In fact, I haven't met anyone who knows much about Owen Quinn or where he comes from. He simply appeared in town one day and bought that hole-in-the-wall restaurant along with that rust bucket of a food truck. That thing is a real eyesore. Everyone says so."

"Yeah, but those same people also say he makes great barbecue."

Even Abby had to admit Quinn had a talent for barbecue. In fact, the local grocery store now stocked jars of his secret sauce and special spice rubs. By all reports, both were flying off the shelves. Well, it would take more than the right mix of chili powder and cumin to earn her trust, especially when it came to Owen Quinn.

When she held out her hand for the popcorn, Tripp set the bucket down between them. As she grabbed a handful, she said, "The ability to cook ribs doesn't provide much in the way of a character reference. Besides, Owen spends far more of his time out on his boat than he does running his restaurant."

In fact, the place was only open on the few days he didn't go fishing. What kind of business model was that? Of course, maybe he'd made tons of money in his prior occupation and could live forever off his investments. There was no way to know that, though, since the man was amazingly vague when it came to the details of his life prior to moving to Snowberry Creek. She leaned in closer to Tripp. "Has he ever said anything to you about what he did before moving here?"

Before he could answer, a wadded-up paper bag came flying at them to bounce off the back of Tripp's head. The attack was accompanied by a familiar voice calling out, "Will you two please shut up? Some of us want to see how the movie turns out."

Tripp winked at Abby as he lobbed the bag right back at Gage Logan, the local chief of police and a personal friend. "Sorry, Gage. Didn't know you'd find cartoon characters so riveting!"

The brief conversation stirred up some more grumbling from other quarters, so they lapsed into silence while the rest of the movie played out on the makeshift screen strung between two trees. Abby knew most of the dialogue by heart, but that didn't make it any less funny. The fact that the humor in the movie worked on multiple levels was one reason that she'd recommended it for the last film in the town's summer movie-in-the-park series.

As the credits rolled, the people around them began packing up their blankets and lawn chairs. She and Tripp remained right where they were for a few more minutes. Since she was the one in charge tonight, she had to stick around to help with cleanup. When the crowd had thinned out, Tripp offered Abby a hand up off the ground. As she folded their blanket, she asked, "Well, did you like the movie?"

The former soldier looked a bit sheepish as he reluctantly nodded. "Yeah, way more than I expected to. It's been years since I watched a kids' movie, but evidently they've gotten a whole lot funnier."

She wasn't surprised that he hadn't kept up with animated films, considering he'd spent twenty years bouncing all over the world's hot spots as part of the Army Special Forces. It hadn't been all that long ago since he'd retired from the military in his late thirties to enroll at the local college to finish his degree. In fact, he'd arrived in Snowberry Creek only a short time before Abby moved there herself.

"Well, I own a few more you might enjoy. Maybe we can watch one the next time we have a beer and pizza night."

Tripp looked around to make sure no one was listening before he answered. "Sure, as long as you don't tell anyone I agreed to such a thing."

She couldn't resist teasing him a bit. "Afraid you'll damage your tough soldier image?"

"Very funny."

Yeah, it was. But to make him feel better, she pointed out that several of his friends from the local veterans group were also there. "I think your reputation is safe considering Gage Logan, Leif Brevik, Pastor Haliday, and Spence Lang are all here tonight."

That information didn't seem to impress him much. "I'll go dump our stuff in my truck and then come back to help."

He started to walk away but stopped to add, "And for what it's worth, your mom is headed this way, and Owen is with her. Be nice."

She almost stuck her tongue out at him but took the high road instead. After pasting what she hoped was a genuine smile on her face, she turned to face her mom and her companion. "Did you two enjoy your evening?"

Owen grinned. "Very much."

Somehow Abby doubted he was talking about the movie, but she wasn't about to ask for clarification. Besides, it was time for her to get to work. "I've got to help the cleanup crew, Mom. It shouldn't take long, and then we can head back to the house."

Owen glanced around them. "What do you need us to do?"

Great. She should've known it wouldn't be that easy to get rid of the man. "We have to do a final sweep through the area to make sure that all the trash has been picked up. I've got the necessary supplies."

She paused to pull a flashlight, plastic bags, and disposable gloves out of her backpack. "We're supposed to separate the recyclables from the trash and keep an eye out for any personal items that got left behind."

Tripp was back, so Abby offered him gloves before putting on her own. He looked past her to where some of the volunteers were breaking down the tables that had served as refreshment stands. "Owen, want to give me a hand carrying some of those tables back to the parking lot?"

"Sure thing." He handed the plastic bags back to Abby's mom. "Phoebe, I'll catch up with you when we're done."

"I'll hang out with Abby until you get back."

After the two men headed off, Abby said, "It's nice of Owen to help, but it really isn't necessary. We already have a full contingent of volunteers."

Her mother stared after the two men. "Owen knows I wanted to help, and he's my ride home."

Abby knew she was losing the battle, but she couldn't seem to stop trying. "There's plenty of room in Tripp's truck for the three of us."

Her mother sighed. "Abigail, you're my daughter, not my chaperone. I want to ride with Owen. Deal with it."

Then she pulled on her gloves and looked around. "Now that we've got that settled, where should we start?"

Conceding the battle for the moment, Abby set her backpack down on a nearby picnic table long enough to put on her own gloves. From what she could see, the rest of the volunteers were already hard at work on the lower side of the slope. "It looks like we should cover the top of the rise up near the trees. If you'll go left, I'll go right and meet you in the middle."

"Sounds good."

From the look she gave Abby before starting up the slope, her mother wasn't particularly happy with her right now. It might take some groveling to get back into her good graces, but there would be time to worry about that later. Right now, she was ready for this evening to end. She'd really been looking forward to enjoying something close to a real date with Tripp.

Then, from out of the blue, her mother had called to say she was taking a couple of weeks off from her accounting job to drive down from Seattle to spend time with Abby. If that's what she'd actually done, Abby might've appreciated the thought. However, ever since her mom had met Owen Quinn a few weeks back at his restaurant, it was clear that he was the real reason her mom suddenly wanted to spend so much time in Snowberry Creek.

Admittedly, Owen Quinn was a handsome man, physically fit with silver-gray hair and sky-blue eyes. It was no wonder that her mother found him attractive. And to give her mom credit, Phoebe McCree was a good-looking woman in her own right. Thanks to her hairdresser's best efforts, there wasn't even a hint of gray in her dark hair, which she wore in a flattering short bob. Abby knew there was a strong family resemblance between her and her mom. Although Abby wore her hair longer, they both had the same reddish-brown hair coupled with hazel eyes.

Even she had to admit that her mom and Owen actually looked good as a couple, but that didn't mean Abby was comfortable with the way the pair had gone from zero to sixty in such a short time. But, as her mom had pointed out, Abby wasn't their chaperone.

Rather than worry about something she couldn't control, she concentrated on the job at hand and dutifully began scanning the ground for anything that had been left behind. Two pop cans and a popcorn bucket later, she'd almost reached the center point where she was supposed to meet up with her partner in trash gathering.

Her mom was making steady progress in Abby's direction. As she walked, she kept her flashlight focused on the ground, swinging it back and forth in big arcs and pausing only when there was something to pick up. Abby resumed her own search, slowly closing the distance between them.

When they finally met up, her mom said, "Sorry to take so long. I noticed several people were sitting just inside the tree line during the movie, so I've been scanning the ground a short distance into the woods along the way."

Darn, Abby hadn't been that thorough. "Thanks for reminding me. I'll do a quick sweep as we head back."

They'd only gone a short distance when she spotted someone sitting in a lawn chair about ten feet into the trees. If she hadn't happened to shine her light in just the right direction, she might not have noticed him at all. The man was slumped down in the chair with a hat pulled low over his eyes, making it seem likely he'd dozed off during the movie. The empty beer cans scattered at his feet might've had something to do with that.

Her mom moved up beside her. "Oh my. Should we leave him to sleep it off, or try to wake him up?"

Abby considered their options. "The park ordinarily closes at sundown. The city council made an official exception just for the movie-in-the-park program this summer. I'd hate to have him get in trouble just because he dozed off."

They continued to study the sleeping man, still maintaining a safe distance from him. "Do you know who he is?"

"I don't think so, but it's hard to tell with his hat covering half his face like that."

Abby was picking up some bad vibes about the situation, but that was probably just her own nerves talking. After stumbling over three dead bodies since she'd moved to Snowberry Creek, she'd developed an unfortunate tendency to imagine the worst. Even so, it never hurt to err on the side of caution. "Maybe we should get Tripp or Owen to deal with this."

"There's no use in hauling them all the way up here before we try to wake him up ourselves." Before Abby could stop her, Phoebe called out, "Hey, mister, the movie is over. Time to go home."

When he didn't respond, she tried again, this time a little louder. "Sorry to bother you, sir, but the park is closing. You need to pack up your stuff and head out."

She glanced in Abby's direction before creeping forward several careful steps to stand beside the still motionless man. Abby kept the flashlight aimed in their direction as Phoebe reached out to shake his shoulder. "Mister, it's time to head—"

Then she jerked her hand back. "What the heck?"

Abby hurried forward. "What's wrong, Mom?"

Her mom grimaced. "Sorry to startle you. I wasn't expecting his shirt to be wet."

Abby looked around. "How would it have gotten wet? It hasn't rained tonight. Did he spill one of his beers?"

"Maybe, but regardless his whole shirt is soaked."

She had stepped back as if unsure what to do next. When she started to give his shoulder another shake, Abby stopped her. Her instincts were screaming that it was well past time to call in reinforcements.

"Mom, wait a minute. I need to call Tripp."

For some reason, that only increased her mother's determination to get the job done herself. "Nonsense. We can handle the situation ourselves. He's just a sound sleeper."

When Phoebe started to give his shoulder another shake, Abby followed the motion with the flashlight. As soon as the beam hit her mother's hand, she almost screamed, "Stop, Mom! Look at your hand!"

Phoebe froze in midmotion. "What about it?"

Then she looked at it herself. The palm of the blue glove was covered in dark red streaks. "Good lord, is that . . . is that what I think it is?"

The note of hysteria in her voice snapped Abby out of her own growing panic. "Stand back, Mom. Let me check him."

She stepped over a couple of tree roots to stand on the other side of the man's chair. Shining the flashlight directly on him, she pressed her gloved fingers against the side of his neck and prayed she'd feel the steady thump of his pulse. No such luck.

"Mom, you need to step away while I make some calls."

It was hard to tell if her mother had yet grasped the truth about the situation. At least she immediately retreated to the edge of the woods. From there, she watched as Abby pulled out her cell phone. "Are you calling Tripp?"

Abby nodded. "Him, too, but I need to talk to Gage Logan first."

That clearly surprised her mom. "The police chief? Why him?"

Seriously? Could she not connect the dots for herself? Turning her back on the man in the chair, Abby met her mother's gaze head-on. There was no use in sugarcoating the situation, especially when things were likely to get a lot worse before they got any better.

Wishing she had a more palatable explanation for the necessity of dragging Gage back to the park, she said, "I'm sorry, Mom, but calling the cops is the first thing you do when you find a dead body. Unfortunately, I've had some experience with this kind of thing."

CHAPTER 2

After a short, unhappy call to Gage, Abby immediately moved on to the next name on her list. She quickly summarized the situation, talking fast to keep Tripp from interrupting her. "And there's one more thing. Gage wants you to ask everyone who is still around to wait until he gets here before leaving. He'll need to get at least preliminary statements from them."

It was no fault of Gage Logan's, or his deputies, but one of Abby's biggest regrets was how much circumstances had forced her to learn about police procedures since moving to Snowberry Creek. However, since she was in charge of tonight's event, she had no choice but to help get the investigation off on the right foot.

She also needed to stay strong until she could surrender control of the situation to Gage and bolt for the sanctuary of her home. Once there, her plans included a stiff drink—or maybe several—to be followed by a good cry in the shower. Until then, she drew a calming breath and continued talking. "I'll stay up here with my mother to make sure the crime scene doesn't become more contaminated than it already has been."

When Tripp finally managed to get a word in, the ensuing roar coming from his end of the call had her holding the phone out at arm's length until he ran out of breath. If she were forced to pick a winner in tonight's Shout at Abby McCree Contest, Tripp would take the grand prize. Not only had he hollered at her on the phone, he would soon have physical proximity, giving him an unfair advantage over the chief of police. Gage had left right after the movie ended, so all he could do was rail at her over the phone until he'd finally hung up to rally his troops. As soon as she told Tripp what they'd discovered, he snarled several of those words he always ended up apologizing for as he pelted up the slope with Owen Quinn in hot pursuit.

It was hard to judge how well her mother was handling the situation as they waited for the two men to reach them. Realizing her mother still had on the bloody gloves, Abby pointed the flashlight at her mother's hands. "Why don't you peel those off? I'm guessing Gage will want them."

Her mother stared at the bloody gloves and shuddered. After she stripped them off, Abby held out a clean glove from her pack. "Here, stick them inside this."

Then she glanced back down the hillside. "Please don't get upset with Tripp for anything he might say or do when he gets here. He doesn't take it well when stuff like this happens to me."

Her mother latched on to Abby's arm, her facial expression a volatile mix of emotions. "And you think I'm any happier about it? Correct me if I'm wrong, but isn't this the fourth dead body you've found since you moved here?"

The fact that her mom spoke in a low voice didn't make her worry and anger any less potent than that of the police chief or the man who was now only a few yards away and closing fast. Feeling a bit defensive, Abby said, "It's not like I go looking for trouble, especially this kind."

She aimed that comment at her mother, but Tripp was the one who responded. "Maybe not, but it sure seems to find you anyway."

Abby didn't bother to deny it. Besides, all that experience that she'd mentioned to her mother didn't mean this time was any easier than the last. She took a tentative step forward and was relieved when Tripp immediately enfolded her in a breath-stealing hug. She wasn't as happy to see her mother turn to Owen Quinn for the same kind of comfort. But under the circumstances, she cut the pair some slack.

Meanwhile, sirens and the flicker of emergency lights announced the arrival of law enforcement. Abby allowed herself a few more seconds to absorb some of Tripp's warmth and strength before stepping back. He remained close by with his arm around her shoulders as the four of them watched several police cars cruise into the parking lot below. At least the full moon cast enough light to make it easy to recognize Gage. He and two of his deputies immediately headed up the hillside while others scattered like ants to take charge of the people still lurking in the parking lot.

Abby waved her flashlight to draw Gage's attention. He cut across the grass at an angle, making good time on his approach. The gentle curve of the slope made it a perfect location for the movie nights. Sound carried well, and even those seated in the back had a clear view of the movie screen.

Of course, none of that was important right now.

Gage wasn't even breathing hard when he finally reached them. He nodded at both Tripp and Owen before focusing his attention on Abby and her mother. "Are you two all right?"

Abby briefly debated whether or not to put on a brave face, but this was Gage. He would know she was lying if she claimed to be unaffected by the situation. "Not particularly, but we don't plan on giving in to a fit of the vapors anytime soon."

Her mother nodded in agreement but added, "I really wish I could turn back the clock on tonight." Then she held out the bloody gloves safely tucked inside the clean one. "Abby thought you might want these. I was wearing them when I shook that man's shoulder to wake him up. That's when we figured out something was wrong . . . that he was . . . well, you know."

When her voice cracked, Owen immediately tugged her back against his chest and held her close. It hurt to see her normally unflappable mom so upset. "I'm really sorry you got caught up in this, Mom."

When she didn't immediately respond, Owen spoke for her. "Phoebe knows none of this is your fault, Abby."

No, it wasn't, but that didn't stop her from feeling pretty darn guilty anyway. She turned her attention back to Gage. "What do you need from us?"

"For starters, a brief rundown on what exactly happened here. Start from when movie ended and go from there. Once I've heard the basics, you can head back to your place. I'll come by later to take a full statement." He glanced at his watch. "Considering how late it is, I probably won't get there until tomorrow."

Actually that was kind of a relief. "That's fine. We'll be home."

He nodded and looked around the area. "We'll close the park for the time being and secure this area while we start processing the evidence. Let me get my deputies started on things, and then we'll talk."

After a brief call to whoever he'd left in charge down below, Gage turned his flashlight on the victim while he and the two deputies studied the body without going any closer. Finally, he put on a pair of gloves and stepped closer to tip up the man's hat long enough for everyone to get a good look at his face. "He looks familiar, like I've seen him around town. No name comes to mind, though. Anybody else recognize him?"

Owen took a closer look and grimaced. "His name is . . . was Mitchell Anders. He took over Don Davidson's insurance business after he passed away a few weeks back."

One of the deputies must have been assigned the job of taking notes. He jotted down the name as Gage continued his preliminary examination. He was about to step back when he hesitated and then leaned forward as he aimed his flashlight toward something on the ground. Abby wondered what had caught his attention that had him looking even more grim. "Okay, Abby, start at the top and tell me what happened."

She tried her best to give Gage a succinct summary of the events since the movie had ended, aiming to give him just the bare-bones facts. She might've even succeeded if Tripp, her mother, and even Owen hadn't kept interrupting to add their two cents' worth. Did they think he really needed to know how many pop cans her mother had found or that Owen had stopped to make sure his assistant had locked up his food truck on the way to help Tripp load the tables into someone's pickup? None of those things had a darn thing to do with Mr. Anders's death.

She was nearly breathless by the time she finished her narration. "And that's when I called you."

"Thanks, Abby. That's enough for now." Gage looked past her to Tripp. "You can take her home. Like I said, I'll come by in the morning, say around ten."

"See you then." Tripp took her hand in his. "Come on, Abs. I'll fix you some of that special tea you like on nights like this. I'm betting that sounds pretty good about now."

He was right; it did. This wouldn't be the first time he or Gage had fixed her a cup of Earl Grey tea laced with the expensive brandy she kept for such emergencies. She let him guide her back down the hillside, expecting Owen and her mother to follow right behind them. About halfway down the slope, she realized they weren't coming.

"Tripp, we should wait for my mom and Owen."

When he kept walking, she planted her feet hard in an attempt to slow him down, but Tripp wasn't having it. After a quick look back up the hillside, he tugged on her hand hard enough to restart their forward progress. "Let's go. They're still talking to Gage, but I'm sure they'll be along shortly. Owen already said he would drive her back to the house."

Then he marched on down the hillside, giving Abby no

choice but to cooperate or risk being dragged the rest of the way to the parking lot. Before climbing into the truck, she looked back one last time to see if her mom and Owen were finally on their way, but a row of tall Douglas firs blocked her view.

"Are you getting in or not?"

She resigned herself to leaving her mother behind and hoisted herself up into the cab. Tired beyond belief, she leaned back against the headrest and closed her eyes. Right now she'd give anything to erase the past hour, taking them both back to when she'd been teasing Tripp about watching kids' movies or even earlier when he was giving her a hard time about her mother canoodling with Owen.

Abby reached out to rest her hand on Tripp's arm. She needed that small connection but wished that right now the distance between them didn't feel far greater than the width of the center console. "I'm sorry our evening turned out this way."

He nodded but remained silent until they were several blocks away from the park. Finally, he sighed as he covered her hand with his much bigger one. "Me too. God knows the last thing you needed was to stumble across another murder victim. I seriously hate that this kind of sh—"

Tripp visibly bit back the need to curse and tried again. "I'm sorry this kind of stuff keeps happening to you."

And did he think she didn't hate it just as much? "If I knew how to avoid it, believe me, I would."

He just kept driving. When they'd reached her driveway a few minutes later, Tripp pulled around back to park the truck near the small mother-in-law house he rented from her. The silence between them had grown heavier with each passing second. Maybe it was time for them to each go their own way. She removed her hand from his arm to unfasten her seat belt and was out the door, heading across the lawn toward her own back door without waiting for him. She could make her own darn tea.

Thanks to his much longer legs, Tripp caught up with her before she reached the porch steps. She kept walking, hoping he'd take the hint. However, stubborn determination defined the man right down to the bone; that, as well as a sense of honor that didn't allow him to shirk anything he saw as his duty. It would be a major battle to convince him that she'd be all right on her own. Right now, she didn't have the energy to launch an opening salvo, much less sustain the fight for the length of time it would take to wear him down.

Wordlessly, she unlocked the door and stepped back out of the way to avoid being run over by her furry roommate. Zeke would never deliberately hurt her, but these days the mastiff mix weighed in at a solid ninety-five pounds of pure muscle. In his excitement to see both her and his best buddy, it would be all too easy for him to send her tumbling to the ground. Luckily, Tripp's ninja-fast reflexes allowed him to haul back on Zeke's collar and bring him under control.

"Settle down, dog. Abby's already had a rough time of it. She doesn't need you bowling her over to cap off the night."

It was always hard to guess if Zeke actually understood what was being said or if it was the dead-serious tone of Tripp's voice he picked up on. Either way, the dog immediately plunked his backside down on the porch with a soft whine. Tripp patted him on the head. "That's better. Now go patrol the perimeter and report back."

Abby did her best to hide a smile, but it always tickled her when Tripp treated Zeke like a new recruit. Her companion picked up on her amusement. "What are you laughing at?"

She led the way into the kitchen and flipped on the overhead light. "I was just wondering if you were going to teach Zeke how to salute next."

Tripp grinned just a little. "Maybe. He already follows orders better than you do."

Then he pointed toward her usual chair at the big oak table that held pride of place in the kitchen. "Sit down before you fall down."

"I would remind you that you're not the boss of me, but right now I'm too tired to argue."

Besides, it felt really good to let Tripp fuss over her a bit. He was well acquainted with her kitchen and could make the tea without having to ask a bunch of pesky questions about where she kept things. He filled the kettle with water and set it on the stove to heat. Next, he got out Earl Grey tea and the bottle of brandy she kept in the cabinet over the refrigerator. After dumping a dollop of honey and a purely medicinal dose of brandy into two mugs, he added the teabags and waited impatiently for the kettle to finally whistle.

Abby's eyes felt gritty, and her neck muscles were a solid knot of tense pain. Rather than sit there and stare at Tripp's back, she folded her arms on the table and laid her head down. A minute or two later, a soft scratch at the door signaled that Zeke had completed his assigned patrol and was ready to report in. When she started to get up, Tripp stopped her. "I'll let him in."

As usual, he also had a couple of treats ready to reward Zeke for all of his hard work in keeping the world a safer place for the people in his pack. After gulping them down, the dog abandoned Tripp to come sit beside her chair. He shoved his head under her arm to rest his jowly face on her thigh. She freed up one hand to scratch between his ears.

A few seconds later, Tripp set a steaming mug of his special tea recipe in front of her. "Drink up. It'll cure what ails you."

"And if it doesn't, I won't care, especially if I have seconds or even thirds."

"True enough."

She sat upright and breathed in the fragrant steam before risking a sip. It burned all the way down, but that had more to do with the amount of brandy he'd put into the mug than it did the temperature of the water. Not that she was complaining.

"Boy, that hits the spot."

He'd filled a plate with some of the gingersnaps she'd made the day before and set it down between them on the table. "Eat a few of those with your tea. I've heard ginger is good for the digestion."

She reached for one. "Well, you're a surprising font of all kinds of useful information. Don't tell me you're going to turn into a health nut."

He laughed as he finished off his first cookie and picked up a second. "Nope, but it gives me an excuse to eat far more of these than is reasonable."

After washing the last bit of her cookie down with another swig of her tea, she stared at the clock on the stove. "What do you think is taking Mom and Owen so long?"

Tripp's mouth quirked up in a small grin. "Maybe they stopped off on the way to indulge in some more canoodling."

"Very funny." When he started to pick up yet another cookie, she slid the plate out of his reach. "For the record, I do not find that idea amusing."

"Okay, okay. I won't yank your chain anymore about it for tonight. Now, can I have another cookie?"

She pretended to give the matter some serious thought before finally pushing the plate back within his reach. As she did, the sound of a car in the driveway caught their attention. Zeke barked and charged down the hallway when someone rang the front doorbell.

Tripp asked the obvious question. "Who would be dropping by this late at night? Gage said he wouldn't be here until tomorrow morning."

"Maybe Mom forgot her key."

They headed for the front of the house. Past experience had taught Abby to never open the door without looking to see who was standing on the other side. Zeke wasn't pitching a fit, but she preferred to err on the side of caution. Seeing her mother's distraught face through the narrow window by the door, she unlocked the dead bolt and threw the door open wide. As soon as she did, a police cruiser backed out of the driveway and drove away. Where was Owen Quinn and why would Gage have one of his deputies bring her mother back to the house?

Tripp gave voice to the questions running through Abby's head. "Mrs. McCree, what happened? Where's Owen?"

Her mother's chin quivered as she tried to answer. "That man we found. He was murdered."

Puzzled, Abby said, "We already knew that much, Mom."

She hadn't meant to upset her mother, but the simple statement sparked the woman's temper. "Yes, but what we didn't know was that he was stabbed with a chef's knife."

Abby had a bad feeling about what was going to come next. Bracing herself for the worst, she asked, "And that's important why?"

By that point, her mother's eyes were flashing with fury. "Because that Podunk police chief claims the knife belongs to Owen. They hauled him off to jail, and God knows what they're doing to him right now, hoping he'll confess to something he didn't do."

CHAPTER 3

Up until that ridiculous comment, her mother was the last person Abby would've accused of being a drama queen. Granted, the woman barely knew Gage Logan, but she knew full well that both Abby and Tripp had great respect for the man and trusted him implicitly. Apparently their opinion on the nature of his character didn't carry much weight right now. Phoebe McCree clearly was in no mood to be reasonable when it came to anything to do with Owen Quinn.

Regardless, Gage would never mistreat a prisoner, much less browbeat Owen into making a false confession. Heck, when Gage had been forced to lock Tripp up a while back, he'd allowed Abby to bring his prisoner cookies, and even let Zeke come along for a few visits. He'd also spent hours playing chess with Tripp to keep him from going stir-crazy.

She wasn't the only one who felt compelled to defend Gage, because Tripp was frowning big-time. "I don't know what's going on, but you can trust Gage to do right by Owen. And he's not always been a small town cop. He had years of experience as a homicide detective in Seattle and a distinguished military career."

Gage's impressive credentials clearly didn't satisfy her mother. "Neither of you were there tonight when he all but accused Owen of killing that man. Now, if you'll excuse me, I need to call my attorney."

When she pulled out her cell phone, Abby tried to snatch it out of her hand. "Mom, just stop."

Phoebe backed away, still brandishing her phone. "Why should I?"

"Well, for one thing, it's the middle of the night, and cousin David won't appreciate being dragged out of bed at this hour. For another, if Owen does end up needing legal advice, he'll want a criminal attorney. Unless something's changed, David specializes in estate planning and wills."

Some of the air seeped out of her mother's balloon full of righteous indignation. "But I have to do something to help Owen."

"And you will, Mom. Just not tonight. Why don't we go sit down at the table? Tripp can make us all a fresh cup of tea. Then you can tell us more about what happened, and we'll make plans."

Tripp took the hint and hustled down the hall to the kitchen. He was already serving up three more helpings of his special recipe when they caught up with him. Abby waited until her mother sat down before she took her own seat. Tripp set a mug of the steaming brew in front of each of them before getting his own. After adding a few more cookies to the plate on the table, he finally joined them.

"Mrs. McCree, you'll want to drink that tea slowly. I may have been a bit heavy-handed with my secret ingredient."

Her mom dutifully took a small sip and then another. For the first time since walking in the front door, there was a small glint of humor in her eyes. "That's some special ingredient, Tripp. No wonder Abby likes how you brew tea. You'll have to give me your recipe."

Okay, the brandy must be hitting her mom pretty hard if it had her cracking a joke so soon after her near meltdown over Owen's trip to the police station. "Mom, eat a couple of cookies. You don't want to drink too much of that tea on an empty stomach."

Abby took one for herself, mainly to set a good example. Okay, that wasn't true. Somehow gingersnaps partnered perfectly with the heady combination of Earl Grey laced with brandy and honey. She waited until her mother had made serious inroads into her tea and finished off two cookies before directing the conversation back to what had happened after they'd left the park. "So, I take it they found the knife at the scene."

"That's what they're claiming. I never saw it, and I was standing right over the body . . . I mean, that poor man." Her mom set the mug down on the table with unnecessary force. "I assume you would've said something at the time if you'd spotted it."

Abby put down her own drink with a great deal more care. "Mom, I know everything that's happened has upset you a great deal, and that's understandable. However, I would really appreciate it if you would stop insinuating that Gage and his deputies have mishandled the situation.

They would never twist the facts or allow an innocent man to take the fall just to close a case quickly."

Phoebe remained unconvinced. "Well, they sure jumped on the chance to point the finger at Owen. I tried telling them that he was with me all evening, but that didn't carry any weight with them at all."

Tripp added more hot water to his tea. "There must be a reason they thought the knife belonged to Owen. If so, Gage would need his help to figure out who else had access to the knife and when Owen last saw it. That fact alone might be the key to the whole case."

Her mother held out her mug for him to top off hers as well. "Even if that makes sense, they could've simply asked him all of that out at the park. Why take him to the police station?"

Drawing on her own experience, Abby did her best to explain. "Gage might take a preliminary statement at the scene, but he'll also need a more formal one from key witnesses. The police have to nail down all the details while the events are fresh in the witnesses' minds. That's why he'll be here first thing in the morning to talk to us."

Which meant they should all get some sleep. She picked up her mug and carried it over to the sink. "I don't know about you two, but I'm calling it a night."

Tripp was already up and moving. "Zeke and I will do one last patrol before turning in. I can let him back inside and lock the door, so no need to wait up for him."

That left her mother sitting alone at the table, her shoulders slumped as she fiddled with the tag on her tea bag and stared at her cell phone as if willing it to ring. As much as Abby ached to climb in bed and ignore the world for a few hours, she couldn't bring herself to abandon her mother right now.

"Mom, are you coming?"

Phoebe sighed and moved as if to follow Abby, when her cell lit up and chimed. Her mom swiped the screen and asked, "Owen, are you all right?"

Abby postponed going to bed until she learned what Owen had to say. Rather than listen in on their conversation, she decided to join Tripp and Zeke out on their patrol. It took her a few seconds to spot Tripp sitting on the steps of his front porch. Then a movement near the trees caught her eye. Zeke had his nose to the ground, no doubt following the trail of some varmint.

She made her way across the yard to take a seat next to Tripp. He bumped her with his shoulder. "I thought you were turning in for the night."

"Mom and I both were, but that plan got derailed when Owen called. I decided to wait up to see what he had to say. You know, in case Mom decides to break him out of jail or something else equally crazy."

"Good idea."

As they waited, she let the peaceful night sounds calm her ragged nerves. The small frogs that inhabited the stretch of wetlands a couple of blocks east of her house were belting out a rousing chorus of their favorite song. There was no telling what it was about, but she had to admire their nightly enthusiasm for sharing it with everyone in the neighborhood.

Tripp pointed toward the top floor of Abby's house. "Looks like your mom's off the phone. The light just came on in her bedroom upstairs."

A few minutes ago, Abby couldn't wait for this night to end, but that sense of urgency had faded. Chances were her mom wouldn't want to rehash the night's events again anyway. "I think I'll stay right here until she's had time to get settled before I go in."

She glanced at Tripp, "That is if you don't mind some company."

"It's fine, Abs." His smile wasn't all that it could be as he added, "I'm really sorry how things turned out tonight, and especially that the two of you found that guy. It's been tough on your mom, but I'm more worried about you."

He wrapped his arm around her shoulders and tugged her in closer to his side, a brief reminder of how she'd hoped the evening would've played out for the two of them. Instead, everything had gone off the rails through no fault of their own. "I don't know why stuff like this keeps happening around me, and I sure don't mean to keep dragging you into my messes."

He huffed a small laugh. "At least things are never boring around you."

"Very funny."

Zeke wandered by on his way toward her back porch, pausing long enough to glance in their direction before climbing the steps to wait by the door. Must be his bedtime as well. When Abby didn't immediately leap to her feet to follow him, he jumped up to put his paws on the railing and woofed.

"Looks like you've been given your marching orders."

"Yeah, I can take a hint."

Tripp stood first and offered her a hand up off the steps. "Come on. I'll walk you home."

Like she couldn't make it across the yard on her own, not that she was going to give up even a few more minutes in his company. Meanwhile, Zeke bounded back down off the porch to help Tripp herd her in the right direction. She patted the dog on the head, enjoying the company of the two men in her life.

When they reached the steps, Zeke charged ahead of them to stand by the door, clearly anxious to get inside. She couldn't blame him. It had been long night for all of them. "I'm coming, I'm coming."

Evidently Tripp had other plans. "Give us a minute, buddy."

The dog stretched out on the porch with a heavy sigh, his much put-upon air making his two humans laugh. After Zeke settled in for the duration, Tripp stepped between Abby and the porch, blocking her from going inside. If he had something to say, she wished he'd get on with it.

She would need a decent night's sleep to face everything that tomorrow morning would bring. Giving a formal statement to the police would never be on her list of favorite things to do, but she wasn't concerned about dealing with Gage herself. No, it was shepherding her mother through the process that had her worried.

Before she could ask him what was going on, he cupped her cheek and gently tilted her face up to look her straight in the eye. "I want you to know that despite everything, I enjoyed tonight."

Her pulse picked up speed. "So did I."

"So we'll do this again sometime soon."

"I'd like that," she answered, even though he hadn't exactly framed his comment as a question. At least his words had eased the niggling worry that he might've had his fill of hanging out with a woman who somehow attracted trouble.

"The night started off great, even allowing for some

unappreciated canoodling. It was only that last part that wasn't any fun." His eyes stared down into hers. "So I'm thinking we should rewrite the ending a little. Maybe finish the night on a high note."

That sounded like a fine idea to her. When his hand dropped away from her cheek to land at her waist, she inched closer to him and slid her hands up to his shoulders. Never slow to take a hint, Tripp immediately leaned down and brushed his lips across hers. It was a nice start, but not nearly enough to wipe away the taint of finding another body.

"Tripp, no teasing."

He smiled at her impatient demand for more and had just started to kiss her again when a sudden flicker of light nearly blinded them both. Her brain took a second to realize the porch light had just come on. It immediately blinked off before coming back on twice in rapid succession. Tripp glared at the offending light. "Did you put that thing on a timer or has the wiring suddenly gone bonkers?"

"No, I didn't, and the wiring is fine."

She almost wished it wasn't, because right now she was flashing back to high school when she still lived at home. Bracing herself, she counted down the seconds until the further humiliation that was bound to come next. Sure enough, the door opened to reveal her mother. "Abby, isn't it time you call it a night?"

Abby dropped her head forward to rest against Tripp's chest. "Mother, please let Zeke inside. You don't need to wait up for me."

Instead of retreating, Phoebe stepped out onto the porch. "I'm sorry, but morning will be here before you know it. We'll both need a good night's rest to deal with the police tomorrow."

It was no surprise the woman wouldn't give up easily. Back in the day, the blinking porch light had been her mother's code that Abby had spent enough time alone with her date. Maybe her mother was feeling extra protective because of everything that had happened, but Abby was no longer a teenager subject to her parents' house rules.

Abby turned to face the woman directly. "For Pete's sake, just go back inside."

"But—"

Praying for patience, she added, "Now, Mom."

And when that didn't convince the woman to finally back off, Abby threaded a lot more temper in her next words. "While you're at it, turn off that stupid light."

With that, her mom disappeared back into the house, closing the door hard enough to rattle the windows. Abby closed her eyes and drew a deep breath. Did she really want to see Tripp's reaction to that whole embarrassing fiasco? No, but since he was still standing right beside her, there was no way to avoid it.

He smirked as he gave the back door a pointed look. "I guess I know where you got your stubbornness."

"That's not funny—or true."

"You're wrong on both counts. However, your mom was right about one thing. It's way past your normal bedtime. Tomorrow is shaping up to be a long day for all of us."

As he spoke, he once again wrapped her in his arms and leaned in close for one last kiss. "Now, let's see if I can get it right this time."

And bless his heart, he did. She was still smiling half an hour later when sleep finally claimed her.

CHAPTER 4

The warm press of a heavy body tucked in next to Abby's helped make a really great dream even better. The good times lasted right up until reality hit with the slurp of a tongue accompanied by a heated blast of doggy breath. Surrendering to the inevitable, she opened her eyes just far enough to squint at her furry companion. "Sorry, Zeke, but it's way too early to be awake."

After everything that had happened last night, she was in no hurry to get out of bed. When she snuggled down further under the covers, Zeke plopped his huge head down on his paws, his brown eyes full of disappointment. She relented and patted his wrinkled forehead. "Sorry, big guy, but I'm not ready to face the day."

He seemed content to stay beside her in exchange for her scratching that spot behind his ears that always had him sighing with doggy pleasure. The two of them had almost drifted back to sleep again when she heard the un-mistakable sound of footsteps coming down the stairs from the third floor. When they paused on the landing outside her door, Abby remained perfectly still in the foolish hope her mother would walk on by.

She should've known better. Phoebe McCree had al-ways been a cheerful morning person and couldn't under-stand why anyone else might have a different opinion on the subject. Back when Abby had been part of the work-force, she'd learned to drag herself out of bed at the crack of dawn out of simple necessity. But since her divorce and subsequent move to Snowberry Creek, she'd fallen back on old habits. Well, except on the days when one of her elderly friends decided to call her before the sun had cleared the horizon. At least when that happened, she had the option of letting the call go to voice mail.

Not so with her mother, who now stood right beside the bed. "Abby, I'm heading down to start breakfast. How do bacon and eggs sound?"

Zeke lifted his head and woofed softly, voicing his ap-proval. Clearly there was no use pretending to be asleep. However, that didn't mean she would bound out of bed just because everyone else in the house was awake and hungry.

"Fix whatever you want, Mom, but nothing for me. I'll have cereal or yogurt later whenever I decide to get up."

To make it clear she wasn't leaving her bed anytime soon, she added, "Zeke will be glad to keep you com-pany, though. Please close my door on your way out."

Her mother was nothing if not determined. "You know the police chief is coming over this morning at ten."

"So wake me up at nine thirty if I'm not already up by then."

Her mother stepped even closer to the bed, not a good sign. "I invited Owen to join us for breakfast at eight. That's just over thirty minutes from now, so you need to get moving."

That did it. Abby rolled over onto her back and glared up at her mom. "First of all, that man is coming to see you, not me. Second, I would appreciate it if you showed me the courtesy of asking me before you invite some stranger into my home, especially at this ungodly hour."

Her mother wasn't having it. "Seven thirty is a perfectly reasonable time to get up. Besides, Owen isn't a stranger, Abby, and you know it. He's my . . . my friend, and you will make him feel welcome here."

Zeke picked up on the tension between the two women, and it was making him unhappy. Abby reached over to pat his back and reassure him that everything was under control. For her part, she'd noticed the slight hesitation in her mother's voice before she'd finally decided to claim Owen was simply a friend. What other labels had she considered before settling on that one?

Abby didn't want to know.

Surrendering to the inevitable, Abby gave Zeke a gentle shove to get him off the bed and threw back her covers. "Fine, Mom. I'll get up this time, but I meant what I said. I don't appreciate having unexpected guests being sprung on me with no notice."

"I would've told you last night if you hadn't ordered me to go back inside."

Tired of being at a disadvantage, she stood up to meet her mom on more equal footing. "And about that—don't ever flash the porch light at me like that again. You embarrassed me in front of Tripp, and I didn't appreciate your ridiculous behavior one bit."

Her mother crossed her arms over her chest and glared right back at her. "I simply wanted to tell you I'd invited Owen over for breakfast. If you'd come inside in a timely manner instead of hanging around outside until all hours, I wouldn't have had to use the light to get your attention."

Abby rolled her eyes, something she knew would set her mom's teeth on edge. "You could've easily left me a note, Mom. I'm also an adult, not a teenager with a cur-few."

Phoebe took a step back, but Abby didn't mistake it for any kind of surrender. Sure enough, her mom did her best to make Abby out to be the unreasonable one in the room. "I'd forgotten what you're like before your first cup of coffee. I'll be downstairs. I could use some help cooking breakfast, so don't drag your feet getting dressed."

It was so tempting to slam the door and crawl back into bed after her mom finally left, taking Zeke with her. However, that would be like throwing gas on a fire. While she and her mother normally got along pretty well, it had been years since they'd spent much time under the same roof. The two of them needed to set some bound-aries before they managed to damage their relationship permanently. Until they did, it wouldn't hurt to have someone else besides Owen to act as a buffer between them.

With that happy thought, Abby reached for her phone and sent Tripp an invitation to join them for breakfast.

Abby's mood had improved only slightly by the time she came downstairs. She paused at the bottom of the steps to determine who her mother was talking to in the kitchen. When there was no response, she figured it had to be Zeke. Maybe if she hurried, she could be on her second cup of coffee before their company arrived.

Upon reaching the kitchen, she stopped long enough to feed Zeke before filling a mug with her favorite dark roast. One sip helped chase away the last cobwebs that came from going to bed too late and waking up way too early. At least her mother had put the thirty minutes since they'd parted company to good use. The table was set for three, there was a pitcher of orange juice sitting on the counter, and she'd just filled the cast-iron skillet with bacon.

Abby pulled another plate out of the cabinet and set it on the table. When she opened the cutlery drawer, her mother sighed. "I take it Tripp will be joining us."

"Yep, so you'll need to double up on everything. That man can really eat."

Her mother adjusted the heat under the skillet. "Maybe he wanted to sleep in this morning. He had a late night, too, you know."

So other people could sleep in, just not her.

Abby didn't bother pointing that out as she filled the toaster with slices of bread. "Tripp rarely sleeps late. He runs five miles at an ungodly early hour every morning, rain or shine. It's a habit left from his years in the army."

Meanwhile, her mother added several more strips of bacon to the already crowded skillet. "Owen texted just now to say he is on the way, so I hope Tripp won't keep us waiting."

The man only lived on the other side of the backyard, but her mother knew that. Besides, one glance out the window verified he was already headed in their direction. Rather than stand there and trade barbs with her mother, Abby unlocked the back door and stepped out onto the porch. Zeke shoved past her to charge across the grass toward his buddy. Tripp immediately stopped to send a stick sailing through the air. Zeke woofed his approval as he lumbered across the yard to retrieve it. The pair continued the game for several more tosses before finally heading back in her direction.

She stepped down off the porch to meet him in the middle of the yard. "Thanks for coming."

He studied her face for a few seconds and then looked past her toward the house. "I take it you and your mom are having a tough time of it this morning."

"You could say that."

It probably wasn't fair do dump all her anger on Tripp, but she needed to blow off some steam before facing her mom again. "To start with, I planned to sleep in this morning, but Mom didn't give me that option. She not only feels it's perfectly fine to invite a strange man over for breakfast without asking me first, but she also expects me to drag myself out of bed to play hostess. She didn't take it well when I told her never to flash that stupid light again. I also pointed out that this is my house, and I'm an adult."

Tripp crossed his arms over his chest and didn't say a word, which spoke volumes in itself. That he wasn't rushing to Abby's defense made it clear that he didn't think she was the victim in this situation.

"What?"

He arched an eyebrow. "Come on, Abby. Your mom is well aware that you're an adult and that this is your home. I suspect she also knows she was out of line with the whole 'it's time to come in' routine, but look at the situation through her eyes. This is the first time she's stumbled across a dead body, and she's upset that her only daughter is caught up in yet another murder investigation. That's enough to freak her out, but it's obvious that she has feelings for Owen. Even if the evidence tying him to the case turns out to be only circumstantial, it still makes the whole situation that much harder for her to deal with."

Okay, even if Abby didn't like it, he was right. That meant there was one other thing she needed to apologize for. "I shouldn't have asked you to join us just because I need a buffer between me, my mom, and that man. I'll understand if you want to skip out on breakfast with the McCree clan."

Tripp pretended to give the matter some thought. "Let's see—I can stay home and eat cold cereal with slightly outdated milk, or I can eat a home-cooked meal at your place. Gee, that's a tough one."

Okay, that made her laugh. "So bottom line, you're willing to put up with two testy women and a slobbery dog because you're hungry and haven't made it to the store recently."

"Pretty much."

It was hard to argue with that logic and wasn't the first time she'd rescued Tripp from stale cereal and old milk. "Okay, come on in. Owen should be here any minute. Play your cards right, and I might even make pancakes to go with the bacon and eggs my mom was cooking."

"It's a deal."

Owen was coming in the front door just as they walked in the back. Abby headed down the hall to greet her mother's guest, her mood improving considerably as soon as she spotted the logo on the box he held out to her mom. He must have stopped at Something's Brewing on his way to her place. People came from all over the surrounding area to hang out at the popular coffee shop and to enjoy Bridey Kyser's baked goods. Abby was particularly fond of her muffins and brownies, but she wasn't picky. Whatever Owen had brought would be a nice addition to the meal her mother had prepared. It also meant Abby wouldn't have to make pancakes after all.

Her mother peeked inside the box and smiled. "These muffins look great, Owen. You didn't have to bring anything, but thank you."

She surrendered the box to Abby. "I put the eggs and bacon in the oven to stay warm until we were ready to eat. Now that Owen is here, set it all on the table and then arrange the muffins neatly on a plate."

Seriously, did the woman think Abby was going to just dump the muffins out on the table? Clenching her teeth, she walked away rather than snarl at her mom for once again ordering her around in her own home. Tripp trailed after her, leaving the older couple to follow behind. She hoped they stayed there long enough for her to regain control of her temper. That didn't stop her from complaining to Tripp about it. At least speaking through gritted teeth made it easier to keep her voice down. "See what I mean about how she's acting?"

This time Tripp looked a lot more sympathetic as he set the bowl of scrambled eggs on the table. "Yeah, I do. Would you rather go have breakfast at the diner? We can scoot out the back and be gone before your mom can stop us. It would even be my treat."

The idea was tempting, and Abby actually toyed with the idea of making an escape. Finally, she sighed. "As good as that sounds, I won't be driven out of my own home. Besides, we'd have to get back in time to meet with Gage. I can only imagine the fit Mom would pitch if we disappeared and left her and Owen to face him on their own."

With that decided, the two of them made quick work of setting out the rest of the food. When her mom and Owen still hadn't come in, she called, "Breakfast is ready."

Tripp had already settled in his usual seat at the table, and Abby took the chair next to his. When the other couple finally joined them, she tried not to notice that her mom's lipstick was smeared a little. Meanwhile, Owen smiled as he surveyed the table. "Ladies, I would say you shouldn't have gone to all this trouble, but I won't. It all looks delicious."

He was laying it on a bit thick, but Abby carefully schooled her expression. They still had a long, tough morning to get through, and there was no use in making it harder on all of them. She picked up the platter of bacon and passed it to Tripp. He winked at her as he took several strips before passing it over to Owen. "Thanks, Abs."

At least no one seemed inclined to talk much as the food made the rounds. That was fine with her. A lack of sleep combined with her irritation with her mother made for a volatile combination. Unfortunately, the peace didn't last long. When Zeke scooted closer to get her attention, she automatically broke off a small piece of her bacon and fed it to him.

"Abby, we don't feed animals at the table."

That did it. She gave him another, even bigger bite of bacon as she met her mother's gaze head-on. "You might not, but I do. For the last time, Mom, this is *my* home. Zeke's, too, for that matter. If I want to feed my dog at the table, I will. Deal with it."

Phoebe gasped in outrage. "I taught you better manners than this."

Abby's smile was tight and showed a fair amount of teeth. "Nope, I guess not."

Her mother flinched as if Abby had hit her. Tripp was smart enough not to get between the two women and didn't say a word. Neither did Owen, but he quietly took her mother's hand in his in a show of support. Either way, Abby wouldn't apologize. Not this time. Rather than continue the discussion, she picked up her plate and grabbed two strips of bacon for Zeke before heading out onto the back porch to finish her meal.

Tripp and Zeke joined her a few seconds later. The dog stretched out on the floor, happy to hang out with his two favorite people. Tripp set a fresh cup of coffee down beside her before settling into his own chair. He'd brought his breakfast with him, too. Abby let him enjoy his meal in peace. She fed Zeke his bacon and then carefully peeled the wrapper off her muffin before taking a big bite. Peach was her favorite flavor, but it might as well have been sawdust. She washed it down with coffee and then set her plate and mug up on the porch railing.

"I'll apologize to her later."

Tripp shook his head. "I wouldn't."

Okay, that surprised her. "Really? You were the one who pointed out she'd been thrown for a loop last night."

"Yeah, she was. That doesn't excuse her embarrassing you in front of Owen and me. Even if feeding dogs at the table really bothered her for some reason, she should've told you that privately." He paused to give her a considering look. "I don't remember you ever complaining about her before this."

"We had a few rough spots when I was a teenager. Just

normal stuff. I spent most of my time with her after my folks split up. She did most of the parenting, because Dad moved to Oregon and remarried. He and I are still close, but not like me and Mom."

"So what's changed?"

Abby gave the question some thought. "I'm not sure, but I've noticed it since I moved here to Snowberry Creek. She never acted like this when I was still with my ex-husband. Of course, she only came over for an occasional dinner or to spend a holiday with the two of us. No overnight or extended visits."

"Did she think you should've stayed married to him or something?"

"Not that she's ever said. Considering she's divorced, too, she can hardly point fingers on that subject. No, I think it's more the fact that I didn't start looking for a new job as soon as Chad bought out my half of our import business." She reached for her coffee and took another long drink. Thanks to her divorce settlement and her unexpected inheritance from Aunt Sybil, she could afford to take some time to decide what she wanted to do next. "There have also been a few pointed comments about me not diving right back into the dating pool."

There was an amused gleam in Tripp's dark eyes. "Tell me this. Has she also started sending you links to dating sites?"

"Seriously? Your mother actually does that?"

The corner of Tripp's mouth quirked up in a small grin. "Yep, nothing like having your mom offering you tips on how to create a great profile. She thinks I'm not trying hard enough find a 'nice girl' and settle down to give her some grandkids to spoil."

Tripp rarely talked about his family, but he and his

mother were pretty tight. He sounded genuinely amused
by her efforts to marry him off. It also occurred to her to
wonder what his mom would think about her son's
friendship with Abby. Probably not much, considering
the trouble that seemed to follow her around since moving to Snowberry Creek. Rather than ask, she picked up
where their conversation had left off.

"Back before Chad and I broke up, Mom had started
dropping some heavy-handed hints about wanting grandkids, so maybe that's part of it. She's mentioned that it
will be hard to find another guy like Chad in a town this
size." Shaking her head at that thought, she added, "She
actually said it like that was a bad thing. Personally, it's
one of the things I like most about Snowberry Creek."

The last thing she wanted was another man who had
cheated on her for months without ever having the guts to
tell her that he wanted a divorce. Tripp looked as if he
was about to say something in response when her cell
phone beeped. She dug it out of her pocket and glanced at
the screen before answering. "Hi, Gage. What's up?"

She listened for several seconds. "Sure, come ahead.
We've just finished breakfast, but the coffee's still hot.
We also have some of Bridey's best muffins. I'm sure
there are some of those left if you're hungry. See you
soon."

Tripp was already up and gathering their dishes. "He's
early."

"Yeah, but I want to get this over with. Maybe Mom
will calm down once she's given her statement."

Before going inside, Tripp leaned closer to whisper,
"That will probably depend on what Gage has to say
about Owen's knife being the murder weapon."

A chill washed over her as she followed Tripp back into the house. She might not be very happy with her mom right now, but it would really be great if the police had somehow already cleared Owen's name. But judging from Gage's grim voice on the phone, she was very much afraid they weren't going to be that lucky.

CHAPTER 5

Surprise, surprise. Abby's announcement that Gage was already on his way didn't go over at all well with her mother. She clutched Owen's hand and gave him a worried look. He smiled at her and said, "It will be fine, Phoebe."

"But he said ten o'clock. What's happened that he's coming so early?" Turning back to Abby, she frowned. "You should've told him we weren't ready for company."

It was really hard not to laugh at that comment. "Mom, Gage is my friend. That means he is welcome to stop by regardless of the circumstances."

She paused to give Owen and Tripp each a pointed look. "Besides, it's hard to say that company isn't welcome at this hour with the two of them here."

Her mother didn't back down. "It's not the same. No

matter how you personally feel about Chief Logan, he's not making a social call."

"No, he's doing his job, one which is never easy. I'm not going to make it any harder for him by playing stupid games." Then she deliberately softened her voice in an effort to rachet down the tension. "For what it's worth, I know for a fact the sooner you give your statement, the better you'll feel."

She meant her words to offer some comfort. Judging by her mother's reaction, they had the opposite effect. "The fact that you know that just makes me furious. What kind of town is this that you've gotten drawn into multiple homicide investigations since moving here? It's time you move back where you belong."

Okay, they needed to have that discussion about boundaries, and sooner rather than later. "These things can happen anywhere, Mom. Regardless, I love Snowberry Creek, and I plan to stay here. It's my home now."

There was no winning this argument, and both men were smart enough to stay out of it. When Tripp made quick work of clearing the table and washing the dishes, Abby joined him by the sink to dry the few things that didn't go in the dishwasher. She could feel her mother watching them with interest—or more likely disapproval. Clearly nothing Abby did these days made the woman happy. It came as no surprise when she asked, "Do you always make your guests wash dishes?"

Abby closed her eyes and prayed for at least a scrap of patience. Before she could respond, Tripp answered for both of them. "Abby knows my mother raised me that if she cooked, I cleaned up and vice versa. I guess I've never outgrown the habit."

It was hard not to smile. Since he'd played the mom card, there wasn't much her mother could say to that. After hanging up the dish towel to dry, Abby got another cup and plate out of the cupboard and set a place for Gage at the table. Tripp made a fresh pot of coffee while her mom and Owen watched in grim silence. The only sounds were the drip of the coffeemaker and the slow sweep of Zeke's tail on the floor as he watched Abby and Tripp for any sign that they had treats for him.

It was a relief when a knock at the front door gave her an excuse to escape the heavy cloud of tension in the kitchen. After verifying it was indeed Gage, she invited him inside.

"We're all in the kitchen. Like I said on the phone, the coffee is fresh and so are the muffins. Owen bought them this morning on his way over."

Gage frowned at the mention of Owen's name. "I didn't know he would be here. He was going to be my next stop."

She shrugged. "He called Mom last night to let her know that you hadn't thrown him behind bars. Thank goodness for that. I was afraid she'd storm the citadel, and I'd have to bail her out of jail. I didn't know until early this morning that she'd invited him over for breakfast. Tripp's here, too."

For a brief second, the hard edges in Gage's expression softened just a little. "No surprise there. We both know he goes into full protective mode anytime there's trouble."

There was no use in disputing that. Tripp had been there not once, but twice when murderers had her in their sights. She suspected he was still beating himself up for not being on hand when it had happened a third time.

Her mother appeared at the other end of the hall. "Abby, are you going to stand there chatting all day? Some of us have other things we need to be doing."

Like what? Granted, Tripp probably had homework. But as far as she knew, her mother had no firm plans to go back to her own home for at least another few days; and Owen never seemed to keep any sort of schedule when it came to his restaurant. Even if it stayed closed for days on end, his customers miraculously reappeared the minute he flipped the cardboard sign in the window to "Open" again.

Her jaws ached from all the clenching she'd been doing lately. Still, she managed to keep a mostly civil tone in her voice when she finally responded. "We'll be right there, Mom."

Gage, who always saw more than she wanted him to, gave her a quick smile. "Tough night?"

She nodded. "And morning, with no end in sight. She hasn't told me when she plans to go home."

"Well, maybe she'll settle down once I've taken her statement. Even innocent bystanders get freaked out by having to talk to the police."

Again, something she couldn't argue with. Somehow, she didn't think her mother's mood would improve until she knew for sure that Owen Quinn wasn't in Gage's crosshairs for the murder. "We can only hope, Gage. If she keeps this up, I'm going to pitch a fit the likes of which she hasn't seen since the worst of my teenage years."

He actually chuckled. "I'd pay to see that."

Making him laugh improved her own mood. She doubted he'd found very much to be amused about since she'd called him back to the park the night before. They headed down the hall to the kitchen, where Tripp had already poured her a fresh cup of coffee and one for Gage.

They quickly settled around the table and got down to business.

Gage chose a muffin and put it on his plate but made no effort to eat it. "I appreciate all of you being here this morning. I've already taken Owen's statement, although I may have a few more questions for him later today. It will be better if I talk to each of you alone. If you don't mind, we can do that here at the table while the rest of you wait in the other room. I'll call you in one at a time."

Naturally her mother was already shaking her head. She exchanged glances with Owen and then said, "Actually, I don't think we should talk to you at all without an attorney present."

This time Owen responded before Abby could string the words together to explain to her mother just how ridiculous she sounded. "Phoebe, you're a witness, not a suspect. Gage is doing you a favor by coming here rather than making you come down to his office. There's no harm in telling him exactly what happened last night."

"But you—"

"Let me worry about me. Just answer the man's questions." He glanced in Gage's direction before turning his attention back to her mother. "He'll do right by you. By all of us."

"How do you know that?"

"Because that's the kind of man he is and always has been. I trust him, and you should, too."

Now that was interesting. Unless Abby was mistaken, Owen had just admitted he'd known Gage for longer than the time he'd lived here in Snowberry Creek. Had their paths crossed when Gage had been a homicide detective in Seattle, or was it during his time in the army? He and Tripp had known each other back then, but Tripp had never indicated that he'd known Owen before the man opened his restaurant.

At least her mom was slowly nodding. "Fine, I'll answer your questions."

Rather than give her time to change her mind, Abby picked up her coffee and stood. "I think the rest of us will head down the hall to the dining room."

The living room might've been more comfortable, but she'd be able to close the pocket doors that led into the dining room. That would afford Gage more privacy while he did his interviews. He must have guessed that was what she was thinking because he nodded and gave her another of his quick smiles.

A few seconds later, she and her two remaining guests were seated at the dining room table. She'd stopped long enough to grab a container of cookies from the cabinet in the kitchen, not that any of them needed any more sugar this morning. Still, her aunt Sybil, who had left Abby the house and everything in it, had always stressed the importance of offering guests some form of refreshments.

Owen studied the pile of cookies with a hint of amusement. "I didn't realize people served dessert with breakfast. I may need to rethink the menu at my restaurant."

She didn't want to laugh, but she did. "Sorry. It's force of habit. Sometimes it feels like I'm channeling the spirit of my late aunt. I inherited this house from her, and Aunt Sybil had a hard-and-fast rule about offering guests something to go along with their coffee. Feel free to ignore the cookies."

Tripp had already grabbed a couple. No surprise there.

The man thrived on sugar and caffeine. After a brief hesitation, Owen took one, too. "I can use the extra boost the sugar will give me. It was a long night, and today isn't likely to be any easier."

"Do you have to work after you're done with Gage?"

There was a little twinkle in his eyes when he answered. He probably suspected that she'd be relieved when he left. "No, not today. Gage asked me to keep both the restaurant and the food truck closed down, at least for now. He's called in the county forensics team to go through them."

She was about to ask why when the pocket door slid open. She did her best to muster up a smile for her mother. "That didn't take long."

Phoebe shrugged as she walked over to sit next to Owen. "There wasn't much to tell. He wants to talk to you next."

Abby shot Tripp an apologetic look for abandoning him. "I'll be back as quickly as I can."

He just nodded and reached for another cookie. "I'll be here."

She reluctantly left the trio to their own devices and hurried down the hall to where Gage waited. It was hard not to wince when he looked up from his notes as soon as she entered the kitchen. Granted, none of them were in top form this morning, but he definitely looked a bit worse for wear. "Have you gotten any sleep at all?"

He shrugged. "Not much, but it goes with the job."

"How about some breakfast?"

He laughed and sat back in his chair. "You just can't help yourself, can you? Shoving food at people, I mean."

Her face flamed hot. It was the second time in the past

few minutes that she'd had that particular habit pointed out to her. "No, I guess not."

"To answer your question, we sent out for burgers somewhere about four this morning. The muffin and coffee will help, though."

Despite his teasing, she gave it one more try. "When you're done taking my statement, I'll fix you a sandwich. You can take it to go if you need to get back to the office."

"I should tell you not to bother, but I'd actually appreciate it. I have to stop at the crime scene and then check in at . . . well, someplace else."

When Zeke joined them in the kitchen, she grabbed two of his pumpkin treats and set them in front of Gage before taking her usual seat at the table. "I'm guessing you're talking about Owen's restaurant."

Gage dutifully offered one of the organic cookies to Zeke and then patted the big mastiff mix on the head. "You know, that's exactly why I prefer to keep all of the witnesses separated. No one is supposed to know we've connected the murder weapon to Owen at all." He paused to give her a suspicious look, no doubt wondering if she'd been snooping into his business again.

"Mom told me about the knife last night, and Owen just now told us you asked him not to open the restaurant or the food truck today. Neither of them said it was supposed to be a secret, but I haven't told anyone."

Honesty had her adding, "Tripp also knows, though. He was with me when Mom told me about the knife and just now when Owen mentioned why he wouldn't be working today."

Gage let out a slow breath and offered another treat to

Zeke. "Just keep it to yourselves. You know how rumors fly through this town. I don't want anyone jumping to conclusions or pointing fingers at an innocent party. My investigation has barely gotten started, and we have a long way to go."

He picked up his pen. "And with that in mind, I want you to go through everything that happened last night. Start from when you first got to the park, and then take it all the way up until you got back home."

Odd that he cared about events that happened hours before the victim had been murdered, but she'd learned not to question Gage's methods. Had something happened during that time period that had an impact on his investigation? She didn't bother to ask. He wouldn't answer her questions and would likely earn her another lecture on minding her own business.

She started her story with her and Tripp arriving at the park early to help set up everything for the evening's festivities since she was the one in charge. Gage looked up from his notes. "I thought you were trying to taper off on running committees here in town."

"I am, but you know how it is when Connie Pohler gets you in her sights."

He laughed and set his pen back down on the table. "Yeah, that woman is amazing. The mayor definitely hit the jackpot when she hired Connie to be her assistant. She keeps that whole office running like clockwork, and there's no denying that getting people to step up to do what she wants them to is Connie's superpower."

Abby had learned that the hard way. "True enough. This time I tried a new maneuver, hoping it would work. When she strongly hinted that she wanted me for the lead role on the movie committee, I volunteered to be the secretary instead. I figured that way all I'd have to do was take the minutes and help out with the grunt work as needed."

She shook her head sadly. "Mr. and Mrs. Henley eventually agreed to head up the committee and did a great job organizing everything. Unfortunately, they had to leave town suddenly to help out a daughter who's having a difficult pregnancy. Since this was the last movie night left, it didn't seem like any big deal to take over for them. Sure didn't turn out that way."

A chill washed over her skin. "I swear, Gage, somehow I've become a dead body detector."

Gage fed Zeke his last treat. "I can see why you might feel that way."

After giving the dog a thorough scratching, he picked up his ballpoint pen and clicked the top a couple of times to signal that it was time they got back down to business. "So everything ran smoothly before the movie began?"

"Yes, the food trucks arrived right on time, and the other vendors got set up to sell popcorn and soft drinks. No alcohol was allowed at the park. Some folks thought we should allow beer and wine, but the committee voted that idea down. We were aiming to make the movie nights a family event and thought it was better to err on the side of caution. That's why they had volunteers to check the bags and coolers that people brought into the park. I understand they plan to revisit the idea of allowing alcohol if the town council decides to continue the movie series next summer."

And none of that really mattered right now. On second thought, maybe it did. "It looked like Mr. Anders managed to drink most of a twelve pack. How did he get beer past the inspection station with no one noticing?"

Gage didn't look particularly concerned. "Maybe he bypassed the parking lot entrance and walked into the park from the trail that leads through the national forest. We're still trying to trace his movements for that entire day. We'll see if anyone happened to notice him coming from that direction."

It was another reminder that it was early days in the investigation. Abby picked up where she'd left off, letting the events play out in her head like a movie. "Anyway, Tripp and I spread our blanket just down the hillside from where you were sitting."

"And your mother and Owen were nearby, too."

Images of the pair snuggling on their blanket flashed through her mind. "Yeah, they were."

She thought she'd controlled the amount of snark in her voice, but Gage picked up on it anyway. "You don't approve of your mom dating Owen?"

How honest should she be? It wasn't as if she had any concrete reason for her misgivings about the relationship, and Gage seemed to like the man. So did other people in town. She settled for saying, "It's more that I wish I knew more about him. I've tried asking Mom about where he came from and what he did for a living before coming to Snowberry Creek, but she just brushes me off. I swear, it's like his prior life is some deep, dark secret."

"Could it simply be that your mom doesn't think she needs her daughter to vet her dates for her? She's a grownup, you know."

Did he have to be so logical about everything? "Yeah, she is. But she's also a woman who hasn't dated very much in the years since her divorce. I want her to be happy, but I think she should be cautious about trusting a man whose whole life is a big mystery for some reason."

"Would you like her poking her nose into your business?"

Maybe it was time to point out the obvious. "She already does, something the two of us are going to have a long talk about, and soon. But back to my issues with Owen—I'm guessing there's a reason you asked the forensics team to check out his restaurant and the food truck, not to mention you also kept him at police headquarters for hours last night."

Rather than answer her questions, the irritating man went back to asking more of his own. "Over the course of the movie, did you or Tripp leave the area for any length of time?"

She crossed her arms over her chest and leaned back in her chair. "Tripp went up to the refreshment stand to get popcorn. I asked him to switch sides with me when he got back. When he cracked up because I wanted him to block my view of my mother and Owen, you threw a wadded-up bag at him for making too much noise."

Gage didn't deny it. "And you never left?"

"Nope."

What was the point of this line of questioning? Neither she nor Tripp were persons of interest in the murder. Meanwhile, Gage moved on to his next question.

"How about your mother? When did she arrive, and did she wander around during the movie?"

"She rode to the park with Tripp and me, so Owen met her there. From what I understand, he'd been at his restaurant to help set up the food truck. His assistant drove it over to the park. He followed in his own car, because he planned to give my mother a ride back to the house after the movie ended."

Gage's pen scratched across the paper as he took

notes. She paused to give him time to catch up and then picked up where she'd left off. "I had work to do, and Tripp trailed along with me. I didn't see Mom or Owen until after we'd staked out our spot on the hillside. They showed up a few minutes later and sat off to our left. You should've been able to see them from where you were sitting."

Gage didn't respond. While he continued writing, she decided to pour herself another cup of coffee and topped off his while she was at it. As she did, she said, "After the movie started, Owen must have gone somewhere for a short time, because he wasn't on their blanket when I happened to look in their direction."

He looked up from his notes. "Any idea what time that was? Or how long he was gone?"

"Not exactly, no. If I had to guess, I'd say he left when the movie was about half over. I couldn't swear to that, though. It was definitely before Tripp went to get our popcorn, because Owen was back by then. I can't be more specific than that."

"That's okay, Abby. You're doing great."

Despite his encouraging words, Gage had a decidedly grim look on his face. Had something she'd said upset him? When she couldn't think of anything, she wrote it off to the fact he was once again dealing with a murder investigation. "We watched the rest of the movie. After most people were gone, Tripp asked Owen to help him load tables and stuff while Mom and I picked up trash. Other people were working on the lower part of the hillside, so we took the top. That's when we found the body. I called you and then Tripp."

"And when Tripp came running, was Owen with him?"

"Yes, he was. You got there just minutes later."

"Thanks, Abby. That's enough for now. Would you ask Tripp to come in next?"

There were so many things she would've loved to ask Gage, but now was not the time. After making the sandwich she'd promised him, she packed it up in a paper bag along with some chips and cookies. That done, she took her coffee and the carafe down the hall to the dining room. She tried to ignore the white-knuckled grip her mother had on Owen's hand, instead keeping her focus on Tripp. "Gage says you're up next."

As he passed by her on his way out of the room, he gave her a sympathetic smile. "This shouldn't take long. Once Gage cuts us loose, do you want to take Zeke for a walk?"

"I'd love that."

After he left and closed the door, she turned her attention back to the couple seated at the table and held up the carafe. "Either of you need some coffee?"

They both silently shook their heads. When her mother finally looked directly at her, her complexion appeared ashen. Was she not feeling well, or had something happened in the brief time Abby had been gone? If something was wrong, surely Tripp would've given her a heads-up before he'd left the room. "Mom, are you okay?"

Her mother glanced away. "I'm fine."

That was clearly not true. When she showed no interest in continuing the conversation, Abby sat down and entertained herself by staring at the clock on the wall and counting off the minutes until Tripp returned. She couldn't wait, because the tension in the room was becoming unbearable. The second Gage cut Tripp loose, the two of them and Zeke would make good on their escape. A long walk would clear her head and help put the events of the previous evening behind her. Maybe they could also make a quick stop at Something's Brewing to let Bridey's excellent coffee work its wonders.

Sadly, after another glance in her mother's direction, she was very much afraid it wasn't going to be that easy.

CHAPTER 6

While the silence dragged on, Abby drew comfort from the familiar surroundings. She loved all the antiques that had come with the house her aunt had left her, but the Seth Thomas mantel clock sitting on the sideboard was a particular favorite. She could still remember the first time Aunt Sybil had allowed her the privilege of winding its mechanism. To this day, she took pleasure in twisting the key just the right number of turns to keep the clock running for another week.

Right now, though, it ticked off the passing seconds with excruciatingly slow precision. Finally, footsteps were headed their way from the kitchen. She was so ready to grab Zeke's leash and bolt out the door with Tripp. She was already halfway out of her seat when the pocket door slid open. To her surprise, it was Gage standing there. A second later, Tripp eased into sight just behind Gage's left shoulder. While Gage looked to be in full-on chief of police mode, Tripp shot a hard glance in her mother's direction before finally dragging his gaze back to Abby.

Something was wrong. Seriously wrong if she was reading their body language correctly.

"Gage, what's up?"

For a brief second, his demeanor softened. "I'm sorry, Abby, but I need to talk to your mother again."

Her stomach did a slow roll. She might not be happy with the woman right now, but she couldn't imagine what Phoebe had done to incur Gage's wrath. "Why?"

She wasn't sure if he would tell her. But before she could demand answers, her mother spoke out, her voice ringing across the room with self-righteous indignation. "Sorry, but you've already taken my statement, Mr. Police Chief. If you have any more questions, call my attorney. I'm done talking to you."

Great. Her mom had just succeeded in triggering Gage's normally slow-to-burn temper. "Fine, Mrs. Mc-Cree. If that's how you want to play it, we'll take this discussion down to headquarters. You can wait for your attorney there."

Her mother blanched. "Not so fast, mister. I'm not going anywhere with you."

Abby stared at her mom as if she'd never seen her before. "Mom, that's enough. Gage did us a favor by coming here. I won't stand for you insulting him in my house. He's only doing his job."

Her defense of Gage immediately drew her mother's ire in her direction. "Abigail McCree, quit defending that man. I was right when I warned you he would try to railroad Owen for a crime he didn't commit. I can't believe you'd take his word over mine. I'm your mother, and you *will* listen to me."

Throwing her hands in the air, Abby snarled right back. "No, actually I won't, not when you're talking all crazy like this."

"That's enough, Abby. I'm going to call my attorney right now." Then her mom pointed at Gage. "Meanwhile, tell him to leave. My lawyer will contact him only when and if I have anything else to say to him."

It was as if the two of them had drawn a line in the sand and were daring each other to cross it. Okay, Abby would take the first step. She pointed at Owen. "If anyone needs to leave, it's your friend there. You've been acting like a lunatic ever since you met him. Maybe when he's gone, you'll calm down and start making sense again."

By that point, Tripp had shoved his way past Gage to join her at the table. He put his hand on her shoulder, maybe in a show of support. More likely he was trying to make sure she stayed right where she was. "Abby, Mrs. McCree—can we take this discussion down a notch?"

Then he shot a look at Gage before sitting down next to Abby. "I'm just guessing here, but I suspect there's a small discrepancy in your mother's version of what happened last night and what you . . . no, make that what *we* told him."

Her mother's outrageous behavior made it difficult to make sense of what Tripp was trying to tell her. But if Abby understood him correctly, it could only mean one thing.

"Mom, why would you lie to Gage?"

Her mother's face flushed bright red this time, but it was impossible to tell whether it was due to anger or embarrassment at having been caught out. Considering the woman didn't try to deny it, the answer was obvious. "You tell him the truth right now."

"Stop bossing me around, Abby. I won't have it."

Rather than argue with her anymore, Abby shot her one more disgusted look. "Gage, you have my permission to lock her up until she comes to her senses."

Okay, judging from the slack-jawed look on her mother's face, she'd succeeded in shocking her maternal parent. "You don't mean that."

"I do, Mom. With you in jail, at least I'll get to sleep late tomorrow morning."

Owen, who'd remained oddly quiet through the entire discussion, finally spoke up. "Phoebe, Abby is right. You're only acting like this out of a sweet but rather misguided effort to protect me."

He gently turned her mother to focus her full attention on him. "What kind of man would I be if I let you get in trouble with the law to protect my own hide? Worse yet, I don't want to come between you and your daughter. Right now, you're on the edge of destroying that special relationship you've always had with her. Don't let that happen. Not because of me."

He brushed a lock of her mother's hair back from her face. "I swear I didn't kill that man, but Gage has to follow where the investigation leads him. He also can't prove my innocence if he doesn't have all the facts. Misleading him only makes me look as if I have something to hide. Please, for all our sakes, tell the man what he needs to know."

For a minute, Abby thought her mom would refuse. As Tripp had pointed out the night before, stubbornness was a trait both she and her mom had in common. Suddenly all the starch went out of her mother's sails, and her shoulders slumped in defeat. She avoided looking in Abby's direction, but at least she sounded a great deal more respectful when she spoke to Gage.

"Chief Logan, it would appear that I need to amend my earlier statement."

Abby held her breath until Gage slowly nodded. "Fine. Let's go to the kitchen."

After her mother followed him out of the room, Abby and the two men all let out a slow breath, letting the last of the tension dissipate. She probably owed Owen an apology, but she didn't have it in her to offer one right now.

To her surprise, he was the one who expressed his regrets. "I'm sorry my relationship with Phoebe is causing problems for the two of you, Abby. For what it's worth, I did not ask your mother to cover for me with Gage. I would never put her in such an awkward position. Besides, he already knows I left for a short time during the movie to check on my food truck. My assistant is new and also dealing with the loss of her father. It was just the two of them, so this is a rough time for her."

"I'm sorry to hear that."

She might as well bite the bullet and offer up her own excuse. "I shouldn't have asked you to leave. Having you here is helping Mom deal with what happened last night. These things are never easy."

Then she shuddered. "Believe me, I know."

His eyebrows shot up. "Your mom said you'd been through something similar before this."

Tripp had started to grab another cookie but rerouted his hand to settle on top of Abby's. He gave it a quick squeeze as he responded to Owen's comment. "Yeah, our girl here has inadvertently discovered several new cases

for Gage to investigate, so things have been more interesting for the local police department since she moved to
town. It's a real talent."

Abby appreciated that he was trying to keep things
light, but that didn't stop her from nudging him in the ribs
with her elbow. "It's actually more of a curse. I'm sure
Gage and his people would be happier if things went back
to the way they used to be."

He reached for one of the gingersnaps. "Maybe, but
they'd also miss out on all those cookies you bake for
them when this stuff happens."

Owen picked up one as well. After taking a bite, he
smiled at her. "I can see why they'd appreciate the cookies if they're all this good."

Her face flushed a bit hot at the compliment. "Thanks.
I'm not all that fond of cooking, but I do enjoy baking,
especially when I'm stressed out over something. Lately,
my freezer is almost always jam-packed with containers
full of cookies, but at least I have a tenant with a major
sweet tooth who's willing to take some off my hands."

Tripp leaned back in his chair with a satisfied smile on
his face. He patted his stomach as he said, "Yeah, it's a
major sacrifice on my part, but I do what I can to help."

Owen took one of the last two cookies and then
pushed the plate across the table closer to Tripp. "Well, if
you ever find that it's too much for you to handle alone,
let me know."

Maybe it was time for a peace offering. She smiled at
Owen. "Remind me before you leave, and I'll give you a
couple of containers to take home with you. I've got
more of the gingersnaps, but there are also some sugar
cookies and maybe some oatmeal raisin."

Then she frowned. "No, I take that back. Tripp took

the last of the oatmeal raisin cookies to his veterans group meeting the other night."

"Don't worry. I'm not picky. I don't think there's any such thing as a bad cookie."

Owen winked at her as he spoke, but then turned his attention back to Tripp. "I'm guessing that's the veterans group Pastor Jack started. I've heard good things about it."

Tripp nodded. "Yep, that's the one. It's a pretty active group. Interested?"

Abby waited to see how Owen would react. If he actually admitted to having served in the military, it would be the first scrap of information she would've learned about his mysterious past. He looked as if he were about to answer when he turned his attention toward the door. Sure enough, a second later her mother walked back into the room with Gage following closely behind. He held up the brown-bag lunch Abby had made for him earlier.

"Thanks again for this, Abby. I'll be going now." Then he paused as if considering what else he wanted to say. Finally, he added, "At this point, Owen, take this as a suggestion. Now is not the time for you to disappear on one of your long fishing trips."

Her mother immediately tensed up, but Owen didn't look particularly concerned. "Don't worry, Gage. I'll be around. If anything comes up to change that, I'll let you know."

Abby followed Gage out onto the front porch, with Zeke following close behind. When she stopped moving, the dog sat down and leaned in hard against her leg, nearly knocking her over. She appreciated his show of support but really didn't need a tumble down the front steps to cap off an already stressful day.

"I want to apologize again for my mother's behavior,

Gage. Even if she's trying to help Owen, that's no excuse for the way she treated you."

Gage had gone down the steps to the sidewalk, but he turned back to face her. "You don't have to apologize for your mother, Abby. She's an adult and makes her own choices, and she probably wouldn't appreciate your speaking on her behalf. Like Owen, I don't want to cause any problems between the two of you."

The weariness she'd noted in his eyes earlier was back in full force. "Besides, it comes with the job. People aren't always at their best in these situations, especially if they feel like someone they care about is being threatened. Your mom is worried about you getting caught up in another murder case, but also that the facts of the case might cause problems for Owen."

Abby knelt by Zeke and gave him a tight hug, mainly for her own comfort. "Is she right to be worried?"

Gage rocked back on his heels as he shifted his focus to some point in the distance, his mouth set in a hard line. Whatever he was seeing inside his mind wasn't good. Finally, he shook his head as if to clear it and started walking away. When he reached the police cruiser parked in front of the house, he waved. "We'll talk more soon."

She was pretty sure that sounded ominous. Even if he hadn't answered her question directly, she suspected he'd still managed to tell her that there was more trouble to come.

CHAPTER 7

Just back from their walk with Tripp, Abby unhooked Zeke's leash and set him free. After she patted him on the head, the dog wandered over to his favorite spot in the shade and stretched out for what would likely be a long nap. She should probably go inside to check on her mom, but she wasn't quite ready for that. Instead, she sat down on the porch steps and smiled up at Tripp. "Thanks for getting me out of the house."

She'd left room for him to sit beside her, but he remained standing. "Glad I could help, but I need to get going. I want to go over to the university library to work on my paper. Text me if anything important comes up."

Then he dropped his voice to add, "Especially if you need me to run interference between you and your mom. I'll distract her with some slick moves I learned playing high school football so you can grab Zeke and make a run for it. We'll rendezvous at Gary's Drive-In, where you can reward my craftiness by feeding me a couple of Gary's Number Three Specials."

It was hard not to laugh. She'd seen Tripp on one of his burger binges before. At least he wasn't threatening to use his more lethal Special Forces skills on her mom. "I can probably handle her on my own. However, having one of Gary's burgers for dinner tonight does sound good."

"Yeah, and it would for sure beat eating another one of Jean's tuna casseroles."

Abby groaned, although she couldn't say she was surprised. Their elderly friend had a bit of a crush on Tripp, and the octogenarian was always coming up with another new version of her favorite recipe to share with him. Abby thought it was rather sweet that he always politely thanked Jean for her generosity. He even ate the casseroles no matter what secret ingredients she decided to try next.

"I didn't know she'd brought you another one."

He gave a heavy sigh and nodded. "I really don't want to hurt Jean's feelings, but I'm not sure how much more of this I can take. Can people develop allergies to tuna?"

Without waiting for her to answer, he rubbed his hands together, clearly shaking off the gloomy specter of another night of warmed-over tuna and noodles. "Anyway, I can pick up dinner on the way home, unless you want to take Zeke for another walk along the river."

She gave the matter some thought. "I should probably check with Mom before I make any plans. Can you give me a call before you leave campus? Depending on what she has to say, we can either give you our orders or even meet you out there. It might do her some good to get out of the house for a while, too."

"Sounds good. I'll catch you later, then."

Right after he disappeared into his own place, the door behind Abby opened. Without looking around, she patted the step where she was sitting. "Have a seat, Mom. It's a nice day out."

Her mother approached cautiously, as if unsure of her welcome. When she came down the steps, she handed Abby a glass of iced tea and then set Zeke's water bowl down on the ground where he could get to it. He immediately lumbered to his feet and trotted over to slurp up half of its contents. His next move was to lay his head on her mom's lap, letting her slacks soak up the extra water he always stored in his jowls for just such an occasion. Instead of protesting, her mom smiled and patted Zeke's wrinkled forehead as she pulled two chunks of his favorite jerky from her pocket.

In an unexpected show of good manners, he immediately sat and waited patiently for her to formally offer his treats. When she held them out in her palm, he picked the first one up with great care and then did the same with the second one. Then, Zeke being Zeke, he stared down at her hand and then up with a hopeful look on his face.

Her mother just laughed. "Sorry, boy, that's all I brought out with me."

He accepted the disappointing news with good grace and headed back to his spot in the shade. Predictably, he closed his eyes and immediately dropped off to sleep, the soft rumble of his snores bringing a smile to Abby's face.

"Doesn't his snoring keep you awake at night?"

It was a fair question. "It did when I first moved down

here after Aunt Sybil passed away, but I didn't have the heart to shut him out of my room, considering he'd just lost his best friend. Now it's like white noise and kind of soothing."

Her mom sighed. "After the divorce, I hated sleeping alone. I got used to it, but once in a while I still wake up and wonder where your father is."

That was news to Abby, so she did a little sharing of her own. "It was an adjustment to live alone after Chad and I split up, but he was already emotionally long gone before he actually left. It wasn't all his fault that we both got so caught up in the whirlwind of starting up our business. I just wish he'd let me know he was that unhappy before . . . well, before he found someone else."

Her mom patted her hand. "I know Chad wasn't a bad guy, but I'd still like to punch his lights out for making my baby girl cry."

Abby couldn't help but laugh at that. "I would've bought tickets to watch."

They sat in silence for a few minutes until the sound of Tripp's truck starting up drew their attention. "Tripp's heading over to the university to work on a paper. He . . . actually we both thought it would be a good night to have burgers from Gary's Drive-In for dinner. You, me, and Zeke can meet him there and then maybe walk along the river after we eat. If you'd rather stay in, Tripp offered to pick up whatever we want and bring it home. It's up to you."

Her mother winced. "Thank him for the offer, but I already have plans. Owen wants to grill a couple of steaks at his place. I was going to ask if it's okay if I make a tossed salad to take with me."

Although she still wasn't sure how she felt about her

mom and Owen spending so much time together, it wasn't her decision to make. Besides, it would give her some time alone with Tripp. "Use whatever you need, Mom. I also have several bottles of my favorite red wines if you want to take one along."

Her mom brightened up at that offer. "Thanks, I will. Just let me know how much it cost so I can reimburse you."

"That's not necessary."

Then she nudged her mom with her shoulder. "Just promise you'll text me if you're not coming back tonight so I don't worry."

When her mother looked scandalized, Abby gave in to the urge for a little payback after her mother's behavior the previous night. "Also, do we need to have 'The Talk' before you go?"

"Now you're being mean. Owen and I are just friends."

Looking at her mom's bright pink cheeks, Abby laughed. "Yeah, right."

After giving Tripp's house a pointed look, her mom said, "If I'm not mistaken, you've said the same thing about you and your handsome tenant."

"Fair enough."

Abby took a long drink of her water to buy enough time to decide what she wanted to say next. "Friendship aside, you seem to like Owen. I mean really, *really* like him. I've never seen you act this way about any other man you've dated."

"And you're not pleased about that."

True enough. "I don't actually dislike him, and I do want you to be happy. My main concern is that I don't know much about him."

No one seemed to, but she didn't point that out again. "Also, it bothers me that you were willing to lie for him. He said he would never ask that of you, so why did you feel the need to try?"

Her mother looked away, staring across the lawn to where Zeke slept. "Because he's not the kind of man who would kill someone like that. I was afraid that your police chief would take the fact that Owen disappeared for a while, and that the murder weapon belonged to him, and decide not to look any further."

"And I've told you Gabe wouldn't do that."

When her mom started to protest, Abby held up her hand to stop the possible tirade. "Let's not rehash that argument right now. Just remember that Gage is well respected in the law enforcement community and by everyone here in Snowberry Creek. Even Owen seems to trust him to do the job right."

"Fine, but I'm still not convinced." Her mom stood up and stretched. "I think I'll go take a short nap before I have to get ready for tonight."

"Go ahead. I'll be in soon. If you'd like, I'll put the salad together and make a vinaigrette dressing you can add after you get to Owen's house. Do you want to pick the wine or would you rather I do it?"

"I'll trust your judgment."

On wine, evidently, but obviously not when it came to men. That was a discussion for another day. Right now, she was too tired to deal with it. "Enjoy your nap."

Once her mom was safely back in the house, Abby texted Tripp that she and Zeke would be joining him for dinner. He answered a minute later, saying he'd let her know when he was about to leave the library.

With her plans made for the evening, it was time to

make that salad for her mother. She picked up Zeke's bowl to carry it back inside, which drew his immediate attention.

She patted her leg to call him. "Come on, boy. Let's go."

Inside, as she gathered the ingredients for the dressing and salad, she caught herself yawning. She gave her furry companion a look. "After we get done here, what do you say we both take a nap?"

Judging from the quick wag of his tail, Zeke thought that was a fine idea. "Okay, first we make the salad, and then we sleep."

As usual, Gary's burgers were perfectly cooked, the perfect combination of grease and salt. Abby tossed her last fry to Zeke and then dumped all their trash in a nearby garbage can.

That done, the three of them headed for the path that followed along the river's edge. Tripp held Abby's hand as they turned left to head upstream, and they let Zeke set the pace. The evening air was pleasantly cool, the perfect temperature for a slow ramble.

When they reached the water's edge, Tripp asked, "Did you and your mom have any more heated discussions while I wasn't there to referee?"

"No, actually. In fact, we had a nice chat right after you left. I even made a salad for her to take over to Owen's and even gave her a bottle of my favorite red wine for good measure. I still wish I knew more about him, but I guess all I can do is trust her instincts about him."

She gave Tripp a teasing look. "I guess we McCree women are drawn to men of mystery."

That earned her a frown. "What's that supposed to mean?"

"Well, for example, Owen's interest in the veterans group sort of hinted that he might've served in the military. He stopped short of admitting that, though. Makes me wonder what there is in his background that he's so reluctant to share."

Maybe she'd touched on a nerve, because Tripp didn't look particularly happy right now. In fact, it was as if he was no longer with her. "Tripp? What's wrong?"

He kept walking for a few more steps before he finally answered. "Abby, some memories are a burden no one else should have to carry."

Okay, this conversation had gone off track. "Look, your memories are yours to share or not, as you see fit. I was going to tease you about the fact that I still have no idea what your major is at the university."

She knew the crisis had passed when the corners of his eyes crinkled just a bit. "That drives you crazy, doesn't it?"

"Yep, like I said—you're a man of mystery. I spend a lot of time thinking about all the possible different directions you could go."

He looked curious now. "What are your top five guesses?"

"For starters, a business major, maybe, but I really don't think so. Psychology is a strong possibility, though."

"Why? Oh wait, I know. It's so I can figure out how that quirky mind of your works."

Abby rolled her eyes. "Hey, you're the topic of this conversation, not me. Anyway, another strong possibility would be history, but only because I know you find it interesting. The same with biology."

"Okay, that's four. What's your top idea?"

It was a struggle to keep a straight face, but she thought she pulled it off pretty well when she said, "Kindergarten teacher. I can just see a line of camo-wearing five-year-olds saluting as they march into your classroom."

Tripp's laughter rang out in the night air. While he still didn't give her the slightest hint if she'd come close with any of her guesses, she didn't care. What mattered was he was still chuckling half an hour later when they finally returned to where they'd left their vehicles parked.

Always the gentleman, he walked her all the way to her car instead of veering off to where his truck was parked on the other end of the lot. After letting Zeke into the back seat to get comfortable, Tripp started to wrap his arms around Abby, but then he stopped to look around. Puzzled, she asked, "Is something wrong?"

He shot her a quick grin. "Just checking for flashing porch lights."

"I'm never going to live that down, am I?"

"Nope, probably not." He took her hand and tugged her in close. "However, since the coast is clear, what do you say we pick up where we left off last night?"

When she lifted her face in invitation, he pressed her back against the driver's door and took his time kissing her, doing a thorough job of it. Both of them were breathing hard when they finally came up for air. He remained motionless, as if waiting for her to say something. Unfortunately, he'd managed to fry her brain, so the only thing she could come up with was a heartfelt "Wow."

Evidently that was enough, because he grinned and stepped back. "Wow pretty much says it for me, too."

She was about to suggest going for seconds when her phone started beeping. It was tempting to ignore the call, but her conscience demanded she at least peek at the screen to see who it was. As soon as she did, she wished like crazy that she hadn't.

"It's my mom. I swear that woman has the worst timing."

Tripp took another step back, their special moment clearly over. The insistent beeping was as much of a mood killer as the flashing porch light had been.

"Aren't you going to answer it?"

"Why do I feel as if I'm about to regret this?" Surrendering to the inevitable, she swiped her finger across the screen. "Hi, Mom, what's up?"

Whatever her mother was trying to tell her came bubbling out in an incomprehensible rush. "Slow down, take a deep breath, and then tell me again. I'm with Tripp, so I'm going to put the call on the speaker."

The sound of her mother breathing hard and fast came through loud and clear as they waited for her to regain control of her emotions. Finally, she tried again, this time with more success and a whole lot more anger.

"You were dead wrong about Gage Logan, Abby. I told you he couldn't be trusted. He just showed up unannounced and hauled poor Owen back down to that jail of his. Now, what are you going to do about it?"

Good question, but one Abby had no answer for. Already knowing she would regret it, she said, "I'm on my way, Mom."

And if she drove really slow, maybe she'd come up with a brilliant idea, but she wouldn't bet on it.

CHAPTER 8

The need to get back to her mother had Abby flirting with getting an ugly speeding ticket. Unfortunately, she still hadn't come up with a plan of action that would keep her mother from doing something that might end up with her in the cell right next to Owen's.

Her mom was on the front porch when Abby pulled into the driveway. Tripp was right behind her, so she drove around back to park so he could leave his truck in its usual spot by the garage. Bracing herself for another maternal explosion, she got out of the car and let Zeke out of the back seat. She waited for Tripp to catch up with them, figuring she would need his calming presence to get through the next few minutes. They'd barely started down the driveway when her mom came charging around from the front of the house.

Abby paused to pet Zeke and muttered, "Oh brother, she's definitely got fire in her eyes right now."

Tripp leaned in close to whisper, "Brace yourself, because I've seen that badass look before. It was when you faced down Detective Earle when he tried to run you off the first time you visited me in jail."

"Very funny."

Tripp looked dead serious. "Who's laughing? I'm telling you straight up that you McCree women are tough, especially when you get all riled up trying to protect someone you care about. It's scary enough to make battle-hardened soldiers and homicide cops tremble in their boots."

Actually, she kind of liked that he saw her that way. Hopefully it was true, because she'd need every scrap of determination to get through the confrontation headed their way.

Her mother planted her hands on her hips and glared at her. "Well, what do you have to say now? Still going to claim that your good buddy will treat Owen fairly?"

Praying for patience, she said, "Mom, if you're going to insist on yelling rather than having a calm discussion, let's take it inside. I prefer not to provide my neighbors with their evening's entertainment."

"Fine."

With that, her mom spun around and marched toward the back door, leaving Abby to follow. Not that she wanted to. Before taking a single step toward what she knew was going to be a major fight, she offered Tripp a chance to miss out on the fireworks. "Why don't you take Zeke back to your place for a while? No use in the two of you getting caught in the crossfire of a McCree family argument."

To her surprise, he fell into step right beside her. "Don't worry about us. We can take care of ourselves. Besides, you might need help restraining her if she decides to go after Gage just for doing his job."

Tripp was right about how she'd acted back when he'd willingly gone to jail rather than let Detective Earle arrest someone Tripp had believed to be innocent. In her efforts to help, Abby had done a little investigating on her own and almost got herself killed in the process. Assuming her mom was right about Owen being innocent, that meant the real killer was still on the loose and wouldn't appreciate anyone asking too many questions.

Abby had been there and done that. There was no way she wanted her mother drawing that kind of danger in her direction. When their little parade reached the kitchen, she tried to buy herself a little more time to think by putting on a pot of coffee. Her mother plopped down at the table to watch.

"I know what you're doing, Abigail, but delay tactics won't work. Besides, it's too late for caffeine if any of us hope to get to sleep at a decent hour."

Abby turned on the coffeemaker and sat down across from her mother. "I drink coffee this late all the time, Mom, but then I'm sure your definition of a decent bedtime is different than mine."

Her mother sniffed in disapproval. "Well, some of us work for a living and have to keep a regular schedule."

"Luckily for me, I don't. For the record, I plan to sleep in tomorrow."

Tripp looked like he was at a tennis match, his head swiveling back and forth as the two women lobbed snarky comments back and forth. Zeke whined and laid his head in Abby's lap, another indication the McCree women were once again making a spectacle of themselves. She did her best to tamp down her temper and redirect the conversation. "So, why don't we start by you filling us in on what happened after you went to Owen's tonight."

"Like I told you, Gage Logan and his deputy showed up to take Owen into custody. They wouldn't let me come with him or tell me why they were arresting him."

Then she pointed a finger at Abby. "I should've never trusted you. Now look what's happened."

Up until then, Tripp had been relaxed, but no longer. In the blink of an eye, he leaned forward and slammed his hands down on the table as his dark eyes shot sparks at her mother. "That's enough, Mrs. McCree. Stop hammering on Abby for something that isn't her fault, or this conversation is over."

Her mom's eyes went wide with shock. "Abby, are you going to let him talk to me like that?"

Good question.

Yep, she was. "He's right, Mom. I get why you're upset, and I'm sorry you got caught up in this mess. I'm even sorry that Owen has as well. That doesn't mean I'm willing to let you tear into me like this. When you want to discuss the matter like a reasonable adult, fine. Otherwise, we're done here."

Then she poured coffee for Tripp and herself. She handed him his mug and jerked her head in the direction of the back door. "I'm going to drink this out on the porch. You're welcome to join me, but I won't blame you if you want to take it over to your place and barricade yourself inside."

He accepted the coffee. "Yeah, I'd better head home to work on my paper. You're welcome to hang out over there with me if you'd like."

Her mom continued to fume in stony silence. Maybe a better daughter would have groveled and begged for forgiveness for snarling back at her mother, but Abby wasn't that person. She followed Tripp and Zeke out the door. "Thanks for inviting me over to your place. If I have to talk to that woman again right now, I won't be responsible for my actions."

"Sure thing."

He slung his arm around her shoulders as they made their way across the yard. Once they were safely inside his cozy living room, she did her best to shed the last of her anger. "I can't help her when she goes on the attack like that."

She watched as Tripp filled the water bowl he kept on hand for Zeke. When he was done, he motioned her to sit down on the love seat. "Enjoy your coffee, unless you'd prefer something stronger."

She briefly considered the offer. "Tempting, but I'd better keep my wits about me. Don't let me being here interfere with your plans for the evening. Once I've calmed down a bit, I'll head back home."

"No rush. Meanwhile, I'll give Gage a call to see what's going on. I'd rather hear it straight from him. Even if he won't tell us much, maybe we'll learn something that will reassure your mom."

"That would be great, unless that's going to get you in trouble with him for even asking."

Tripp picked up his coffee and joined her on the love seat. "The worst he can do is tell me to butt out of his business."

The small size of the sofa put her in close proximity to Tripp, not that she minded. After dialing Gage's number, he leaned in closer, probably hoping she'd be able to eavesdrop on the conversation without the police chief being any wiser.

Gage answered on the second ring. "I'm busy, Blackston. Make it quick."

Tripp rolled his eyes but kept his voice low and even. "I know, Gage. I just wondered what you can tell me about why you took Owen into custody."

Abby winced. How could silence convey anger so easily?

When Gage finally spoke, the chill in his voice left her shivering and ready to apologize for bothering him. Tripp, however, was made of sterner stuff. "Gage, listen. I'm not asking you give me all the nitty-gritty details. Just enough so I can tell Abby what's going on. She needs some ammo to talk Mrs. McCree down off the ledge."

He paused for effect and then added, "It's either that or you need to get that cell you used to threaten Abby with ready for her mom. And if that happens, I don't have to tell you that you'll need a third one for Abby and a fourth for me."

His comment would have been funny if it weren't so true. She waited to see which way Gage would go. Fortunately he chose to see the humor in the threat. "Well, at least that way I could be reasonably sure the McCree women would be someplace safe until I can nail down what happened out there at the park."

"True enough, but then you'd also have the entire quilting guild camped out in your office demanding you set their leader free. I'm envisioning protest marches, sit-ins, and phone trees to call in reinforcements."

Then his grin turned wicked. "And if you're not careful, I'll tell Jean that you're jealous of all the tuna casseroles she's brought me."

By this point Abby was having a hard time not laughing out loud as Tripp continued. "Yeah, I can see it now. There'll also be open rebellion among your staff for creating a hostile work environment when you foist the casseroles off on them."

"You can be a real jerk sometimes, Blackston."

Tripp snorted. "Yeah, but you know Special Forces soldiers do whatever it takes to get the job done. Don't forget, you were one, too."

Gage's big sigh came through loud and clear. "Fine. Owen is sitting in a cell because he both lied and withheld crucial evidence. I'm giving him a chance to rethink his poor choices. You can tell Mrs. McCree she's welcome to visit him tomorrow morning. Maybe she can talk some sense into him."

"Will do."

"And, Abby?"

She winced. She should've known he'd guess she was listening in. "Yes, Gage?"

"Tell your mom some chocolate chip cookies would go a long way toward smoothing the feathers she ruffled when she insulted both me and my department. She'll need to do that to get past the front desk if she wants to actually visit with my prisoner. You should also let her know that while I've got a pretty thick skin when it comes to myself, I don't appreciate anyone insulting the hardworking men and women who serve this town."

The glacial chill was back in his voice, but she didn't blame him for feeling the way he did. Her mom had been out of line. "I'll tell her, Gage, and I'm sorry."

"Not your problem. See you tomorrow."

Tripp set his phone on the end table. "Well, that went better than I'd hoped. I can't imagine why Owen would lie to Gage or what kind of information he could be holding back."

After pondering the idea for a matter of seconds, she shrugged. "I can only come up with two scenarios. The first, and admittedly most unlikely, reason is that he actually did kill Mr. Anders and isn't ready to confess."

Despite her misgivings about Owen's mysterious past, she couldn't quite imagine him slipping away from her mother at the movie to commit murder. Even if he'd wanted the man dead, why do so in a way that would mark him as the chief suspect? He could've bought a different knife anywhere, and only a complete idiot would've used a weapon that would point directly back at him.

And while she wouldn't admit it to her mom, there was something about Owen that reminded her of both Tripp and Gage, like maybe he'd worn a uniform at some time in the past. She wasn't naïve enough to assume that all former members of the military walked the straight and narrow, but men like Gage and Tripp wore their sense of honor like a second skin. She suspected Owen did as well.

If true, then there was only one alternative as to why he was sitting behind bars. She angled herself to be able to look directly at Tripp. The more she thought about it, the more she was convinced she was right. "He's sitting in that cell for the same reason you did. He's another stubborn idiot trying to protect someone."

Tripp smiled. "I was wondering how long it would take you to connect the dots."

"I notice you don't deny it's a stupid move on his part."

"Yeah, well, sometimes a man's got to do what a man's got to do."

"Leaving his woman to clean up the mess."

When his eyes flared wide in shock, she replayed what she'd just said. Had she just called herself his woman? Yeah, she had. Her cheeks burned hot. "I was talking about Mom and Owen."

Mostly, anyway.

Rather than sit there and dwell on the big heap of awkwardness she'd just unleashed between them, she gulped down the last of her coffee before bolting for the door. "I'd better get back to Mom. We've got cookies to bake."

Tripp watched from his spot on the love seat. "Don't you already have a freezer full of cookies?"

"Yeah, but not chocolate chip. I know Gage would probably be okay with whatever Mom offered him. Under the circumstances, it would be smarter to bring exactly what he asked for."

"Makes sense."

She reached for the knob to let Zeke and herself out. The dog managed to make his escape, but she wasn't quite as lucky. Tripp was up and moving right for her, trapping her between him and the door. "One more thing, Abby."

"What's that?"

"This."

Then he gave her one of his patented hit-and-run kisses. In her opinion, it was over far too quickly but still packed quite a punch. She managed a small smile. "We seem to have developed a habit of doing this."

Not that she was complaining, nor did he deny the truth of her accusation. He twirled a lock of her hair through his fingers. It looked as if he were about to say something, but he must have thought better of it. Evidently they weren't going to discuss either what she'd said or what he'd done. Fine with her. It was getting late, and she wasn't up to handling any more drama. Eventually they were going to have to figure out where this thing between them was headed. First, though, she needed to help her mom deal with her own set of problems. She might not be real happy with the woman right now, but the bottom line was that the McCree women stood together. "Good night, Tripp. I'd better get to baking, and you've got a paper to do."

He followed her outside. "Let me know how it goes with Gage and Owen tomorrow."

"I will."

Abby was almost halfway across the yard when he called after her, "I noticed you didn't say whether it was a good habit or a bad one."

"I'll let you know when I decide."

His laughter followed her the rest of the way to her back door.

Back inside, she noticed the television was on in the living room. Rather than heading down the hall, she dug out the ingredients needed to make their bribe. She slammed a few things down on the counter louder than necessary, knowing eventually her mother's curiosity would send her wandering in Abby's direction. She figured it would be less than three minutes before she had company in the kitchen.

It didn't even take that long. Her mom now hovered in the doorway, staring at the row of cookie sheets Abby had set out on the table.

"Do you always do your baking this late?"

Abby kept measuring the dry ingredients into a large

bowl. "Nope, only when my mother needs to apologize to the local chief of police."

Without giving her mother a chance to get a word in edgewise, Abby kept talking. "Which I suggest said mother should do if she wants any hope of visiting a certain prisoner tomorrow morning."

Her mother seemed to shrink in on herself. "So Owen really is in jail."

"Yeah, he is." Abby did her best to act as if that were no big deal. "Can you hand me a bag of chocolate chips from the cabinet over there? After that, chop a cup of walnuts for me. I have some in the freezer."

As her mother followed orders, Abby offered up what little she knew about the situation. "From what I understand, your buddy Owen is sitting in that cell for two reasons, neither of which is that Gage really thinks Owen killed that man."

Her mom dropped the package of chocolate chips on the counter within easy reach. "So, in other words, he's holding him for no good reason."

"No, he's holding him because Owen has either lied to him or he's withholding important information regarding the case."

Having laid out the basic facts, Abby turned to point her spatula at her mother. "That's the same stupid stunt Tripp pulled a while back that resulted in him sitting in one of Gage's cells. I swear men can be total idiots sometimes, especially if they're trying to protect someone else. Believe me, I know. I've also learned that a woman can never go wrong by showing up at Snowberry Creek's police headquarters armed with fresh-baked cookies as a . . ."

She hesitated, briefly hoping to come up with the best way to finish that statement. In the end, she went with the truth. "Well, frankly, as a bribe. However, I wouldn't recommend calling it that in front of Gage. I'd go with something like they might like to give us some feedback on a new recipe."

Her mom reached for a cutting board and a chef's knife. "If it gets me in to see Owen, I'll call it whatever you want."

They worked side by side for a few minutes before her mom spoke again. "Maybe we should make a double batch. I suspect I owe Tripp an apology, too."

Abby reached for the sugar to measure out another cup. "Smart thinking, Mom. We'll need more chocolate chips and walnuts."

Zeke had been watching their every move and finally whined just a little. Her mom glanced in his direction. "What's he need? His water bowl is full, and he was just outside."

If only it were that simple. "That's not what he's asking for."

When he whined again, Abby sighed and admitted defeat without bothering to argue with him. "You're right, Zeke. We're getting low on your favorite peanut butter treats. We'll make a batch once we get these in the oven."

The dog sighed happily and went right back to sleep. Offering her mother a rueful smile, she said, "Sorry, but it looks like we're in for a long night."

To her surprise, her mom smiled right back. "I was just thinking that it's been a long time since we've hung out and done something like this together. I've missed it. I might hate the reason for needing the cookies, but I don't regret the chance to spend time with my daughter."

Feeling better about things than she had all day, Abby turned on the mixer and got lost in the familiar rhythms of turning common ingredients into something delicious. If only it was as easy to combine all the bits and pieces of what had happened at the park into a cohesive whole. If only some little detail would point Gage in the right direction.

No one would sleep well knowing a murderer was once again stalking the streets of Snowberry Creek.

CHAPTER 9

"Tell me again why we had to pack up five separate containers of cookies for one bunch of cops."

Abby had been about to open the door that led into the lobby shared by city hall, the town's library, and the police department. She was sure she'd been clear the first time her mother had asked, but there was no reason not to go over their plan one last time.

"The desk sergeant sits out in the lobby and may not get back to the bullpen before all the cookies we leave there are gone. The second one is for whoever is on guard duty by the jail cells, and Gage deserves his own since he's the one you insulted yesterday. The fifth container is for Owen."

Her mother wrinkled her nose. "Okay, but I've never heard of anyone offering up cookies to buy time to visit a prisoner."

It was hard not to laugh at her reaction. "Seriously, Mom. How many times have you visited someone in jail? But you're probably right. I'm guessing normally it's not done. However, as I've told you, I consider Gage a personal friend. I've also gotten to know some of the other officers as well, and I like them. Maybe it's a small-town thing."

To forestall any further discussion on the subject, Abby opened the door and motioned her mom to go ahead. As usual, Sergeant Jones was manning the front desk. He looked up from his computer and smiled as soon as he spotted her. Then he gave the bag in her mother's hand a—dare she say it?—hungry look.

"Ms. McCree, it's been a while since you've graced us with your presence. We've missed you."

She grinned back at him. "Tell me, Sergeant Jones, is it me you really miss or is it the cookies I always bring?"

Her assessment had him laughing. "Let's go with a little bit of both."

"That's what I thought." Abby dutifully signed the visitors' log and then took the bag from her mother so she could do the same. "We're supposed to check in with your boss. Is he available?"

While he gave Gage a quick call, Abby dug a small container out of the bag and set it on the desk. The sergeant eyed it with a smile. "Yes, sir, and they've come bearing gifts."

He hung up and pointed to the door behind him. "He's in his office. Go on back."

Pointing to the container, he asked, "Are those just for me, or do I have to share?"

"All yours, Sergeant Jones. I brought more for the bullpen and for Gage."

The cookies instantly disappeared behind the counter. "Thank you, ladies. Enjoy your visit."

Her mother followed close on her heels as they made their way down the hall toward the area that housed the rest of the department. Abby stopped long enough to set the largest container of cookies by the coffeepot, where the staff would find it soon enough. From there they headed toward the door to Gage's office. He was on the phone, so she knocked on the door frame in case he wanted privacy. He looked up and motioned for them to come on in. She and her mother took seats and waited until he finished up his call.

As soon as he hung up, Abby raised one eyebrow and gave her companion a pointed look. Her mother's smile wasn't all it should be, but at least she was trying. She set one of the remaining containers of cookies on Gage's desk.

"Chocolate chip as requested, Chief Logan. I apologize for my poor behavior yesterday. I offer no excuse other than to say I've never seen someone I care about arrested before. I felt helpless and didn't handle it very well."

Abby held her breath as Gage sat quietly for several seconds before finally nodding. "Apology accepted. I do realize that it was a stressful situation for you."

The laugh lines around his eyes deepened just enough to signal the tense moment was over. "If it's any consolation, your daughter wasn't any happier with me back when I invited Tripp to take up residence in our deluxe accommodations."

She gave Abby a quick glance. "So she said. I understand he was there for similar reasons."

"Close enough."

He picked up the cookies. "I'll put these out for my people."

Abby rejoined the conversation. "Actually, those are for you. I already put another bunch out by the coffee-maker for the rest of the crew. We also brought some for whoever is on guard duty today."

Gage leaned back in his chair, looking far more re-laxed than he had when they first arrived. "Your buddy, Deputy Chapin, will be happy to see you."

Abby would be glad to see him as well. They'd met back when Tripp had been locked up. The young deputy had gone out of his way to make things easier for Abby, even letting Zeke come hang out with his buddy. The dog had serious abandonment issues, and Tripp's abrupt dis-appearance had left the mastiff mix confused and hurting. It had done both dog and man good to spend time to-gether, even if Zeke hadn't understood why his friend couldn't come home with them. Looking back, she had to wonder if Zeke thought Tripp had been in a people shelter waiting to be adopted.

Back to the matter at hand. She had no desire to in-trude on the limited time her mother would have with Owen. Hopefully, Deputy Chapin wouldn't mind if Abby hung out with him instead.

"Tim knows to let both of you in, so there shouldn't be any problems." Then Gage gave her mom a considering look. "If you have any influence on Owen, convince him to tell me whatever it is that he's holding back. The sooner he does, the sooner you can have the stubborn idiot back where you want him."

Abby was already heading for the door when Gage

added, "Besides, I'm tired of people complaining because his restaurant is closed. Evidently, they want their barbecue back."

"Are you done scoping out the place for evidence?"

"Yeah, we have everything we need"—Gage paused long enough to open the lid of the container and snag two of the cookies—"except answers."

"We'll try, Gage, but no promises. I never had any luck talking sense to Tripp."

Before he could respond, the phone rang. She glanced back one last time before walking out the door. He held the phone a couple of inches from his ear with one hand and pinched the bridge of his nose with the other as if fighting a headache. The two cookies lay abandoned on his desk next to an empty coffee cup. The poor guy had probably been running full tilt since they'd first stumbled across the body.

"Mom, give me a second."

She headed for the coffeemaker and picked up a clean mug. After filling it with coffee, she added a splash of cream and two sugars. Gage gave her a look of pure gratitude when she set it down on his desk. She waved and slipped back out the door.

"Okay, let's go."

The walk down to where the cells were located didn't take long. Her mother coasted to a stop as soon as she spotted the wall of metal bars right behind where the deputy on guard duty sat. Abby could remember feeling the same horror the first time she'd passed this way. As promised, it was Tim Chapin who rose to his feet to greet them.

"Ms. McCree, it's good to see you again."

"Please, it's Abby. And this is my mother, Phoebe Mc-Cree. She's here to see Owen Quinn."

"Yeah, the boss said she could stay twenty minutes."

He got the keys out of the desk drawer. "You know the drill, Abby. After you put your things in the locker, I'll take you two the rest of the way."

Her mother removed the last two containers of cookies from the bag and folded it up. "One of these is for you, Deputy. I'd like to take the other one to Owen, if that's acceptable."

His face lit up as he accepted her offering. "It's fine, ma'am, and I appreciate your thoughtfulness in bringing me some, too."

Abby hung back as he unlocked the door. "I'll wait here, Mom, unless you need me to come with you. I will let you know when it's time to leave."

"Don't worry. I'll be fine." Her mother didn't sound convinced of that, but she drew herself up to her full height, clearly bracing herself for what came next. Then she followed the deputy around the corner to where the cells were.

When they were out of sight, Abby parked herself in the chair in front of the deputy's desk and waited for him to return. She heard the scrape of a heavy chair being dragged across the floor, which made her smile. No doubt Deputy Chapin was doing his best to make her mother comfortable in a place that was anything but. At least her mom could sit down while she talked to Owen.

If the man was anything like Tripp, he was probably telling her she didn't belong in a place like this. That much was true, but she suspected her mom's response to that would be much the same as Abby's had been. As long as Owen was going to be there, he'd just have to put up with her coming to check on him. She'd have to remember to mention that the other bribe that worked well was dinner from Gary's Drive-In. It had worked wonders on morale when she'd smuggled in burgers and shakes for Gage, the deputy, and their prisoner.

Deputy Chapin was back. When he closed the door and turned the key, locking her mother inside, it sent a chill through her. As if sensing Abby's discomfort, he grimaced. "Sorry, Abby, but I have to follow regulations. Mr. Quinn is the only prisoner right now, so she's safe enough."

She tried to lighten the moment. "I know. It's just that I never envisioned bringing my mother on a field trip to the local lockup."

He snickered. "Yeah, you'll find us listed on all the best tours here in town."

Then he offered her one of the cookies, and they chatted until it was time for her to retrieve her mother.

"Do you want me to go fetch her?"

She shook her head. "No, I'd better do it. Mom can get testy when it comes to Owen. I'd rather she not take her temper out on my friends."

That he didn't argue made it clear that her mother had already earned a questionable reputation in the local law enforcement community. If so, it probably meant there'd be a lot more baking going on to restore the peace.

She deliberately walked a little heavier than necessary to warn her mother and Owen that she was headed their way. The scene as she rounded the last turn was all too familiar. Her mother was sitting facing Owen's cell, so they could hold hands through the bars. He was the first to acknowledge Abby's presence. His smile looked tired, which didn't really surprise her. He probably hadn't gotten much more rest than Gage had over the past two days. Couple that with sleeping on a rock-hard cot in strange surroundings, it was no wonder he looked a bit haggard. Besides, few people looked good in a garish orange jumpsuit. Tripp certainly hadn't.

"I told your mother she shouldn't have come, but I am grateful to you both for making the effort. I also appreciate the cookies. I can't complain about the food here since it comes from the Creek Café. However, chocolate chip cookies are my favorite, so thank you."

"You're welcome." She turned her attention to her mother. "Sorry, Mom, but we have to go. We shouldn't overstay our welcome, especially if there's a chance you'll want to visit again."

As she spoke, she gave Owen a questioning look, hoping he would suddenly be overcome with the urge to confess all to Gage. The corner of his mouth quirked up briefly, as if he knew exactly what she was thinking. Meanwhile, her mother reluctantly released her death grip on his hands.

"I'll try to come back tomorrow, Owen. Is there anything I can bring you?"

"I'm fine, Phoebe. And although I know you won't listen, I'll say it again. This is no place for you to be."

Even if Owen didn't recognize the stubborn set to her mother's chin, Abby did. "I'll be coming back every chance I get until you walk out of that cell."

She stood up and put the chair back where it had come from. As she did, Owen paced the short length of his cell, finally coming to a stop back in front of the door with his hands gripping the bars. "Don't forget to check in with my assistant, Jada Davidson, for me. She takes classes at the university, so she might not be home. It would be easier if you could call first, but I don't know her number. She's in my list of contacts, but they took my cell phone when they brought me here."

"Don't worry, Owen. We'll find her." Then by way of explanation, her mother added, "He wants us to let her know she'll still get paid even though the restaurant and food truck are both closed right now."

That was generous of him. "Do you know her address?"

Owen frowned. "No, but I've given her a ride home a couple of times after work. She lives on Madrone Place out near the grocery store. Her street is a loop that hits the main road twice, a block apart. If you turn at the first entrance, hers is the fourth house on the right. It's a cream-colored rambler with green trim. There's a huge vine maple out front."

"We should be able to find it." Abby frowned. "Just in case, Mom, have you ever met Jada?"

"Not exactly, but I've seen her from a distance. I'm sure I'll recognize her."

"Good. We'll stop by her house on the way home. If she's not there, we can leave a note asking her to call us. If that doesn't work, we'll do another drive-by later this evening."

Owen looked considerably happier. "Thanks, Abby. Dinner's on me after all of this is over. We should invite Tripp, too, despite the amount of food that boy can devour. You should've seen him the last time he and some of his fellow veterans showed up for all-the-ribs-you-can-eat buffet. My bottom line took a direct hit that night for sure."

If true, it certainly didn't seem to concern him overly much. But then, nothing about how Owen ran his business made sense to Abby. Reminding herself that it wasn't her problem, she ushered her mother toward the exit. "We really need to go, Mom. We're already past the time limit Gage set for this visit, and we don't want to push our luck."

"Bye, ladies."

Owen remained standing as they walked away. Abby glanced back one last time before turning the corner. By that time, he'd stretched out on the bunk and was staring up at the ceiling.

He might not be her favorite person, but he was slowly winning her over. She liked the fact that he cared more about his assistant getting paid than he did his current predicament. If they couldn't spring him from that cell, the least they could do was check on his employee.

Deputy Chapin made quick work of processing them out. Her mother thanked him for his courtesy and said she would likely see him again soon. When they skirted the edge of the bullpen, Abby hesitated for a second to decide if they should stop by Gage's office on the way out. She hadn't had a chance to debrief her mom about what, if anything, Owen had told her about why he wasn't cooperating with the police investigation. All things considered, it would be better to make themselves scarce.

Once they were in the car, Abby braced herself in case her next question didn't go over well. "So, did Owen tell you why he's sitting on his backside in that cell?"

Her mother shook her head. "No, other than he's hoping Gage will find the killer sooner rather than later."

She stared out the side window. "It's like you thought. He's either worried that he's done something that ties him to the killer or he's protecting someone."

Abby reached over to pat her mother's hand. "I won't bother telling you not to worry, because you will, no matter what I say. Just know Gage and his people will do everything they can to get to the truth about what happened. They can also call on the county sheriff's department for any assistance they might need."

It wasn't clear if that made her mom feel any better about the situation, but Abby had done her best. Meanwhile, they were almost to the neighborhood where Jada Davidson lived. After turning on Madrone, she counted the houses. Sure enough, the fourth one down matched the description Owen had given them. Abby pulled over to the curb to study the house and noted the driveway was empty. "I can't tell if anyone's home. Let's go ring the doorbell."

When they didn't get an immediate response, Abby pressed the button one more time. Still no answer. If any of the neighbors had been outside, she would've asked them if they'd seen Jada. However, the only sign of movement on the entire street was a dark blue SUV driving away from a house two doors down. It was headed in the wrong direction for her to wave the driver down. Turning back to her mother, she said, "We'll have to leave a note."

Her mother pulled a notepad out of her purse and was hunting for a pen when someone turned into the driveway. After the garage door rolled up out of the way, the car disappeared inside. It was hard to decide what to do next when the garage door slid back down. Abby was about to knock when she heard footsteps approaching the door from the inside. A few seconds later it opened, revealing a young woman, presumably Jada Davidson.

She looked more wary than friendly. "Can I help you?"

"Ms. Davidson, I'm Abby McCree, and this is my mother, Phoebe McCree. We're friends of Owen Quinn. He asked us to stop by to make sure you were doing all right."

Jada's whole demeanor changed dramatically, although she certainly didn't look any happier. At least she opened the screen door, "Won't you come in? Can I get you something to drink? I have bottled water, pop, and iced tea. I could also make coffee."

Abby smiled. "Actually, I'd love some water. How about you, Mom?"

"I'm good, but thank you for offering."

Jada led them into the living room off the entryway. "Make yourselves comfortable. I'll be right back."

Abby chose one of the two easy chairs and her mother took the other one. The furniture was a bit worn but comfortable looking. There were several framed photos on the mantel over the fireplace. Most were of Jada and an older man, most likely her father considering the strong family resemblance. There was only one picture that included a woman. Guessing from how young Jada looked, it had been taken at least ten years ago. Did that mean that both of Jada's parents were gone? If so, she had to be reeling from the recent loss of her father.

Jada came back with two bottles. After handing one to Abby, she sat down on the sofa and unscrewed the top on her water and took a long drink. "I've been trying to call

Mr. Quinn, but it keeps going to voice mail. I was wondering when he'd be able to reopen the restaurant. I'm scheduled to work this evening."

Abby exchanged glances with her mother. "Actually, that's why we're here. Owen wanted you to know that you'll be paid your usual salary even though the restaurant is closed for the foreseeable future."

"But why? I know the police were checking the place out, but they finished yesterday."

Did she not know where Owen was right now? Evidently not, and Abby hated to be the one to deliver the bad news. "I'm sorry, Jada, but Owen is in police custody right now."

The younger woman's face turned pale. "Why would they arrest Owen? He didn't do anything wrong. They need to let him go. It's my fault he's in there. I'm the one who . . ."

Jada didn't finish her sentence, which had alarm bells going off in Abby's head. "You're the one who what?"

When she didn't immediately answer, Abby tried again. "What happened that night, Jada?"

"Nothing happened. I worked at the food truck just like I was supposed to do. I also kept the door locked at all times, just like Owen taught me, so no one could've gotten in. That's what I told the police."

Maybe that was true, but there something about the way she spoke the words that made it sound as if she'd rehearsed the statement over and over to make sure she got it right. Right now, Abby had no idea what had really gone on at the food truck, but she strongly suspected that the facts of the situation only marginally lined up with what Jada was claiming. If that was true, it also made it likely that Jada was the one Owen was trying to protect.

She leaned forward to make more direct eye contact with Jada. "Ms. Davidson, are you sure there's nothing you want to tell us?"

Tears started tumbling down Jada's cheeks, and she looked both guilty and terrified. Abby gripped the arms of the chair hard, to resist charging over to hug the poor girl. They really needed to hear what she was struggling to find the words to tell them. It was hard but necessary to wait for Jada to regain control and find the courage to speak the truth, whatever it might be. Unfortunately, her mother broke first and gathered the still sobbing girl into her arms. Jada started crying even harder as she took comfort from a total stranger. Maybe she just needed to get it all out of her system.

Abby watched and waited and hoped like heck that Jada wasn't about to confess to having murdered Mitchell Anders.

CHAPTER 10

As the deluge of tears slowed, Abby got a damp paper towel from the kitchen. A wet washcloth would've been better, but she didn't feel comfortable rooting around in the bathroom or linen closet to find one. She handed it off to her mother and sat back down to resume her vigil.

Finally, Jada hiccupped twice and straightened up. Phoebe handed her the towel and scooted back, putting a little distance between them as Jada dabbed at her red, swollen eyes. Her breathing remained a bit ragged while she rebuilt her control little by little. "Sorry, I didn't mean to fall apart like that."

"That's okay. I'm sure all of this comes as a bit of a shock."

Well handled, Mom. It was tempting to join the conversation, but she waited to see what her mom would do next. It was probably wiser to let her lead the conversation since she and Jada had made a connection of sorts.

Jada wiped her face one last time and tossed the paper towel in a decorative bowl on the end table. After that, she took a long drink of her water and set the bottle aside. "I'm sorry, I don't remember your names. I'm not normally this much of a mess, but things have been a bit rough lately."

"I'm Phoebe McCree, and this is my daughter, Abby. She lives here in Snowberry Creek, and I came down from Seattle to spend a few days with her."

Her mom pitched her voice low and calm, giving Jada a chance to get comfortable with two total strangers sitting in her living room. Once they established some common ground, it would be easier to get down to the nitty-gritty of what had happened the other night at the park. Her mom continued talking. "I've visited this area before, of course, because we had family here."

Jada frowned briefly and then her eyes widened as she looked at Abby and back at her mother. "That's right. You're the lady Owen has been dating. He was meeting you at the park on movie night."

"That's right. Abby was there, too, with her friend, Tripp Blackston. I don't know if you've met him, but from what Owen has told me, Tripp really loves the ribs at Owen's restaurant."

By that point, Jada definitely looked more relaxed. They were no longer strangers, but two women with connections to both Owen Quinn and the town as a whole. It was time to edge the discussion back in the direction of the murder. It felt a little like kicking puppies to continue pressing Jada for details, but it was important to find out what they were dealing with here if they were going to help Owen and Jada herself.

Her mom stepped into the breach and launched right in. "So, Jada, you said the police shouldn't have arrested Owen because of what happened the other night. I happen to agree with you, and so does my daughter. We both think he's protecting someone else. He must care about that person an awful lot to let himself be locked up like that. I've gotta tell you, it really hurt to see him in that tiny cell today."

Wow, suddenly Abby flashed back to her teenage years when she'd committed some transgression that she'd hoped her mother wouldn't find out about. The sneaky woman had used that same reasonable, calm tone to lull Abby into a false sense of security before pouncing. Almost without fail, Abby would find herself confessing anything and everything she'd done.

It was frightening how well the technique worked. Obviously, Jada was within her rights to tell them to get the heck out of her house and leave her alone. Abby knew how Gage would react if he found out they'd been poking around in his investigation—and he always found out. They were supposed to convince Owen to admit what was going on, not go out and dig up the information themselves. The smart thing to do would be to leave before they went any farther down this path. However, even if she was willing to go, she'd have to drag her mother out the door, kicking and screaming each inch of the way.

Better to strike hard and fast and get this over with. Her mom shot Abby a questioning look. When she nodded, Phoebe dove right back in. "Jada, honey, I know this situation is difficult. But hiding important information will only make things worse for both you and Owen. I know you don't want that."

Jada slowly shook her head, but she still didn't exactly looked convinced, either. She also didn't immediately confess, but Phoebe was nothing if not determined. She primed the pump with the facts as she knew them.

"Owen met you at the restaurant that night to get the food truck ready. Once it was all stocked up, you drove the truck to the park while he followed in his car. That's because he and I had plans for after the movie."

By that point, Jada had gone completely still, as if aware she was being stalked and really hoped that if she didn't move the predator would pass on by. Fat chance of that happening, not when Abby's mom had Jada in her sights. "Once you two had everything set up, he helped serve the people who wanted to get their food before the movie. When the rush was over, he left you at the truck and tracked me down. I'd ridden to the park with Abby."

She paused and waited for Jada to nod and acknowledge that much of the story was correct. That had been the easy part. Now, they were circling closer to the crux of the matter. "When the movie was about to start, Owen and I found a place to sit on the hillside near Abby and her friend Tripp. Neither of us had ever seen the film before, and we were surprised by how entertaining it was."

Another pause had Jada stepping in to fill the silence. "I've seen it before. It's really funny."

Abby felt compelled to add, "It's one of my personal favorites."

Her mother brought the conversation back on target. "During the film, Owen left to check on you and the truck, because it was the first time you were on your own. I'd guess he was gone about twenty-five, maybe thirty minutes."

She momentarily looked in Abby's direction. "Does that sound about right?"

Abby hadn't actually timed Owen's absence, but she was surprised he'd been gone that long. Regardless, she was willing to go along with her mother's assessment of the situation. "Yes, it does. I do know he was with you for the majority of the movie."

They both turned their attention back to Jada as Abby took charge of the interrogation. "Allowing for the time it took him to walk down to where the food truck was parked and back again, that leaves about twenty minutes unaccounted for. Can you help us with that?"

Jada shrank in on herself as her face turned pale. Abby was pretty sure the girl's hands were shaking, and her eyes darted from side to side as if searching for the nearest escape route.

Abby tried again. "Of course, I suppose he might've stopped off at the restroom or to talk with someone along the way. Can you give us an idea of how long he was actually at the truck?"

Jada bit her lower lip as she pondered her answer. Finally, she said, "I don't know if he spoke to anyone or if he stopped anywhere along the way."

Then she abruptly stood up. "Look, I don't mean to be rude, but I've got groceries to put away, and I also have to finish the reading for my next class. Please tell Mr. Quinn to let me know if there's anything I need to do at the restaurant. Otherwise, I'll wait to hear from him about when I can return to work. Thank you for coming."

They really had no choice but to leave. Her mother looked really frustrated, but the last thing they should have done was make Jada feel threatened by their continued presence. One call to Gage at the police station, and both of them would be in big trouble. Visions of matching mother-and-daughter orange jumpsuits flashed through her head as she stood up and motioned for her mother to do the same.

When they reached the door, she smiled at Jada. "Thanks for talking to us. If there's anything we can do to help, let us know. Or if there's anything you'd like us to tell Owen."

Then she waited to see if Jada would point out that she had no way of contacting them since she didn't have their phone numbers. When she didn't, Abby acted as if the realization had just hit her. "Oh, I'm an idiot. Calling me would be easier if you actually had my phone numbers. Do you want me to write them down or do you want to add them to your contacts?"

Either would work, but she wanted Jada to be able to reach out to her if she felt the need. Maybe Jada had friends to support her, but for some reason Abby doubted that. There was an air about her that spoke of profound loneliness, maybe because of the recent loss of her father. Regardless, if Jada did call Abby, she'd come running.

Meanwhile, Jada quickly keyed in the numbers for Abby's cell and landline. As she finished up, Abby had her own phone at the ready to add Jada's information to hers in return. With that done, it was time to hit the road.

As soon as the door closed behind them, her mother started to go into a full meltdown. "Why didn't you—"

Abby cut her off mid-tirade. Pitching her voice in a soft whisper, she said, "Wait until we're in the car. I suspect she's watching us from the front window. If not, and she really did head out to the garage to bring in groceries, she'll hear every word we say."

At least her mother waited until Abby started the car and was headed down the street before she tried again. "I know she was hiding something, and so do you. Why didn't you press her on the matter?"

"Because she asked us to leave, Mom, and because we can't actually force her into talking to us. We pushed as hard as we could, maybe too hard. I'm guessing something we said panicked her. If that's true, we'll be lucky if she doesn't call Gage and report us. Believe me, you don't want that to happen."

She waited for the intersection to clear before pulling out into traffic. It was time to head back to the house. It was probably bad on her part, but she really wished her mom would decide to return to her own home for a few days. Abby could only speak for herself, but she could really use a break from her mom's company. With Owen in jail, it didn't take a genius to guess that wasn't going to happen.

When she pulled up to a stop sign, she gave her mom a quick look to gauge her mood.

If she had to guess, it wasn't good. She was no doubt frustrated and angry that they hadn't gotten more out of Jada. Couple that with her worry over Owen, and it was a pretty volatile mix. Maybe a change of pace would help.

"Is there anywhere you'd like to stop? Maybe at Something's Brewing for a latte and a piece of gooey butter cake."

Her mother continued to stare out the passenger window and sighed. "Maybe another time. Right now I just want to go home."

She turned to look at Abby. "Your home, I should've said. I can't go back to my place until I know Owen is going to be all right."

Knowing it would do no good, Abby pointed out the obvious. "Mom, you've already done everything you can for him. If he wasn't involved, Gage will have to let him go eventually. I think the limit is something like forty-eight hours."

Abby regretted her words the second they slipped from her mouth. It had been like throwing gas on the fire. "What do you mean *if*, Abby? You can't possibly think Owen killed that man."

"No, I don't. I worded that poorly, but it doesn't change the fact that there's nothing more we can do. Any inter-ference on our part might only make it harder on him."

Her mother's grim expression made it clear Abby's words had fallen on deaf ears. As they drove along Main Street, her mother kept her gaze focused on something in the distance. Finally, she sighed. "It's just now sinking in that Snowberry Creek really has become your new home."

Abby tightened her grip on the steering wheel. "And that's a problem why?"

Her mother briefly glanced at Abby. "After your di-vorce, I figured you'd find a place to live in the same gen-eral area as the condo you and Chad shared and then start looking for a new job, something you'd find challenging. That got derailed when Aunt Sybil passed away and left you to deal with her entire estate. After that, I told myself you were only moving into Sybil's place because that was the easiest way to get it ready to put on the market."

Gesturing toward the buildings that made up the main business district in Snowberry Creek, she continued, "Instead, you've obviously made a lot of friends here and gotten really involved in the community."

"Again, Mom, what's wrong with that? It's not like I moved halfway across the country or anything. Even in heavy traffic, I'm less than a two-hour drive from your house. And while Snowberry Creek is a small town, especially in comparison to Seattle, I like living here. The people are great and have gone out of their way to make me feel welcome. I also love being so close to the Cascades and being able to see Mount Rainier in the distance. It's a great place to live."

"That's true, but this is all far off the trajectory I thought your life was on. You always focused on whatever goals you'd set for yourself, but I don't see that you have any plan of action now. It's as if you're hiding down here."

When Abby started to protest that assessment of the situation, her mother held up her hand to stop her. "I'm serious, Abby. I know what happened with Chad hurt you badly. Believe me, I'm aware how difficult it is to pick up the pieces and start over, but you're strong enough to do it."

And here Abby thought she'd been doing exactly that, which was why her mother's assessment of her current situation hurt so much. It was tempting to lash out, to point out the fact that her mother hadn't let any man get close for years after her own divorce.

Worse yet, her mother wasn't finished. "And then there's the fact you've gotten caught up in all of these murder cases. Forgive me for reacting like a concerned parent, but it scares me. You can make new friends back in Seattle, and the job market is bound to be better there. Seriously, don't you think it's time you moved on?"

Once again her mom lapsed into a dark silence. Right now it was a toss-up if her bad mood was because of Owen or because Abby hadn't reacted well to the criticism of her recent life choices. Either way, it was just more proof that the two of them needed some time apart. There was only one problem with that. Short of throwing herself on Tripp's mercy and begging him to let her hide out in his house, she really had no place to go. It was also clear that her mom had no intention of leaving until Owen was a free man again. Heck, she might not leave even then.

Abby shuddered at the thought.

Evidently the silence had only been the calm before the storm, because her mom picked up right where she'd left off. "Look, I didn't mean to hurt your feelings, Abby. But as your mother, it's my duty to let you know when I think you need to rethink some of your decisions."

It was tempting to slam on the brakes and order the infuriating woman out of the car, but Abby didn't have it in her to do that. She settled for a little plain speaking of her own. "Your opinion is duly noted, Mother. It will also be ignored. I'm a grown woman, capable of making my own decisions. While I will admit at times I'm still feeling my way in this new life I'm building for myself, on the whole I am happy. That should be enough for you."

More silence.

When her mother drew in a breath as if to start in again, Abby braced herself. "I'm not sure if that's really true. I can't believe hanging out with a group of women in their eighties and doing a bunch of busywork for different groups here in town is enough of a challenge for a woman with your education and abilities."

Abby immediately pulled over to the curb and shut off

the engine. When she opened the car door, her mom caught her arm. "Wait, where are you going?"

"I'm getting out of here."

"But why?"

Abby tossed the car keys in her mom's lap. "Let's see—first you told me you don't approve of my life choices, and then you basically call me a liar for saying I'm happy. Sorry to be such a disappointment, Mom. Rather than stay here and see what other constructive criticism you might have to offer, I'm going to walk home."

Then she got out, slammed the door closed, and stalked off down the street.

CHAPTER 11

A few seconds later, the car started. Abby didn't even bother to glance in her mother's direction as she drove by. Maybe she'd just thrown the adult version of a temper tantrum, but too bad. She really needed to walk off her anger—and hurt—before facing off with her mother again. It was less than a mile to her house, but she could always do a couple of extra laps around the block if she was still fuming by the time she reached her own street.

She'd only gone a few blocks when two familiar figures came into sight, headed straight for her. Maybe it was a coincidence that Tripp had chosen that moment and that particular route to take Zeke on an outing, but she doubted it. She kept walking at the same deliberate pace until they met somewhere in the middle. To avoid making immediate eye contact with Tripp, she bent down to pat

Zeke on the head. Finally, when she thought she could speak without crying, she asked, "What did she say to send you out on a search and rescue mission?"

"That you weren't very happy with her right now and had stormed off in a huff."

She straightened up, still keeping her hand on Zeke. Right now she needed that connection with his unconditional love to keep herself grounded. "That's putting it mildly. As it turns out, she doesn't like me living in Snowberry Creek. Seems it's not ambitious enough to satisfy her high expectations for her daughter. When I pointed out I was actually happy living here, she essentially said I was lying. Not sure if she meant I was lying to myself or her."

Too restless to stand still, and not sure she wanted to hear Tripp's response, she started walking, letting him and Zeke follow as they would. They fell into step beside her, but Tripp didn't say a word when she bypassed the most direct route back to where they lived.

After another two blocks he finally spoke. "I'm sorry she feels that way, Abby. I swear your mom and mine must be reading from the same playbook."

"Seriously? Your mom doesn't want you to stay in Snowberry Creek?"

"Yeah, recently she's been waging a campaign to get me to move back East. I've told her the highway runs in both directions. If she wants us to live closer together, she's free to pack up and come out here."

"Think she will?"

"No, she wants to be close to my sister and her kids, which is why she wants me to move home. In short, it would be easier to uproot my life since there's only me."

At the next cross street, Abby turned left, taking them

farther from their neighborhood. She had to ask, even if she wasn't sure she wanted to know the answer. "Are you thinking about it?"

It was a huge relief when he answered, "No, I'm not. I like this area, which is why I moved here in the first place. I also can't switch schools without losing credits, and I really want to finish my degree as soon as possible."

He paused a second and then added, "Mostly, though, it's the people here I would miss. She's been threatening to come out for an extended visit to see what's so wonderful about this area that it keeps me from moving back."

The snarled knot of tension Abby had been trying to untangle eased up. Hopefully she was one of the people keeping him anchored right where he was. "You do know that if your mom ever wants to come visit, she'd be welcome to stay at my house. I've got plenty of room."

After all, his house had only the one bedroom. Why had her offer made him break out in laughter? "What so funny?"

"Heck, you can't get your own mom to leave. What if mine moved in, too? Just think what our lives would be like if they double-teamed us. Snowberry Creek would never be the same."

She shivered. "I hadn't thought about it in that way. The offer still stands, but only if you help me get rid of my mom first. We'll need a plan, though."

They both pondered the situation for the next block. Then she thought about Jada and wondered what secret she was hiding. It had to be substantial if owning up to what had happened that night had her running scared and left Owen sitting in that cell.

Tripp stopped when Zeke paused to inspect some azaleas to see if some other dog had stopped by there recently. After circling the shrubs a second time, Zeke left his own mark on them. Mission accomplished, he snorted and gave himself a good shake. Then, with a wag of his tail, he proudly started on down the sidewalk, dragging his two humans in his wake.

Once they were in motion, Tripp shook his head. "I might be stating the obvious here, but I figure the only way to get your mom to leave is to clear Owen's name. Did Gage give you any idea about how his investigation is going?"

"No. You know how he is about that kind of stuff."

Gage wasn't the only one who didn't like Abby poking her nose in matters best left to the police. Tripp also didn't like surprises, especially when it came to her safety, so she owned up to where she and her mom had gone after leaving the jail. "There is one thing, though. Owen has an employee, a college student named Jada Davidson. She's the one who worked in the food truck the night of the movie. Owen asked us stop by and let her know she'd get paid even though the restaurant is closed right now."

"That's decent of him, but I'm guessing there's more to it than that."

"Yeah, supposedly she's the reason he disappeared for nearly half an hour at the movie. He told Mom that Jada had never worked the truck by herself, and he needed to make sure she hadn't run into any problems."

"Seems reasonable."

"Yeah, but when we asked Jada about it, she acted pretty evasive. Mom explained we were trying to figure out the timeline for that night. Then she laid it all out for Jada, at least as far as what we already knew. We figured it was a five-minute walk to where the truck was parked and the same amount of time to get back. If he was gone thirty minutes, that left twenty minutes unaccounted for. That's as much as we know at this point."

"So what's the problem?"

"When we asked Jada to fill in what she could about the rest of the time, she suddenly asked us to leave. She's hiding something, but I don't know what it could be. She doesn't strike me as a killer, but our questions definitely freaked her out."

They turned the corner, this time circling back toward the house. "Has your mom asked Owen these same questions?"

"I waited with Deputy Chapin until it was time to leave. I have no idea what they said or did while they were alone."

She frowned. "I do know she believes he went to check on the truck."

The house was now in sight, so she slowed her steps. "Maybe Owen is just the nice guy Mom thinks he is, but I keep thinking there's a whole lot more to the man than he lets on."

Tripp tugged on Zeke's leash and coasted to a stop. "Yeah, there's been a couple of times when Gage has said something that hinted he and Owen had crossed paths at some point in the past. I've never pressed him on it, because we both served on missions that we couldn't talk about. Still can't, for that matter."

No surprise there. Both men had been in the Special Forces, although she didn't know the specifics. Tripp didn't talk much about what he'd seen and done, but those memories sometimes kept him up, prowling the yard until the wee hours.

"Do you think there's any chance what happened to Mitch Anders had something to do with Owen's past?"

Tripp was frowning big-time. "Possibly, but it seems unlikely. When he identified the man for Gage, he only said Anders was an insurance agent who had recently moved to town. There was no indication he knew anything else about him."

True, but she had to wonder if Owen had told Gage more about the victim when Gage had taken Owen down to the station to give his statement. The police chief was pretty good at reading people. Something about Owen's story had set off alarms of some kind or else he wouldn't be behind bars right now.

Their path forward seemed clear. Like Tripp had said, getting her mother out of her hair was dependent on clearing Owen's name. She couldn't very well interrogate Owen while he was in jail without Gage having a hissy fit. If they couldn't learn more from him, then she needed to learn more about the murdered man. Uncovering the facts was the only way to unravel a mystery. Maybe she could ask a few questions around town without drawing too much attention to herself. Although it was Gage's job to solve the murder, sometimes people didn't like talking to the police.

"You're planning on investigating on your own again."

There was no use in denying it. Tripp wouldn't believe her if she tried. "Not exactly. I thought I'd see what I could learn about Mitchell Anders. No one will be surprised that I'd want to know more about him, considering I'm the one who found his body."

No sooner had the words left her mouth than Tripp had her hand in a death grip, as if that alone could prevent her from moving forward with her plan. "You're not going to get mixed up in another murder investigation on your own, Abby. I'm not sure my heart can stand the strain."

She might've thought he was exaggerating, but right now her fingers felt as if they were being crushed in a vise. Looking back, maybe he hadn't been kidding on the past occasions when he'd claimed that the dangerous situations she'd gotten caught up in had taken years off his life. Sadly, there was no way for her to walk away from the situation. She made the only promise she knew she could keep. "I plan to be careful."

His grip on her tightened even more. "And how did that work out for you the last time? And the two times before that?"

Even if she conceded that he had a point, what was she supposed to do? Her mother was miserable. They might have their problems, but she didn't like to see her so unhappy. "I mean it, Tripp. I will only ask people I know and trust about Mr. Anders."

The pressure eased up slightly. "Considering he's only been in town a short time, chances are no one knows a lot about him."

"Then I won't learn anything, but at least I can tell Mom I tried."

Tripp's hand dropped away from hers. "Who are you planning to talk to?"

She gave the matter some thought. "Bridey, for sure. A lot of people in town talk to her when they're waiting for their coffee. And there's a meeting at my house for the quilting guild board tomorrow, so I'll ask Glenda, Jean, and Louise while I have the chance. I doubt they'll know much, but I could be wrong. I never knew gossip could travel that fast until I met the three of them."

She gave Tripp a teasing glance. "When I send out a

reminder about the time, do you want me to tell Jean she can pick up her empty casserole dish while she's here? Maybe bring you another tuna surprise in exchange?"

Tripp's scowl was impressive. "Sometimes I forget you have a nasty mean streak. What time is the meeting, anyway?"

"Why? Do you want to come hang out, drink tea, and eat cookies with us?"

He actually shuddered. "No, I'll drop the empty dish off at your place. I also plan to be gone while they're at your house. If you won't tell me the time, I'll just hang out in the school library for the day."

She nudged him with her shoulder. "The meeting starts at nine. We're usually done by eleven. They like to get to the Creek Café in time for the early-bird lunch special. I'll let you know when the coast is clear."

They walked the last block in silence, letting Zeke set the pace for them. Abby was in no hurry to get back home, but at least the combination of good company and exercise had taken the edge off her temper. Hopefully she and her mother could make it through the rest of the day without ripping into each other again. If not, well, she could always lock herself in her bedroom and watch a movie.

Maybe her mom would calm down when Abby told her about her plans to do a little sleuthing on her own. To delay having to face the woman for another few minutes, Abby walked around to sit on the back porch instead of heading directly inside. If Tripp guessed what she was up to, he didn't say anything. He let Zeke off his leash and then handed it to her. "I'd better go back to my place and work, but call me if you need a referee. Maybe I'll even invite the neighbors and sell popcorn."

She shouldn't have encouraged him, but it was impossible not to laugh. "And I could call your mom and tell her that you got this whole thing going on with a lady in her eighties." She paused to waggle her eyebrows. "That she brings you lavish gifts of tuna and pasta."

"Like I said earlier—huge mean streak." He pretended to glare at her, but there was too much humor in his eyes to take him seriously. "But two can play at that game. How do you think Gage would react if someone let it slip that you were breaking out your deerstalker hat and magnifying glass again?"

When she'd gone to the town's Halloween Festival dressed as Sherlock Holmes, she'd been the only one who thought it was funny. Some people, namely Tripp and Gage, had no sense of humor. Or maybe it had just been too soon after she'd had a scary run-in with a murderer. It was hard to tell.

Either way, it was time the two of them parted ways for the day. "Thanks for coming to check on me. It helped. Good luck with your paper. I know essays about teaching kindergartners must be hard."

Tripp's answering growl as he walked away would've done Zeke proud. She laughed and waved when he reached his porch and glanced back in her direction. He relented and grinned before disappearing inside.

She settled on the top step to ponder the best way to find out what she needed to know about Mr. Anders without drawing unwanted attention from his killer.

CHAPTER 12

Although no apologies had been exchanged, the previous evening had passed without any more drama. After a simple meal of broiled salmon and a salad, Abby had watched a movie while her mother read. There was no way to know if the peace would last, but she appreciated the break from the unrelenting tension. Going to bed relaxed made for much more restful sleep.

The morning started off peacefully, as well. If her mother was surprised Abby was up and dressed by eight o'clock, she had the good sense not to comment. Abby grabbed a container of strawberry yogurt from the refrigerator and warmed one of the muffins left over from when Owen had come for breakfast. Finally, she poured herself a huge cup of coffee before joining her mom at the table. Eyeing the half-eaten piece of toast on her mother's plate, she asked, "Is that enough of a breakfast?"

"I had a bowl of cereal about an hour ago."

Abby studied her mother's face over the rim of her coffee cup. "Did you get enough sleep?"

"Oh, sure. At home, my alarm goes off at five a.m., so I'm used to getting up early. Zeke kept me company, so he's already eaten. Which reminds me—when I let him out, there was nothing on the porch. When he woofed to be let in"—she paused to point at an unfamiliar baking dish sitting on the counter—"that was sitting outside the door."

Abby laughed. "Tripp must have dropped it off when he left for his morning run. It belongs to one of the ladies from the quilting guild."

As she explained about Jean and her infamous tuna casseroles, it felt good to hear her mother laughing so hard. "Poor man, but it's nice that he's so good-natured about it."

"Yeah, it is. He's a great guy."

Her mother cleared her spot, putting the cup and plate in the dishwasher before sitting back down. "So, what's on the agenda today besides visiting Owen? Also, I'm not up on jailhouse etiquette. Do I bring cookies again or was that a one-shot deal?"

If there'd been any snark at all in her voice, Abby would've once again felt obligated to defend Gage and his people. But since her mother sounded genuinely curious, she gave the matter some serious thought. "Why don't I text Gage and ask if you can stop by this morning? I can't go with you, though. I have a quilting guild board meeting here at nine. Will you be all right going by yourself?"

"Now that I've been there and know how it works, I'll be fine. I just need to make sure Owen is doing okay. He'll also want to know we talked to Jada."

Just that quickly, the shadows were back in her eyes, and she looked a little lost. Abby understood how she felt. Her mom had come to town to spend time with Owen and have a little fun. Instead, she was caught up in a murder investigation, and he was in jail.

"I can't promise anything, Mom, but I'm going to ask the ladies from the guild if they know anything about Mr. Anders. I also thought I'd see if my friend Bridey has time to meet me for lunch this afternoon. She hears a lot of local news from her customers. Don't get your hopes up, though. He only recently moved to town, so it's a long shot that any of them will know anything useful."

"I appreciate that you're even willing to try. Should I stay home since you're doing this for me?"

Abby shook her head. "No, that's okay. The ladies might not be as willing to share any gossip they've heard with a stranger." She glanced at the clock. "Whoops, I should get moving. They'll be here soon, and I still need to set the dining room table, make the tea, and lay out the refreshments. And I'd better text Gage and Bridey now before I forget."

Her mother pushed away from the table. "I can set the table for you. How many people are coming?"

"Four, counting me. I use Aunt Sybil's china and silver, because the ladies like the fancy stuff. Oh, and there are matching paper napkins in the top left drawer of the buffet."

She typed her message to Gage and crossed her fingers

he'd let her mother back in to see Owen. If he wouldn't, she was pretty sure her mother wouldn't handle it well. Rather than sit there and stare at the screen, she got out two teapots and arranged a selection of cookies on two depression-glass plates.

Her phone chimed just as she filled the kettle and set it on the stove. Bracing herself for the worst, she peeked at the screen. Whew! Good news. Her mom was welcome to stop by for a thirty-minute visit anytime before noon. That would give Abby a chance to quiz her friends without an audience. She sent Gage a quick "thank you" and then heard back from Bridey a few seconds later. Yay, she was batting two for two. Hopefully that was a sign things were on an upswing.

Her mother was back. "Any news?"

"Yep, Gage said you can come by for half an hour as long as it's before noon. He didn't say why it had to be then, but I was pretty sure that would work for you."

"I'd better go get ready then, or do you still need my help?"

"No, I've got it under control." She handed the cookies to her mom. "Can you set these plates on the table on your way?"

"Sure thing."

Abby filled the tea balls with Earl Grey and Darjeeling tea leaves. "What are your plans for the rest of the day?"

Her mom stopped in the doorway. "Actually, I want to go back home to get some more clothes and pick up my mail. I hadn't expected to stay this long, and I need a few things."

That was both good news and bad. It meant her mom would be gone for hours, giving the two of them a much-needed break from each other's company. The downside was that it also meant her mom planned on staying with Abby for the duration of the investigation. Luckily, the kettle chose that moment to whistle, giving her a way to hide her unenthusiastic response to that thought.

She had to say something. "Traffic is unpredictable, so I'll keep dinner simple. Maybe I'll order pizza."

"Sounds good, but don't wait for me if I run late. I can always reheat it in the microwave."

"Sounds like a plan."

As her mom headed upstairs, Abby carried the teapots and Jean's baking dish down the hall to the dining room. The doorbell rang a few seconds later. Her friends were nothing if not punctual.

"Come on in, ladies, and make yourselves comfortable. I have to grab my notes and the minutes from our last meeting. It won't take me a second."

Her mother was coming down the steps when Abby got back, so she performed the necessary introductions. "Mom, you may already know these ladies since they were all close friends of Aunt Sybil's. But just in case, this is Glenda, Louise, and Jean."

Glenda smiled. "Yes, we met several years ago. I think you'd come down to visit for Sybil's seventy-fifth birthday."

Her mother smiled. "I remember. You made that wonderful rhubarb coffee cake."

The older woman beamed at the compliment. "It was one of your aunt's favorites. If I'd known you liked it so much, I would've baked one for today. Maybe next time."

Abby joined the conversation. "Mom, you'd better get going if you don't want to be late."

Taking the hint, her mother moved toward the door. "It was nice seeing you ladies again. Abby, I'll see you later."

As soon as she was out the door, Abby shepherded her friends toward the dining room. "Why don't we get started? We have a lot to cover."

Most of the time Abby had a lot of patience with her elderly friends, but sometimes keeping them focused was a definite challenge. Today had been worse than usual, but they'd finally reached the last item on the agenda. Before the ladies had coaxed—or actually bamboozled— her into taking over as president of the guild, the group's board meetings had been more like a tea party.

Now, they mostly followed the agenda she presented to them. They'd finally learned that the more they stayed focused on the business at hand, the faster they could get to their favorite part of the meeting, which was catching up on local gossip. For once, Abby couldn't wait.

She held up the teapot. "Anyone else want more?"

Glenda held out her cup and let Abby pour. "I was sorry to hear about the unpleasantness at the movie night. Are you all right?"

She passed the teapot on to Louise, so she could pour tea for Jean at the other end of the table. "I'm fine, but my mother is taking the incident pretty hard."

"I'm sure she is. No one expects to discover a body like that." Glenda sighed as she passed around the cookies. "I swear, I don't know what's going on in this town. We never used to have this kind of stuff going on all the time."

Jean took a sugar cookie and set it on her plate. "I

heard Chief Logan arrested someone in connection to the murder—that Owen Quinn, the man who owns that awful food truck." She gave the rest of them a wide-eyed look as she sipped her tea before continuing. "Naturally he claims to be innocent, but that's what they all say. You know, criminals."

The woman definitely had a flair for the melodramatic. If the situation wasn't so dire, Abby would've laughed. She also knew the best way to get the ladies to share what they'd heard was to prime the pump with a little insider information of her own.

"Remember when Tripp was in jail right before Halloween? It wasn't because he'd done anything wrong, but because he was protecting a friend."

Jean sat back in her chair. "So you think Mr. Quinn knows something he doesn't want to tell Gage?"

"I can't say. You know Gage can't share the details when he's investigating a crime." She paused and drew a deep breath for effect. "What I can tell you is that my mother and Owen have become friends, and she believes him to be innocent of any wrongdoing. But just like Tripp, he isn't cooperating with Gage."

Louise frowned. "Surely your mother has tried talking some sense into the man."

Abby huffed an exasperated laugh. "Yeah, and got about as far with him as I did with Tripp."

"Was Mr. Quinn the friend your mother was on her way to visit?"

There was no use in denying it. "Yeah. Gage said she could stop by for a short time. I think he's still hoping Owen will listen to her. I have to admit, I don't know what to think. All I know about Mitchell Anders is that he only recently moved here. It seems so strange that someone so new to our town would've already made an enemy who was willing to kill."

She gave each of her friends a questioning look. "Unless he had some past connection with someone here in Snowberry Creek that I just haven't heard about."

Jean, who always had the closest connection to the unofficial gossip brigade in town, responded first. "Not that anyone knows about. As far as I've heard, the only reason he moved here was because that nice Mr. Davidson passed away unexpectedly. The home office sent Mr. Anders down here to take over his office, but I never met the man."

Louise joined in. "I have my car insurance through that company. Even though Mr. Davidson was my agent for years, I rarely had to contact him. In fact, when a rock cracked my windshield last year, I never spoke to him at all. It was his daughter who gave me the name of the glass shop to use."

That bit of information was unexpected. "You're talking about Jada Davidson? She worked in her father's office?"

"Yes, although I'm sure it was only part-time. She's a student at the university, I believe." Louise gave Abby a curious look. "Why? Do you know her?"

Abby nodded. "We've met, but only briefly. She works for Owen Quinn now."

Glenda frowned. "That must be a recent change. Jada worked in her father's office up until recently. He was always so proud of her. Had her picture on his desk and bragged about her grades and how hard she worked. Maybe she left because it would be difficult to see someone else sitting at her father's desk."

Before the conversation could continue, Louise's phone

beeped. She picked up and touched the screen. "That's our cue, ladies. You asked me to let you know when it was ten thirty."

She smiled at Abby. "We want to make sure we had time to help you clean up and still be out the door by eleven. We're going to the diner for lunch and have to get there early to get a booth. I swear, that place gets more crowded every day."

They helped carry everything back to the kitchen. Abby had given up telling them she could handle the cleanup by herself. When everything was put away, she followed them back down the hall to get their purses. "Jean, don't forget to take your casserole dish. Tripp had class this morning, so he couldn't be here to give it to you himself."

Jean looked disappointed as Abby helped her down the steps and into the back seat of Glenda's sedan. As they backed out of the driveway, Abby waved. "Enjoy your lunch! Leave some pie for me and Bridey."

Once they were out of sight, she headed back inside to ponder what she'd gleaned from their conversation. Her gut said the fact that Jada had worked in the insurance office was significant. The question was why.

Zeke was waiting for her inside. He whined softly and stared at the door. "Okay, big guy, I can take a hint. Let me grab my keys and your leash. We'll take a quick walk before I have to meet Bridey for lunch."

And while they made the rounds, she'd figure out what to do with the knowledge that there was a direct connection between Jada Davidson and the murder victim.

CHAPTER 13

"So how are you and your mom handling being temporary roommates?"

At least Bridey had waited until Frannie took their orders before asking. Abby debated how much to share but decided venting a little wouldn't hurt. "Not all that great, especially yesterday afternoon. From out of nowhere, she informed me I needed to leave Snowberry Creek and get on with my life. I was so mad, I got out of the car and walked home rather than listen to whatever else she had to say. I don't know what she said to Tripp, but he and Zeke hiked out to meet me. By the time we'd circled the block, I had my temper back under control. Mostly, anyway."

She dragged her finger down the outside of her water glass, tracing a pattern in the moisture that coated its surface. "Maybe she realized she'd overstepped her boundaries, because the evening was pretty quiet. She left this morning to visit Owen at the jail again. After that, she was heading back to her place to get more clothes, so she expects to be here awhile longer."

Bridey grimaced. "Sorry."

So was Abby. "I just hope that Gage gets this mess figured out soon."

"Any idea how the investigation is going? Or why he's still holding Owen?"

Abby sighed. "I still think Owen knows something that he doesn't want Gage to find out about. Have you heard anything?"

Bridey shrugged. "People are upset, of course. It's kind of scary knowing that someone was murdered while we were all so close by, watching the movie. Who does something like that?"

Good question, but one Abby had no answer for. At least not yet. "Did you or your hubby know Don Davidson?"

If Bridey was surprised by the change in direction, she gave no indication of it. "Yeah, Seth and I had several policies with him, personal as well as business. He was well thought of, and folks took the news of his death hard. It was his heart, I think."

That pretty much fit in with what Abby had heard about the man. "I never met him, but I've met his daughter. I understand Jada used to work for the company, too, but not anymore. I guess it wouldn't have felt right working in the same office but without her father."

Bridey leaned forward and lowered her voice. "From what I've heard, leaving wasn't exactly Jada's choice. No one was surprised that they brought in another agent right away, but the first thing Mitch Anders did was tell Jada he no longer needed her services. So in a matter of days, she lost both her father and her job. A lot of folks didn't take kindly to that. For sure it didn't win him any friends."

"I can see why. I suppose the insurance company will be sending in another agent soon."

"They'll have to. Someone has to oversee all those policies and stuff."

Before Abby could think of any other questions to ask, Frannie was back with their food, which ended any chance for further discussion. Bridey was on a tight schedule and needed to get back to her shop before the afternoon rush began. The information she'd given Abby filled in a few more pieces in the puzzle of what had happened to Mitchell Anders. Now all she had to do was start fitting them together. At least she knew why Jada was now working for Owen Quinn.

After making quick work of their meal, they walked out of the diner together. "Thanks again for lunch, Abby. It feels good to get away from work for a little while, but I'd better hustle back before the high school horde descends on the shop en masse."

"Personally, I'm going to go home and catch up on a few things and bask in a little solitude before Mom comes back."

After they parted ways, Abby headed down the street to where she'd left her car. As she strolled along the sidewalk, a sign on the front window of a nearby building caught her eye. On some level, she'd known that the insurance office was in that general area, but she'd never really paid any attention to it as she passed by. Curiosity had her slowing down to take a peek.

Evidently, Mitch Anders hadn't had time to change the sign, because Don Davidson's name was still on the door.

It would likely stay that way until the new agent arrived. The lights were turned off, but enough sunshine filtered in through the windows to allow her to see inside. From what she could tell, it was pretty much how anyone would expect an insurance office to look, everything all neat and tidy.

Deciding there was nothing else to be learned, she started to turn away when she noticed one oddity. Behind the largest desk, there was a rectangular space on the wall where the paint was brighter than the surrounding area. Evidently a large picture had hung there long enough for the paint around it to have faded over time. Interesting, but probably not significant. After all, the office had changed hands recently. No doubt Mitch Anders had been in the middle of personalizing the place to reflect his own tastes.

"Sorry, but I think that office is closed indefinitely."

Abby jumped back at the unexpected comment. She nearly ran into the man standing just behind her shoulder. He immediately offered her an apologetic smile. "Sorry, I didn't mean to startle you."

He was about average height, balding, and looked to be in his late forties. Although not particularly intimidating, his sudden appearance had left Abby a bit shaken. She took a half step back in an attempt to put a little more distance between them. Unfortunately, there wasn't much room to maneuver with the building right behind her. "No problem. I guess my mind was somewhere else, and I didn't hear you approach."

Maybe he realized she wasn't comfortable with having a strange man standing so close because he backed up two steps and apologized again as he nodded in the direction of the door. "Sorry, I was just saying that the office is closed. The agent died a couple of days back, and I guess no one else has stepped in to take over yet."

"I'd heard."

That was putting it mildly, but she didn't want to get into that particular discussion with a total stranger. The expression on his face was rather stark as he looked past her into the darkened office. He scanned the room much as she had, staring briefly at the large desk or maybe the wall behind it. It was tempting to ask if he knew what kind of picture had been taken down, but still she felt hesitant.

"I was friends with the prior agent, Don Davidson. I didn't know the new guy who replaced him." Then he glanced at Abby and stuck out his hand. "I don't believe we've met. I'm Will Swahn."

She reluctantly shook his hand. "Hi, I'm Abby Mc-Cree."

As soon as the words were out of her mouth, his eyebrows shot up. "Hey, aren't you the one who found the body in the park the other night? That had to be hard."

"Yes, it was, even though I had never met him. I guess that's why I stopped to peek in the office, maybe to get some idea of who he was. I didn't know Mr. Davidson either, but I've heard good things about him. I have met his daughter, though."

"Well, there's a coincidence for you. Her dad was my best friend, and I'm Jada's godfather. I bet she's taking all of this pretty hard, poor kid. It doesn't help that she lost her position here at the insurance office when her dad died, and now her new boss is in jail on murder charges. I guess she'll have to start looking for another job."

Owen hadn't actually been charged, but Abby didn't bother to correct him. She could share one thing that might help him feel better about the situation. "Actually, Mr. Quinn promised to pay Jada's salary even though the restaurant is closed for the time being."

That information clearly took him by surprise. "Where did you hear that?"

Okay, maybe it would've been smarter to keep her mouth shut, but now she had no choice but to answer. That didn't mean she had to go into detail. "Mr. Quinn is a casual acquaintance of someone close to me."

Will looked doubtful. "How is he supposed to keep paying her if he's in jail for murder?"

Although his voice sounded as if he were merely curious, there was something in his eyes that made her think that there were deeper emotions in play. Of course that would make sense if Will Swahn and Jada's father had been that close. It would only be natural for him to be concerned about his goddaughter's welfare.

Once again, it was difficult to come up with answers that didn't reveal too much insider information. He didn't need to know about her mother's direct connection to Owen, or that Abby's friendship with the police chief had gotten them inside the jail to visit Owen. Finally, she settled for saying, "You'd have to talk to Chief Logan directly if you want to know more about Owen's situation."

Before he could ask her any other awkward questions, she checked the time. "Oops, I've got to go. I hadn't realize how late it had gotten."

"Same here, Ms. McCree. I'm due somewhere myself."

Without another word, he walked away, leaving her staring at his back. After one last glance into the insurance office, she headed toward her car. It really was time to get back home and do something to relax. Maybe she'd work out in the yard for a while and put all this murder stuff out of her mind. Zeke would probably appreciate the opportunity to bask in the sun while she weeded the flowerbeds.

As she drove the short distance back to the house, she considered the few bits of information she'd gleaned from her brief conversation with Jada's godfather. Once again her mind filled with the image of a bunch of mismatched puzzle pieces that hadn't yet come together to form a cohesive whole. Still, she had more pieces now than she'd had before she left home. If she could fit a few together in her mind, though, maybe they would point her in the right direction to ask further questions.

It might help if she laid it all out for Tripp, to see what he thought. There was one big problem with that idea. The man wouldn't be happy she'd been talking with a total stranger. It might be smarter to keep the information to herself for a while longer.

As she turned into her driveway, she vowed to remain positive about the situation. With all of Gage's experience and training, surely he would be able to figure out how Owen's chef knife had ended up at the crime scene. With luck, the explanation wouldn't end up with her mother's new boyfriend spending the rest of his life behind bars. With that happy thought, she headed inside and changed into her gardening clothes.

When she was done, she called Zeke to her side. "Come on, boy. Let's go outside. You can supervise while I work."

Then she looked around the yard. "And if you don't mind, keep an eye out for any unsavory characters who might decide to pay us a visit."

And bless the big mastiff mix, he woofed his agreement and trotted off to lie down where he could keep watch. Feeling better knowing the dog had her back, Abby gathered up her yard tools and got to work. As she dug in the rich soil, she really wished she could vanquish her concerns about Mitch Anders's death as easily as she could the weeds around the azaleas.

CHAPTER 14

In Abby's experience, phone calls in the middle of the night were never a good thing. Her heart racing, she jerked upright and fumbled for her cell phone on the bedside table. Seeing Gage Logan's name on the caller ID only made it that much worse. "Gage?"

"I hate to bother you, Abby, but I need a favor."

If it had been anyone else, she would've demanded details before agreeing to the request, but Gage wouldn't have called her if it wasn't important. "Sure thing. What do you need me to do at"—she held up the phone to double-check the time—"three in the morning?"

"Sorry, but it's not like I can schedule these things."

Her pulse pounded in her head as she said, "It's okay, Gage. Just tell me what's up."

"I understand you know Jada Davidson. Is that true?"

Was that a trick question? Only one way to find out. "I

met her briefly. Owen asked Mom and me to stop by to check on her for him after the first time we visited him at the jail. That's the only time I've ever talked to her."

There was a long silence before Gage responded. "Interesting. That makes me wonder why she asked me to call you instead of someone she knows better."

Good question. Abby sat on the side of the bed and did her best to gather up her scattered thoughts. "Well, she seemed pretty upset about the situation with Owen, especially coming so soon after the death of her father. I don't know why exactly, but I got the impression she didn't have anyone to talk to. As Mom and I were leaving, I gave Jada my phone number and told her to call me if she needed anything."

She stood up and walked over to look out the window, at the same time bracing herself for the worst. "What's happened to Jada? Is she okay?"

"Not exactly. Someone broke into her house tonight. She wasn't hurt, but Jada is understandably pretty shaken up. I don't blame her. It looks like the perp first tried to pick the lock, but the dead bolt probably kept him from getting in. He finally gave up and kicked the front door off its hinges. The noise alone probably scared her half to death. When I asked if there was a friend she could crash with for the night, she gave me your name."

"Of course she can come here. Tell Jada I'll be there in about twenty minutes."

"Thanks, Abby. I owe you."

After hanging up, she grabbed yesterday's jeans and a clean shirt before heading into the bathroom. She splashed water on her face and brushed her teeth to make herself feel a little more human. Next, she ran upstairs to open her mother's door.

"Mom, sorry to wake you up, but I have to go out for a while. I shouldn't be gone long."

Her mother sat up in bed. "What's happened?"

Abby filled her in on the few details she knew. "Anyway, Gage asked if I could pick up Jada and bring her here. It shouldn't take long, but I didn't want you to wake up and find me gone with no explanation."

"Do you want me to come, too?"

Abby considered the idea but rejected it. Waiting for her mother to get dressed would only delay things. "That's okay. Go back to sleep if you can. I'll let you know when we get back."

"I'll try, but I'm pretty wide-awake now."

"Either way, I'll see you soon."

Abby turned on the outside lights and grabbed her purse off the counter. Tripp was a pretty light sleeper, so it was no surprise when he stepped out on his own porch before she'd even reached her car.

"What's up, Abby?"

"Gage called. Someone broke into Jada Davidson's house. I'm going to bring her back here for the night."

"Give me a minute to put on some shoes and lock up."

He disappeared back into the house before she could protest, not that she really wanted to. Ordinarily, she felt pretty safe in Snowberry Creek. But with both a killer and now a burglar on the loose, it was better to err on the side of caution.

Tripp made it in record time. He was dressed in baggy sweatpants and a plain white cotton T-shirt, probably what he'd worn to bed. She fought the urge to smile at how cute and rumpled he looked with his hair uncombed and his jaw shadowed with a bit of scruff.

"Does Gage have any idea who did it?"

"He didn't say, but I'm guessing not. However, someone kicked the door off the hinges, so Jada's understandably a bit freaked out by the situation."

Tripp muttered something under his breath, probably a couple of those choice words he only used when the situation was dire. She didn't blame him. Abby had her own past experience with coming under attack in her own home. No one deserved to live with that kind of fear.

It only took a few minutes to reach Jada's neighborhood. Even if Abby hadn't known right where she lived, it would've been obvious with all the police cruisers parked out front with their flashing red and blue lights illuminating the entire block. Clusters of neighbors had gathered up and down the street to see what was going on. She hated that poor Jada was going to be the subject of neighborhood gossip through no fault of her own.

Abby parked two doors down, which was as close as she could get. Tripp joined her on the side of the road while they studied the situation before they started walking toward the nearest deputy. Fortunately, it was someone Abby knew, at least by name.

"Deputy Lund, can you tell me where Chief Logan is? He's expecting me."

The woman nodded. "Sure thing, Ms. McCree. He told me you'd be arriving soon. Gage is in the house, but he won't want you to come inside while they're processing the area."

After she made a quick call, Gage stepped out on the porch a few seconds later. He motioned for them to come closer. If he was surprised to see Tripp with her, he gave no sign of it. "Sorry to drag you two out like this, but I really appreciate that you came."

"Anytime."

Abby looked past him at the splintered wood that had formed the frame round the door. It had taken a lot of effort to do that much damage. She shuddered to think how the sound alone must have terrified Jada.

"How is she doing?"

"Not good. As soon as she heard the door slam open, she locked herself in the bathroom and called us. A deputy was only two blocks away on routine patrol and responded almost immediately. Even so, it probably felt like forever to her. Regardless, whoever broke in never got close to her. The perpetrator took off as soon as he or she heard the siren. The EMTs checked Jada over just in case."

He turned back to look inside the house. "Right now, she's with one of my deputies, packing a bag. It shouldn't take much longer, and then you can take her back to your place. I don't know if she'll be able to unwind for a while, but some sleep would definitely help."

"Don't worry, Gage. We'll take good care of her. If all else fails, Tripp can make her a big mug of his special tea."

He dredged up a weary smile. "I could use a big dose of that myself. Seriously, I wish I knew what this town was coming to."

Someone inside called Gage's name. "I'll be back in a minute."

The night air was chilly enough she was sorry she hadn't put on a sweater before leaving the house. She rubbed her arms, which were covered in goose bumps. Tripp must have noticed because he moved closer and wrapped his arm around her shoulders. "Do you have a jacket or anything in the car?"

"No, but I'll start keeping one in there after this."

He shot her an amused look. "Are you planning on having a lot of these late-night adventures?"

"I hope not."

She eyed the thin T-shirt he was wearing. "Maybe I should stash one of your sweatshirts in the car, too, since you seem inclined to invite yourself along on all my escapades."

Tripp grinned. "Good thinking. And while you're putting together an emergency kit, a thermos of hot coffee would be nice, too."

He wasn't wrong about that. What else should be on their list? "How about few of Bridey's peach muffins to go with the coffee?"

"And some lawn chairs. Might as well be comfortable while we wait."

When she laughed, a couple of the deputies glanced in their direction, probably wondering what the two of them could possibly find amusing at a crime scene. Abby winced, wishing she could explain that she knew full well there was nothing funny about this situation. But sometimes humor was the only way to deal with all the bad stuff life threw at people.

She noticed Tripp scanning the area as if something bothered him about it. "Is something wrong?"

"Not sure." He released his hold on her long enough to slowly do a three-sixty turn, his eyes narrowing as he studied their surroundings. "I've spent too many nights out on patrol wondering if someone was out there in the darkness watching my every move. I really hate standing out in the open like this. Even if the guy who did this took off, there's no guarantee he stayed gone. If he did come sneaking back to watch, he's going to know we were here. When Jada gets in your car, it won't take a genius to know that she's going to be at your house. I really wish Gage had left you out of this."

"You're scaring me, Tripp."

All signs of his earlier humor were gone, replaced by a grim expression. "I'm sorry, but I need to know you'll be extra careful. For sure I'll be camping out on your couch the rest of tonight. Longer if necessary."

She knew better than to argue with him when he got all hyperprotective like this, and she wasn't sure she would even try anyway. She'd rest easier knowing he was close by, and Jada would likely draw comfort from knowing someone was on guard.

"I appreciate that, Tripp, although it's doubtful any of us are going to get much sleep tonight."

Gage reappeared on the porch with a small suitcase in hand and Jada standing right behind him. Abby started forward, but he motioned for her to stay where she was. He took Jada's elbow and gently escorted her across the yard to where Abby and Tripp stood waiting. "Ms. Davidson is ready to go, Abby. I'll give you a ring later this morning to set up a time to come by."

Jada definitely looked ragged around the edges, her face pale and her eyes full of fear. "I'm sorry to bother you like this, Ms. McCree, but I didn't know who else to call."

"Not a problem, Jada. I'm glad you did. This is my neighbor and friend, Tripp Blackston. He came along for the ride because, well, to be honest, he's just plain nosy."

That remark earned her an elbow in the ribs from Tripp and a small smile from Jada. "If you've got everything you need, why don't we head out? You've had a rough night, but it won't take us long to get to my place. I have a guest room you're welcome to use as long as you need it. I should warn you that my mom is probably in the kitchen cooking up a storm. In my family, food is the answer to most of life's problems."

Tripp took the suitcase from Gage. "She's not kidding, Ms. Davidson, so I hope you packed your appetite."

The four of them walked down the street to where they'd left the car. Tripp opened the front passenger door for Jada and then settled himself in the back seat. Abby hung back until the other two were inside with the doors closed. Turning her back to the car, she kept her voice low as she talked to Gage. "Don't worry about Jada for tonight. We'll take good care of her."

"I know you will. I feel better about her going home with you than with someone I don't know. Until we figure out what's going on and if this has any connection to what happened the other night at the park, I don't like the idea of her being alone."

He glanced back toward Jada's home. "Especially after this."

"She won't be alone. Tripp already plans to camp out on my couch. He's afraid whoever did this is out there watching us right now and might follow us back to the house."

Gage took off his hat and ran his fingers through his hair, clearly frustrated. "I wish I could say he's wrong about that."

When Abby shivered this time, it had nothing to do with the cool night air. "See you later, Gage. I hope you're able to get some rest, too."

One of the deputies stepped out on Jada's porch and called his name. "I'd better go. Keep an eye out, Abby, and don't hesitate to call if you need us."

"Will do."

Slipping into the driver's seat, she started the car and immediately cranked up the heat. They hadn't been there long enough for the engine to have gotten cold, so warm air immediately poured out of the vents.

"Let me know if it gets too hot in here."

"The heat feels good." Jada shifted in her seat to look more directly at Abby. "I apologize again for dragging you into this. If you'd rather not get involved, you can drop me off at the motel in town. I can afford it."

"Sorry, but that's not happening. Even if Gage wouldn't get ticked off about it, my mother would have my head. As soon as I walked in the door without you, we'd be right back in the car and on our way to retrieve you." She softened her response with a smile. "Seriously, we're glad you had Gage call."

Jada turned away to stare out into the night. "I do have friends, but most are away at school."

But that didn't explain why she hadn't called her godfather. Of course, Will Swahn hadn't actually said that he lived in Snowberry Creek. Now wasn't the time to be asking questions. The poor girl had had a rough night, and she didn't need to face an inquisition from an almost total stranger on top of everything else.

It was time to lighten the conversation. "You've met Tripp and my mom, but I should warn you about my roommate, Zeke. He means well, but he has a few bad habits. For one thing, he drools copiously."

Tripp chimed in from the back seat. "He also sheds like crazy, lives to mooch, and snores like a freight train."

A small smile tugged at the corners of Jada's mouth. "Zeke sounds charming. In fact, better than some guys I've dated. I can't wait to meet him."

Abby turned into the driveway and spotted her mom

and Zeke looking out the front window. As soon as they saw her car, they disappeared from sight, no doubt heading for the back door to meet them in the kitchen. "Well, brace yourself because you're about to."

The car had barely come to a stop when Zeke came bounding across the yard. Jada's eyes flared wide in surprise. "You didn't mention he is huge. What kind of dog is he?"

At least she didn't sound scared. "He was a rescue dog, so we don't know much about Zeke's background. Near as we can tell, he's mastiff mixed with who knows what. I know it's hard to believe, he's actually on the small size for that breed. He weighs about ninety-five pounds, but purebreds can weigh in at a hundred and fifty or more."

She opened her car door and tried to snag Zeke's collar, but he danced back out of reach and charged around to the other side of the car to greet his buddy. Tripp knelt on one knee and held on to Zeke's collar to give Jada time to exit the vehicle without being knocked around by one of the dog's enthusiastic greetings.

"Zeke, meet Jada."

The dog's tail thumped the grass hard to show he was happy to see her, but at least he remained seated. Jada held out her hand for him to sniff and was rewarded with one of the dog's patented slobbery licks. Her laughter eased some of Abby's worry about how the girl was handling the night's events.

"Come on, everyone, let's head inside."

With his uncanny sense of who needed him the most, Zeke remained right by Jada's side all the way into the kitchen and then parked himself right at her feet with his big head taking up most of her lap. Tripp took his usual seat. When Abby sat down next him, she saw that the oven was on and there were a couple of skillets on the stove. Just as she predicted, her mom had been busy cooking, and the air was filled with the tantalizing scents of sausage and bacon.

As her mother handed out plates and flatware, she smiled at Jada. "It's nice to see you again, although I'm sorry it's under these circumstances. I hope you're hungry. I tend to cook when I'm worried."

Jada's cheeks flushed a bit pink. "I don't mean to be a bother."

"You're not a bother at all. Besides, Abby feels obligated to feed Tripp every time he walks through the door. I suspect it's part of his lease."

Abby might've taken offense at that if her mother hadn't winked at Tripp as she said it.

He took the jibe in the spirit in which it had been made. "I do my part to keep her busy and out of trouble."

Now Abby was the one who acted offended. "Hey, now."

The teasing exchange had Jada looking a little more relaxed. To help with that, Abby left the table long enough to grab a few of Zeke's favorite treats. She set them down on the table within easy reach for Jada but far enough from the edge to make it harder for Zeke to sneak one with a quick flick of his tongue.

A few seconds later, the table was loaded with a huge bowlful of scrambled eggs and a platter filled with sausage and bacon.

Tripp took it all in with a happy, wide-eyed look. "I'm impressed, Mrs. McCree, especially considering we weren't even gone an hour."

Her mother seemed pleased by Tripp's comment. She

sat down at the opposite end of the table. "Eat up, every-body. I'm sure this will be another busy day, so we should get some sleep while we have the chance."

She passed the eggs to Jada. "I turned down the bed in the room across from Abby's and laid out some clean towels in case you want to take a shower. "

"Thank you, Mrs. McCree. I appreciate everything you all have done for me, a total stranger."

Her mother smiled. "Not a total stranger, Jada. Even if we hadn't met before tonight, we would've been glad to help. After all, any friend of Owen Quinn's is a friend of ours."

Jada had been about to take a bite of her eggs when she suddenly dropped her fork as her face crumpled and tears started pouring down her cheeks. Before Abby could ask her what was wrong, the girl was up and stumbling down the hall. A second later, the bathroom door slammed shut.

Tripp looked confused. "What the heck just happened?"

Abby shook her head. "I don't know. Maybe she's been putting up a brave front, and everything finally just overwhelmed her. I'll go see if I can help."

After grabbing Jada's small suitcase, she headed the short distance down the hall to the bathroom. She set the case down and listened at the door for a few seconds be-fore knocking. "Jada, can you let me in? I can't help you from out here."

Nothing but silence.

She tried again. "Please, Jada. I know you've been through a lot. If you don't want to talk, that's fine. At least let me take you upstairs and show you where you'll be staying. I should warn you that Zeke is probably going to want to get up on the bed, and he likes to hog all the space he can."

There was a slight movement on the other side of the door, followed by the sound of splashing water. A few seconds later, the door opened just far enough to reveal Jada's face. It was impossible to tell if the few droplets that still clung to her skin were leftover tears or water from washing her face.

"Are you all right?"

Jada didn't bother to lie. "No, I'm really not."

When Abby gently pushed on the door, Jada stepped back to allow her to come inside. "Is it what happened tonight, or something else?"

She was betting it was the latter. The girl had been holding it together right up until the second Abby's mother had mentioned Owen's name. Jada's reaction had been similar when they'd been at her house. When they'd pressed her for details about the unexplained twenty or so minutes he'd been gone during the movie, she'd reacted by asking them to leave. The panicky expression was also the same.

She gave Jada a considering look, aiming for sympathetic and not sure she was successful from the way Jada wrapped her arms around herself and backed away as far as the small room would allow. To ease the tension, Abby dug a clean washcloth out of the cabinet under the sink and wet it with cool water.

"Hold that on your eyes for a little bit. They'll feel better. I left your suitcase out in the hall. Take it and head up the stairs to the first room on your left, which is where you'll be sleeping. There's a bathroom right next door, so you can get ready for bed. Meanwhile, I'm going to go heat up your plate and then bring it up to your room. Maybe it will be easier for you to eat something if you're not having to face all of us at once."

Jada shook her head just a little. "Maybe just some toast. I'm not all that hungry, and my stomach's a little iffy from the stress."

"Okay, I'll bring toast and a cup of the herbal tea that helps when I'm feeling a little unsettled."

Abby started to leave but decided she needed to give Jada something to think about. "Look, I know you don't really know us, but you trusted us enough to have Gage call me. Ordinarily, I wouldn't push, especially considering everything that's happened tonight and the fact none of us have had much sleep."

She paused to let Jada digest that much. "But whatever you're hiding or holding back is only complicating things. Not only for you, but for Owen. Maybe you're protecting yourself or someone else, but that's not going to work long term. Gage needs to know if tonight's occurrence is somehow tied to what happened at the park the other night. He won't stop until he has all the answers. You need to make better choices before your secret blows up in your face."

"I'll think about it."

Abby's words had clearly worried Jada. Good. But rather than press any harder for answers when they were both exhausted and running on fumes, she stepped out into the hall to give Jada time and space to collect her thoughts. Hopefully, she'd pushed just enough to make the girl come to her senses. The only way to tell was to see if Jada would head upstairs to her assigned room or out the front door.

Not that Abby would let her get far, not at this hour, and not with the still very real possibility that whoever had kicked in Jada's door had followed them home. There was no telling how Jada would react to being chased down only to be herded back to the house. If necessary, they could always take her to that motel Jada had mentioned earlier, but that would be a last-ditch choice. Fortunately, Abby had barely made it as far as the kitchen when she heard the bathroom door open again, followed by the tell-tale creak of the steps that led up to the second floor. Good, Jada was smart enough to make at least one good decision.

Her mother and Tripp were still seated at the table when Abby returned. Both of them looked up as she dropped back into her own chair. "That poor girl has hit her limit. I promised to fix her some toast and tea. After that, I'm going to go back to bed. I don't know about you two, but I'm about to crash and burn myself."

"Did she tell you anything?"

"No, but I made it clear that it's obvious that she's hid-ing something. I also told her that's likely to blow up in her face if she doesn't tell someone what's going on."

Her mother frowned. "Do you think that was wise?"

Boy, she really hated being second-guessed. Before she could come up with a reply that wouldn't result in the two of them launching into another major battle, Tripp spoke up. His expression remained calm, but his voice had enough gravel in it to convey his disapproval.

"There are no rule books in this kind of situation, Mrs. McCree. All anyone can do is make the best call with the information at hand. Abby had obviously done something right when it comes to dealing with Jada, since the girl reached out to her for help tonight. Now we wait and see what happens next."

He stood up and headed for the back door. "Zeke,

you're with me. We need to do a quick patrol. I'm going to grab my gear from my place, and then I'll be back to sleep on the couch."

Man and dog disappeared out into the night before either Abby or her mother could respond. Lucky them. Her mother stared at the closed door for a few seconds and then sighed. "I didn't mean to sound critical."

But she had, another reminder that the two of them still needed that talk about boundaries. Now wasn't the time for that, though. "I've got to make the toast and tea for Jada."

She popped two slices of bread into the toaster and put a large mug of water in the microwave to heat. While she waited, she scraped the remaining eggs into Zeke's bowl, knowing he'd appreciate the extra treat. When she had the toast buttered and the tea ready, she set them on a tray. "I'll see you tomorrow morning, Mom."

Then she looked at the clock. "Well, I guess what I should say is that I'll see you later this morning. Gage will be coming by at some point, but he promised to call first. I have my cell, so I'll let you know when I hear from him."

"That sounds good. Should I wait for Tripp to come in before going upstairs?"

Abby crossed over to look out the window, where she could see Tripp and Zeke prowling along the edge of the yard and heading back to his place. "They shouldn't be much longer. There's a pillow and a blanket in the hall closet. I'm sure he'd appreciate it if you would lay them on the sofa for him."

Her mom looked glad to have something constructive to do. Leaving her to it, Abby carried the tea and toast up to Jada's room, only to find the younger woman was already sound asleep. It was tempting to close the door to afford Jada a little more privacy, but she hadn't been kidding about Zeke wanting to keep an eye on their visitor. In fact, she'd leave her own door open a little in case Jada called out during the night.

Rather than let the tea and toast go to waste, Abby curled up in the chair in the corner of her bedroom and enjoyed them herself. As she sipped the tea, she let the quiet of the night settle around her. A few minutes later, she heard the deep rumble of Tripp's voice saying something to Zeke. That was followed by the familiar sound of the dog coming up the stairs. He poked his head into her room long enough to check on her. When she held out the last corner of the toast, he dutifully came in to accept the small treat.

She patted his big head. "As much as I'd love your company, big guy, I suspect Jada needs it more. There's something going on with her, and she might sleep better knowing you were on duty tonight."

As always, she wondered exactly how much the dog understood. Way more than most people would give him credit for, especially when he gave her a quick lick before trotting back out the door and across the hall.

She set her mug and empty plate on the table next to the chair and headed for the bathroom to get ready for bed for the second time in one night. It was bound to be another roller-coaster day, but for now she'd sleep more soundly knowing that both Tripp and Zeke stood between the three women in the house and whoever might be lurking out there in the night.

CHAPTER 15

Being jarred out of a sound sleep for the second time in less than six hours was truly hateful. Abby patted her hand across the surface of the bedside table until she finally located the phone. With one arm over her eyes to block out the sunshine streaming in through the window, she did her best to sound coherent when she finally answered the call.

"Morning, Gage."

At least he refrained from laughing at her grumpy tone. "I'd ask if I woke you up, but the answer to that question is pretty obvious. Sorry, Abby."

She blinked at the phone screen to check the time and saw that it was a little after nine. "It's okay, Gage. I should be getting up anyway, since I've got houseguests."

"I know you do. How did it go with Jada last night?"

How much should she say? Was it wrong to share her

suspicions that Jada was hiding something that had happened on the night of the murder? Yeah, even her sleep-deprived brain knew it was. It would be better to give Jada the chance to tell Gage what he needed to know. She also didn't want to cause the poor girl trouble if the secret had nothing to do with Mitch Anders's murder. Better to err on the side of caution.

"She was understandably shaken up by what happened last night, but she kept it together until we got to the house. There were a few tears right before she went up to bed. However, I'm guessing she made it through the rest of the night okay, although I don't know that for sure. I slept like a rock myself. For sure Zeke didn't raise any alarms, and I think he would have."

"That's good. You can tell her that there was no more trouble at the house last night, and the local handyman I contacted said he would get her door fixed today."

"She'll be grateful that you're helping her out, Gage. I assume you're coming over this morning."

"Yep, but I've got a couple of things to take care of before I head your way. I'm hoping to be there in about an hour. Say, a little after ten. Will that work for you?"

As tempting as it was to go back to sleep, that wasn't practical. "Sure thing. I'll let Jada and everyone else know."

"See you soon."

After hanging up, she stared at the ceiling for a minute or two, giving her body and brain time to get in sync before getting out of bed. Sometimes she waited until after breakfast to shower and get dressed rather than hitting the floor running. Unfortunately, this wasn't going to be one of those days. She didn't care what her mother thought of the faded tank top and flannel shorts she'd slept in; she'd seen Abby in far worse. But throwing Tripp and Jada into the mix, it would be better if she made herself presentable before heading downstairs.

Sighing, she threw back the covers and began her day.

Twenty minutes later, Abby started down the steps. She paused long enough to identify the voices coming from the kitchen as belonging to her mother and Tripp. Where was Jada? The door to her room had been open and the bed made. Either she was being extra quiet or she was gone. Hoping that wasn't the case, Abby hustled on down the stairs to find out. Gage would need to know if the girl had disappeared.

She skidded to a stop just outside the kitchen door. She backed up a step into the hall to buy herself a little time to rein in her panic. Luckily, both her mother and Jada had their backs toward her. Tripp had just turned away from the counter. He briefly glanced toward Jada before turning his attention back to Abby. He screwed on the lid of the to-go cup in his hand as she drew a slow breath and started forward again. Feeling far calmer, she said, "Listen, mister, you better have left enough coffee for me."

After stepping aside to allow Abby easy access to the coffeemaker, Tripp spoke to Jada. "I spent two decades in the Special Forces, and I'm trained in all kinds of combat. With that in mind, believe me when I say there's no way I'll ever again risk getting between Abby and her first cup of coffee in the morning. I won't scare you with the details of what happened the one time I made that mistake, but it was ugly."

Abby rolled her eyes at the imaginary story. "Don't

tell lies about me, Tripp. Everyone knows I'm a morning person."

Her mother snorted. "Since when? Or have you forgotten how much fun your high school years were, when school started at seven thirty in the morning? I swear, some days it took dynamite to blast you out of bed."

"All right, you two. That's enough. I'm not that bad."

That claim had both her mother and Tripp snickering. It was no fun being picked on when she wasn't yet operating at full speed, but at least the conversation had Jada smiling. Abby aimed her next comment directly to her. "Did you sleep well last night or did Zeke's snoring keep you awake?"

The younger woman patted the dog's head and looked a bit insulted on his behalf. "He doesn't snore that loudly. In fact, it was sort of a comforting rumble."

Abby added cream and an unhealthy dose of sugar to her coffee. "I can't dispute that. It's kind of like white noise that blocks out other sounds and makes it easier to sleep."

She took a tub of peach yogurt from the fridge and sat down at the table. "Have all of you already eaten?"

Tripp was the first to answer. "Your mom was nice enough to make oatmeal for the three of us."

He edged closer to the door. "I have class this morning, so I'm going to head back over to my place. I'll be back early this afternoon, but text if you need anything."

"Will do. We should be fine, though. Gage will be here pretty soon." She followed him to the door. "Thanks for staying over last night."

"Anytime. See you later, ladies." He looked toward her mother and Jada and finally at Abby. Maybe she was fooling herself into thinking that he kicked it up a notch when he smiled at her, but she didn't think so. The brief connection brightened her whole mood.

If her mother had noticed, she gave no indication of it. "So, Chief Logan is on his way?"

Abby checked the time. "He called to say he should be here a little after ten."

She took a bite of her yogurt while gauging Jada's reaction to the knowledge Gage was already headed their way. Although she didn't say anything, her hand trembled just slightly as she continued to pet Zeke. If Abby hadn't been sitting so close, she might've been fooled into thinking Jada was not at all concerned about the upcoming discussion with Gage. It would be interesting to see how long that façade of calm held up once he started asking questions.

"Oh, I almost forgot. He said a handyman will fix your door today."

At least that bit of news eased some of the tension that surrounded Jada like a second skin. "That's good news. Once that's done, it should be safe for me to go back home." Her eyes widened. "Sorry, if that sounds like I'm ungrateful for you letting me stay here last night. I just figured you'd be glad to have your house back to yourself."

That was true, but it wasn't just Jada who was cluttering up the place. As far as Abby was concerned, her mother was the bigger problem. To avoid letting any hint of that idea show in her expression, she concentrated on consuming her coffee and yogurt. At least neither her mom nor Jada seemed inclined to indulge in idle chat. She couldn't help but notice that they both kept glancing at the clock, maybe counting down the minutes until Gage arrived.

She finished the last of her yogurt and was washing out the container when the front doorbell chimed. After tossing the empty tub into the recycling bin under the sink, she wiped her hands on her jeans and headed for the door. Zeke got there ahead of her and stood wagging his tail as he waited for Abby to let another of his friends inside.

"Hi, Gage. Come on in."

He rivaled Tripp in size and took up a lot of room as he stepped into the entryway. The man was smart enough to know what was expected of him when Zeke flopped on the floor and rolled over to demand a good belly rub. As Gage knelt by the dog to do a proper job of it, he gave her a questioning look, keeping his face low. "How are things going this morning?"

She shrugged. "Well enough, I guess. Mom and Jada are waiting in the kitchen, but Tripp left for class. By the way, Jada hopes to return to her own place once the door gets fixed. I'm not sure that's a good idea."

Gage straightened up to his full height. "We'll make that part of the conversation. And depending how that goes, she might not have much say in where she spends the night."

Abby closed the door and followed Gage back down the hall toward the kitchen. As his words replayed in her head, all she could think was that his pronouncement didn't sound ominous at all. No, not a bit. Poor Jada.

CHAPTER 16

When Abby and Gage reached the kitchen, her mother and Zeke sat flanking Jada, making their loyalties clear. Both would stand with her against Gage. Abby wasn't surprised by her mother's choice. The woman already had issues with the man because of Owen. Zeke, on the other hand, was most likely picking up on Jada's distress and was doing his best to offer comfort.

Maybe she was overanalyzing the situation, but she didn't think so. Regardless, Abby couldn't bring herself to take the empty seat next to Jada's nor the one closer to Gage, for fear it would make Jada feel as if they were ganging up on her. After pouring Gage some coffee, she leaned against the counter, the closest to a neutral corner she could find within the limited space of her kitchen.

Gage added cream and sugar to his mug before taking

out the small spiral notebook that he always used in these circumstances. The county homicide detective had one that was similar, so she always figured it was a cop thing. After he opened it to a new page, he picked up his pen and leaned forward, elbows on the table.

"So, Ms. Davidson, I want you to walk me through what happened last night. Take it slow, the more detail the better. You never know what will end up being important."

Jada's fingers dug deeper into Zeke's fur as if needing his undemanding support. "I went to bed around ten thirty. I've been sleeping in my dad's room instead of mine. I feel closer to him that way. Like he's not really gone, but just away for a while."

Abby hurt so much for Jada, hating that this was all so hard for her. Jada kept her attention trained on the table rather than making direct eye contact with anyone. "The house was quiet, just the usual night sounds. The next thing I know, I heard a loud bang coming from the other end of the house, like something hit the front door hard. At first, I thought I was dreaming, but then it happened a second time. The third time, I heard wood splintering and a loud crash. Realizing someone had broken into the house, I locked myself in the bathroom and called the police."

Her story coasted to a stop while she took a drink of water. After setting the glass aside, she picked up from where she'd left off. "The dispatcher said an officer was close by and to stay right where I was until Deputy Sotot arrived and identified himself."

She finally looked directly at Gage. "My heart was pounding so hard I couldn't really hear much by that point. I huddled down in the tub with the shower curtain closed until the deputy knocked on the bathroom door. Once he gave me his name and badge number, I came out. You and the others arrived shortly after that."

By that point in the narrative, Abby's mother had a firm grasp on one of Jada's hands, offering what comfort she could. Zeke did his part, too, by keeping his head on her lap and grumbling softly to show his concern.

Gage kept writing until he caught up with Jada's narrative. "I know you didn't have much time to look around last night, but did you notice anything at all that was missing?"

She shook her head. "No, only the stuff that got tossed around in the living room. You know, like the couch cushions thrown on the floor. He also pulled a few things out of the coat closet, like he was looking for something. None of the other rooms looked as if they'd been touched, so maybe he ran out of time before he got that far. I'll be able to say more for certain once I start putting everything back where it belongs."

Gage glanced up from his notes. "You said 'he,' indicating a single male person. Is there any reason you think it had to be a man? Could it have been a woman? Or even more than one person?"

Jada paused to think. "I guess I just assumed it had to be a man since it would take a lot of strength to kick the door in like that. I have no idea if he was alone. Like I said, I couldn't hear much of anything once I locked myself in the bathroom."

After jotting down a few things, Gage picked up where he'd left off. "Can you think of anything specific the perpetrator might have been looking for? Something of value that would explain why the guy didn't simply grab the easy stuff like your laptop, which was sitting out in plain sight?"

Jada's face paled. "No, nothing of special value. My mother had some nice jewelry, but it's in the safety deposit box at the bank. Any important paperwork is in the locked filing cabinet in the bedroom Dad used for his home office. It didn't appear to have been opened, but I can double-check that when I get home. I did a lot of filing for him, so I know what should be there."

"Go back to earlier in the day. What time did you get home and where were you coming from?"

"I'd been at school most of the day. I missed some classes after Dad died, and I'm still playing catch-up." She bit her lower lip and frowned. "I didn't feel like cooking, so I went through a drive-up to get a burger and salad. I went straight home from there."

"When you got to the house, did you park in the driveway or in the garage?"

"The garage. I went inside through the door that leads straight into the kitchen."

Gage kept writing as he fired another question at her. "For the few seconds you waited for the door to roll up out of the way, did you look around at all? If so, did you see anything or anyone in the area? Maybe someone who didn't belong there? Take your time and really think about it."

Jada did as he asked, slowly sipping her drink. "None of my neighbors were outside. Not that I noticed, anyway. I remember a car driving by, though. Normally, I wouldn't have paid any attention. Even though it's a pretty quiet neighborhood, we do get some traffic when people miss their turn on the main road and use our loop to turn around. I only noticed this time because the car was moving slowly, like the driver was looking for an address, but then it suddenly picked up speed and took off. I never got a look at the driver."

"Can you give me any kind of description of the vehicle itself?"

"It was a dark color. Black . . . no, it was blue. One of the smaller style SUVs. No idea what make, though."

"Not a problem. Is there anything else you can think of about that day?"

When she shook her head, Gage quietly set his pen back down. He looked relaxed, but the methodical way he moved made Abby suspect his calm demeanor only went skin deep. Fear for what was going to come next ratcheted up her own tension. It was unclear if her mother had picked up on the dark undercurrents, but Jada looked as if she was about to bolt for the closest exit.

Gage finally leaned back in his chair, crossed his arms over his chest, and stared at Jada with that hard-eyed cop gaze that had no doubt broken many a desperate criminal. Abby hated seeing him use it on Jada, but surely he wouldn't go all tough cop on the girl unless it was warranted.

"That takes care of last night, Ms. Davidson." But before anyone could relax, he added, "But I still have questions about what happened at the park the other night."

Abby's mother rushed to intercede before Jada could respond. "Don't you think she's been through enough for now, Chief Logan?"

Interfering with Gage's investigation was never a good idea. Abby tried to head her off at the pass by stepping toward the table. "Mom, don't—"

Gage waved her back. "Mrs. McCree, it's fine if you

want to sit with Jada. And if I have any questions you can answer, I'll aim them at you directly. Otherwise, remain quiet. If that's not possible, leave."

Her mother's eyes briefly widened in shock before narrowing in pure anger. "Excuse me, but this is my daughter's house, not your police station. If anyone needs to go, it's you."

Abby slammed her coffee cup down on the counter. This time she wouldn't be deterred by either her idiot of a parent or the angry cop in the room. "Mom, that's enough. You're way out of line here."

The woman didn't back down, not an inch. "No, I'm not."

"You're right about this being my house. I decide what goes on here, and I'm telling you to apologize to Gage and then leave the room. He's conducting the interview with Jada here because he thinks it would be less upsetting for her than meeting with him at the police station."

Jada shifted her gaze back and forth between Abby and her mother, her mouth hanging open in shock. Abby didn't check to see how Gage was reacting to yet another McCree family squabble. "Well?"

Hands on her hips, her mother snapped, "I can't believe you're still siding with him against your own mother."

Oh, brother! Seriously, when had the woman become such a drama queen? "Mom, playing the guilt card quit working when I was sixteen. This isn't a case of us versus him. It's a case of right and wrong—or have you forgotten this is a murder investigation?"

Her mother flinched as if Abby's words had delivered a physical blow. She deliberately turned away from both Abby and Gage to focus on Jada. "If you are uncomfortable with anything that man asks you, you are within your rights to ask that an attorney be present to protect your best interests."

Then she stalked out of the room and then up the stairs to the third floor. Even Gage winced when the sound of the bedroom door slamming echoed down the steps. It was tempting to go after her, but Abby stood her ground. She wasn't wrong. Gage had every right to interview Jada.

It was his job, for Pete's sake.

The flurry of powerful emotions left her badly shaken. It was time to sit down and try to restore some sense of calm in her mind. The best way would be to put as much distance between herself and everyone else as she could. But as bad as her mother's behavior had been, she'd been right about not leaving Jada to face Gage alone. She took a seat at the table, careful to make sure her chair was no closer to Jada's than it was to Gage's. "If it's okay, I'm going to stay. Jada, do you want another glass of water before Gage gets started again?"

"No, I'm fine."

The words were spoken without hesitation, even though it was clearly not true. Rather than argue, Abby settled back in her chair, hoping if she faked being calm that it would help keep the tension in the room to a manageable level. For his part, Gage cleared his throat. "Abby, I'm sorry to cause problems between you and your mother."

She waved him off. "It's not your fault. We'll work things out."

Eventually. Maybe, anyway. For now, she would really like to get this interview over with so she could move on to other things. Maybe it was time to break out some food, her patented cure-all for stressful situations. "Zeke needs to go out for a minute. Meanwhile, I'll fix us some snacks."

If Jada thought that was weird, she didn't say anything. At least Gage looked marginally more relaxed, no doubt recognizing her need to play hostess even if this wasn't exactly a social situation. She left the back door open after Zeke charged outside. While she waited for him to return, she made quick work of plating up some cheese and crackers. By the time she had everything ready, the dog was back in position next to Jada.

The small respite seemed to have helped all three of them get back on track. Jada put a few crackers and slices of cheese on her plate. Unsurprisingly, she left the food untouched as she asked, "I'm sorry, Chief Logan, but could you repeat that last question?"

"I need you to go through what happened the night of the murder. Start with leaving your house and go right up until you returned home."

It took a couple of deep breaths before Jada could get going with her narrative. "I met Mr. Quinn at the restaurant, so the two of us could set up the food truck together. I've only worked for him a short time, so I'm still learning the job."

Gage looked up from his notes. "I understand before that you worked for your father."

"That's right. I officially started helping out my dad in his office when I was just sixteen—answering phones, doing the filing, stuff like that. Even before that, I did similar clerical stuff for him in his home office. Our plan was for me to finish my business degree and then come work with him as a junior partner. Basically, I was learning the business from the ground up."

"Did you quit because someone else took over the office?"

"No, that wasn't my intention at all. I just planned to take a few days to get everything settled after Dad's death. I've only got what's left of this summer quarter, and then two more, before I graduate. But when I stopped by the office to see if Mr. Anders had any questions about where things were, he informed me that I didn't have a job."

Abby interjected herself into the conversation. "Why not? You'd think he'd appreciate having someone who already knew the business and the people here in town."

Jada's eyes looked shiny as if she were fighting the urge to cry. "That man actually said I never worked for the company in the first place. At least there was no record of me ever having been hired by the home office. All I can figure was that Dad was paying me himself somehow."

She briefly lapsed into silence as she nibbled on a cracker. Gage seemed willing to give her a little extra time to gather her thoughts. "What happened after that?"

"I went home. I was still too messed up from Dad's death to argue with him. I returned a few days later and told him I'd come to get our things . . . mostly Dad's stuff, actually. All I wanted were the personal items, nothing that belonged to the company. Mr. Anders refused to let me take anything and ordered me to leave. His excuse was that he hadn't had time to finish inventorying the place yet. He said it would take a few days, and then he'd call me to come pick up everything. He never did, though,

and wouldn't return my calls. Meanwhile, I started looking for a job."

Gage prompted her to continue when she seemed to
get lost in thought. "So that's when you went to work for
Quinn."

Jada nodded. "Yeah, I really needed to find another job
right away, and he had a spot open. My tuition will be
coming due soon, and I'm still trying to figure out where
I am financially. I'll probably need to hire someone to
help me wade through all the legal mumbo jumbo."

Gage moved on. "So the two of you loaded up the food
truck. Was everything in place? Did you notice anything
missing?"

"No, I didn't, but I'm pretty new to the business. I'm
still learning how it all works. If Mr. Quinn noticed anything weird, he didn't say so."

"Okay, go on from there."

The rest of Jada's narrative was pretty much on track
with what she'd told Abby and her mother when they'd
asked her the same kinds of questions. It was hard to figure out what Gage was thinking, but there was still something off about the sequence of events as she was laying
them out.

Jada had been looking directly at Gage right up until
when he pressed her on how long Owen stayed with her
when he supposedly checked on her during the movie. At
that point, she stared down at Zeke as if he were the most
riveting sight on earth. For an experienced cop like Gage,
it was like a shark scenting blood in the water, because he
immediately leaned in over the table as if trying to get
right up in the girl's face.

"What did the two of you talk about while he was there?"

"He, uh, wanted to know how many customers we'd had since he'd left me alone and if I thought we were running short of anything. You know, that kind of stuff."

Gage made a couple of notes and then flipped back through the pages in the notebook before launching another salvo. "Well, here's the thing. We've talked to a lot of people who were at the movie or just walking the trails at the park that night. Seems several of them claim to have seen you heading out of the park toward Main Street at just about the same time you and Owen claim to have been together."

He tapped his pen on his notes and then pointed at whatever was written there. "So here's my problem, Miss Davidson. Either all of these fine citizens of Snowberry Creek conspired to mislead me for no good reason, or else you and Owen lied to cover for each other. I regret to say I'm inclined to go with that latter option."

Jada sat in frozen silence with her eyes filled with pure panic and breathing as if she'd been running long and hard.

Gage wasn't done yet. "I have a murder to solve and a burglary that may or may not be connected to it. I swore an oath to protect the people of Snowberry Creek, and I can't do that if people are blocking me at every turn. I'm going to give you one more chance to tell me what really happened at the park, because I can't help but wonder what the two of you were up to that night that makes it necessary for you both to lie to me."

Jada's lack of response only made her appear guiltier by the moment.

"Let me make this perfectly clear, Miss Davidson." By this point, his voice was a low growl. "This is your last chance to convince me I shouldn't take you down to police headquarters and put you in the cell next to Owen's after you call an attorney."

For the first time, Abby understood how silence could be deafening.

CHAPTER 17

The clock on the wall counted off the seconds. Normally, Abby didn't notice the sound, but right now the ticking rattled around the silent room, stretching her nerves to the breaking point. If it bothered her so much, how much worse was it for Jada, the one actually in Gage's crosshairs?

Finally, the girl whispered, "I didn't kill Mitch Anders. I saw him, though, when he entered the park from one of the trails from the forest. He was carrying a lawn chair and a twelve-pack of some kind. As soon as I recognized him, I ducked down to make sure he wouldn't see me."

Her expression was bleak when she looked first at Abby and then at Gage. "You have no reason to believe me, but all of that's true. I never went near the man, and I have no idea where he sat to watch the movie. I never went further into the park than the parking lot where we'd set up the food truck."

She was speaking at a more normal volume now, maybe thanks in part to Gage giving her an encouraging nod. "Once the movie started, I didn't have any customers. It occurred to me that I might be able to retrieve Dad's stuff from the office. It was just some pictures and a few plaques for awards Dad had earned over the years. I mean, why wouldn't Mr. Anders just let me get my things and be done with it?"

Her question must have been hypothetical because she didn't pause long enough for either Gage or Abby to respond. "He'd already insisted that I turn in my set of office keys as well as Dad's, but he didn't know that we also kept a spare set at the house. I'd been carrying them with me in case I ever had a chance to sneak in when he wasn't around. I couldn't risk going during the day or when I didn't know where he was. But when he showed up at the movie, I thought it might be my only chance. I slipped away from the food truck and took a roundabout way to the back entrance of the office. I was inside no more than about ten minutes. He'd dumped most everything in a box in the supply closet."

Had the girl even considered what the repercussions would be if Mitch Anders had ever discovered the items were gone? If Jada was telling the truth, and the only things she'd taken had belonged to her and her father, she might as well have painted a target on her back. One call to the police, and it could've had a catastrophic effect on the girl's future.

It still might, especially if Gage decided to play hardball.

Suddenly curious, Abby asked, "Was one of the items was a large picture of some kind that used to hang in that blank spot on the wall behind your father's desk?"

Whoops, that instantly drew Gage's attention in her direction. At least he looked more puzzled than angry. "And how would you know about a blank spot on the wall?"

She gave Jada an apologetic look. "My current insurance agent is a longtime family friend, so I never had a reason to go into your dad's office. I happened to walk past it the other day. Curiosity got the best of me, so I stopped to look through the front window. The only odd thing I noticed was a big rectangle on the wall where the paint was several shades brighter than the area around it. I figured a large picture of some kind had been removed."

Jada nodded, looking as if that picture was one of the more important items she'd recovered. "My father was proud of the time he spent in the military. It was a photo of him with his unit."

Gage held up his hand before Jada could continue. "For now, let's just say you decided to pay an unscheduled visit to your father's office. Pick up the story from where you went from there."

After giving Gage a puzzled look, Jada did as he asked. "I, um, made a quick trip to my car, which was parked down the street at Mr. Quinn's restaurant. From there, it was a short jog back to the food truck. I stayed there until the movie ended. The only time I saw Mr. Quinn was when he stopped by in case I needed help to finish closing up, but I was already pretty much done. After that, I drove the truck back to the restaurant and unloaded everything that needed to go back inside."

Her forehead wrinkled as if something bothered her about that. Gage noticed it, too. "Something you want to tell me?"

Jada bit her lower lip and winced before answering. "I was surprised he didn't follow me back to the restaurant in case I needed help resetting the alarm. I guess he must have stayed with Mrs. McCree or something."

Abby could fill in that blank for her. "Tripp asked him for his help in packing up the tables we'd set up for vendors. That's where they were when my mother and I found the . . . well, you know. After that, we were all busy giving Gage our preliminary statements."

She didn't know if Jada knew Owen was the only one of them Gage had taken back to headquarters that night, and didn't see the need to bring that up now. While Abby might be getting used to the idea of her mother's relationship with the man, she hated that they still didn't know the depth of Owen Quinn's involvement with Mitch Anders. She still suspected the two men had known each other before Snowberry Creek. She didn't have any hard facts to back that up, but she'd learned to trust her gut feeling in these matters. Whether that relationship was innocent or not had yet to be determined. Either way, that was Gage's problem to deal with.

Right now she was more concerned about the break-in at Jada's house. Until they knew if it was a random event or connected to the murder, she wouldn't feel right letting her go back home, especially alone.

Gage closed his notebook. That left both Jada and Abby staring at him as they waited to see what came next. Finally, he pushed his chair back from the table as if preparing to leave, even though he made no move to do so. He studied Jada for several more seconds and then nodded, maybe to indicate that he'd made up his mind about something.

"For the moment, Jada, I'm not going to do anything about the fact you entered Mitch Anders's office without permission. Assuming you told me the truth about what you took and why, it's pretty much no harm, no foul. He's not around to sign a complaint, and I doubt the home office will care about your father's personal belongings."

For the first time all day, Jada had more color in her face, and her eyes look less haunted. Maybe confession really was good for the soul. It also meant that Gage and, by extension, Abby had a few more facts to piece together. If they accepted that Jada had finally given them the truth about her actions, it cleared her of any involvement in the murder.

That was the upside. The downside was that it left Owen Quinn without an alibi for the time he'd claimed to be checking on Jada. Abby really didn't want to be the one to tell her mother that interesting tidbit. The woman was already skating on the nearside of crazy, and this might just send her tumbling over the edge.

"So what happens next, Chief Logan?"

He left the table to set his empty cup and plate on the counter. "First up, Jada, I'd like you to come back to your house with me. I'm not quite ready for you to put things back in order yet. But if you're feeling up to it, I would really like you to go through the place again to see if anything is missing or if you can figure out what the guy was looking for."

Before answering, Jada gave Abby a hopeful look, a clear hint that she should volunteer to go with her. There was no way she could refuse the simple request. It wasn't as if she had anything better to do, and it would get her out of the house—and away from her mother—for a while. A win-win situation as far as she was concerned.

"Gage, if you don't mind, I'd like to come with Jada. I promise not to interfere, and maybe another pair of eyes might come in handy."

He gave her a considering look. "Fine, as long as you keep anything we talk about or discover at the scene to yourself."

She held up her hand as if swearing an oath. "My lips are sealed, honor bright."

Gage just rolled his eyes. "Fine. Now that we have that settled, let's go."

"I'll grab my purse and keys. We'll follow you there."

There was one more thing. "Jada, since Gage is still investigating your break-in, why don't you plan on staying with me for another night or two?"

The instant relief in the girl's body language was unmistakable, making Abby glad she'd extended the invitation. Even so, it took seconds longer than Abby expected for her to respond. Finally, Jada took a deep breath and let it out slowly. "I have to go back sometime. You know, to stay by myself. I was just starting to get used to the empty quiet since Dad died."

Abby could sympathize. "True, but it doesn't have to be today."

Jada slowly nodded. "If you're sure, I'd really appreciate staying here another night."

Gage had listened to the conversation without interfering, but he also nodded as if he approved of their arrangement. "I'm going to head out. I'll see you at the house in a few minutes. I'll let myself out."

After they heard the front door open and close, Jada

cleared the rest of the dishes off the table. As she worked, she glanced up at the ceiling. "Are you going to tell your mother where we're going?"

Abby didn't want to, but she didn't like to think of herself as a coward. "Yeah, I should. Give me a minute."

She forced herself to walk up the steps at a quick pace, even though it was tempting to go much slower to put off another confrontation as long as possible. It was no surprise to find her mother's door closed. Abby softly rapped on it. "Mom?"

No answer.

She tried again, knocking a little louder. This time she was rewarded with a grumpy, "What?"

"I'm driving Jada back to her house to pick up a few things so she can stay with us again tonight. I thought we could have lunch at Frannie's diner afterward. Would you like me to swing back by so you can go with us?"

As peace offerings, it wasn't much. But to her surprise, the door opened just enough for her to see her mother standing on the other side. "Call me when you're on the way. I'll meet you outside."

"Sounds good, Mom. It could be a while, so don't think I've forgotten you."

Rather than push her luck, she started to walk away. Her mother reached out to catch her arm. "How is Jada holding up?"

"She's stronger than she knows. Gage is going to meet us at the house so the two of them can go through the place together. I invited myself along for moral support."

"That's good. I'm glad you're going to be there for her."

Her mother looked a little wistful. "You know, I

would've liked to have had the chance to be here for you back when you were going through so much. I don't mean just the divorce, but everything that's happened since you moved into this house. Sometimes it feels as if you've cut me out of the important stuff in your life and share it with the people you've met here in Snowberry Creek instead."

Abby's mouth dropped open in shock. "I never meant to do that, Mom. It's just that I needed to prove to myself that I could stand on my own. You know, like you did when you and Dad split up. I wanted to be that strong, too."

Evidently it was her mother's turn to be stunned. "Really, is that how you saw me? As strong?"

"Yeah, I did. I know there were some rocky times, but I always knew we'd make it."

She hated to keep both Jada and Gage waiting, but she suspected they both would agree that her taking a few seconds to hug it out with her mother was worth the short delay. She wasn't the only one blinking back a few tears when she took a step back. "I'll call you when we're done at Jada's. Start thinking about which flavor of pie you're going to want with your meal."

Her mom grinned, looking more like her usual cheery self. "For the sake of my hips, I really shouldn't."

"But you will. We can always walk it off after dinner tonight. Zeke will be glad to go with us."

Her mother wrinkled her nose and gave an exaggerated sigh before once again smiling. "Fine, we'll indulge ourselves this afternoon even if we have to pay the price later."

Abby trotted back down the steps in a lot better mood

than she'd been in going up. Now, if only Owen's and Jada's problems could be solved with something as a simple as a hug or a piece of Frannie's pie.

When they reached Jada's place, it was obvious the repairs were well underway. The shattered wood in the door frame and the door itself had both been replaced. The naked wood was a raw scar on the house, but it was the first step back toward normal.

She smiled at Jada. "Once it's painted, you won't even know it had ever been damaged."

Before they could continue the conversation, Gage came walking around the end of the garage. "I circled around the house to make sure no one has been messing around in the backyard and didn't see anything suspicious, so that's good."

Holding up a pair of keys dangling from a small ring, he nodded toward the front door. "Mr. Smiley, the handyman, said it will be a couple of days before he'll be back to paint. He has a couple of other jobs he couldn't reschedule."

"That's fine. There's no hurry. I'm just glad he could do this much so quickly." Jada headed up the steps to the front door. "Should we get started?"

Gage nodded. "Take your time, Ms. Davidson. I know this isn't easy for you."

She turned the key in the lock and pushed the door open. "What are we looking for?"

"Anything that seems off." He took off his hat and ran his fingers through his hair, looking frustrated. "Look, maybe this was just a random burglary. We don't get a lot of them in Snowberry Creek, but we do get a few. We may never know why your house was targeted."

Abby stepped inside and looked around. "But you don't think that's what this was."

"No way to know for sure." Gage scanned the room with eyes that had seen so much of the darker side of life. "But if our perp was looking for stuff to turn into quick cash, logic says he should've at least taken the laptop. Even allowing for my deputy's quick arrival, he could've grabbed it and a few other items and been out the door in no time."

Finally, Jada started a slow walk around the room, stepping over the stuff that had been scattered on the floor. There was no mistaking the pain in the girl's expression as she no doubt relived the terror of the break-in. Abby knew her fear would gradually fade, but it would take time. No one liked living with the knowledge that their home was no longer the bastion of safety they'd thought it was.

While Jada continued her slow survey of the room, Abby edged closer to Gage. "You think this could be connected either to her visit to her father's office or the murder itself, don't you?"

He didn't seem inclined to answer, but he finally shrugged. "It's more of a gut feeling than anything. It just seems odd the break-in came so close on the heels of the other two incidents. That said, I've never been a big fan of coincidences."

By that point, Jada had made a careful lap through the living room. From there, she walked down the hall and disappeared into a room. Gage waited a few seconds before following after her. Since he didn't tell Abby she couldn't, she joined the parade. Before they'd gotten as far as the doorway, Jada popped back out and waved them forward. "Come take a look at this."

The room held a large desk, a couple of bookcases, and a four-drawer filing cabinet. When Jada pointed toward the lock at the top of the cabinet, they both leaned in for a closer look. There were gouges in the beige paint surrounding the lock, which were deep enough to show streaks of the silver metal underneath.

"Sorry I didn't notice that last night, but I barely glanced around this room because there was nothing obviously out of place. I know for a fact those marks weren't there a few days ago when I last vacuumed and dusted in here."

"I'll send my people back out to go over this room again." Then Gage used his cell phone to take pictures. "Are the files in this cabinet work-related or personal?"

"Both, actually. The top two contain our personal papers. The bottom two were related to his business. Old stuff, though. His active files and things were kept at the insurance office."

She opened the closet and reached up to retrieve something from above the door on the inside. Oddly enough, it turned out to be the small silver key needed to unlock the filing cabinet. Seeing the puzzled look on Abby's face, Jada flashed her a grin. "Dad always said no one ever thinks to look above the door frame when they peek into a closet."

After unlocking the filing cabinet, she did a quick check of the first three drawers, only hesitating when she got to the bottom one. It was easy to see why when she finally pulled it open to reveal a stack of plaques and framed certificates.

Gage leaned down to study them. "I'm guessing those are some of your dad's personal items that you wanted returned."

Jada trailed a finger over the top one, tracing her father's name. "Yeah, Dad was proud of these. It wasn't right that Mr. Anders kept hanging on to them. They meant nothing to him."

But they clearly did to Jada. Abby found herself once again getting angry that Mitch Anders put Jada in a position where the only avenue open to her was to break in to steal back what should've been hers in the first place. Hadn't the man realized they represented an important connection to her late father?

She noted Gage didn't comment on how they'd ended up in the filing cabinet. Instead, he looked around the office as if searching for something in particular.

"Where's the picture? The one that was missing from the wall behind the desk at the insurance office?"

Looking a bit sheepish, Jada returned to the closet and lifted a couple of folded blankets down off the top shelf. She handed them off to Gage, who laid them on the desk. From where Abby stood, the shelf looked empty, but maybe the picture was pushed too far back for her to see it. But maybe she wasn't wrong, considering the increasingly frantic way Jada started patting the shelf.

"What's wrong, Jada?"

She looked back at Gage, panic rolling off her in waves, as she pointed toward the empty shelf. "It's not here. The picture is gone."

CHAPTER 18

G age frowned as he motioned for Jada step away from the closet. "Let me look, just in case it got pushed too far back for you to reach."

It didn't take him long to verify the picture was nowhere to be found. "Was it still in the frame?"

Jada clenched her hands in white-knuckled fists at her sides. "Yes, and I swear that's where I put it. I wouldn't lie about that."

Gage put his hand on her shoulder, doing his best to offer her a bit of comfort. "I believe you, Jada."

Abby moved up close enough to offer Jada a tissue to blot the tears threatening to spill down her cheeks. After giving her a few seconds to regain control, she said, "For the moment, let's keep going through the house. Maybe the picture will still turn up."

Then she checked the time on her cell phone. "And don't forget, we still have to pick up my mom before heading to the diner for lunch."

Jada dried her eyes and shoved the tissue into her jeans pocket. Throwing her shoulders back in a show of determination, she drew a slow breath and managed a shaky smile. "That's right, and we don't want to get there too late for pie."

"Boy, I'm jealous," Gage said, offering them an unhappy smile. "I wish I had time to go with you. I hear Frannie has strawberry rhubarb this week."

His comment seemed to brighten Jada's mood a little. After one last worried glance back toward the closet, she headed down the hall to the next room.

It took another twenty minutes to finish going through the entire house and the garage. Gage checked all the high spots while Jada and Abby covered everything else. The downside was that the picture was nowhere to be found. The upside was that it looked to be the only item the thief had taken. The couch cushions were strewn on the floor and a few things knocked over on the book-shelves, but nothing else had been disturbed. When they'd completed the circuit, Gage got out his ever-present note-book and asked Jada for a detailed description of the picture.

She closed her eyes as if seeing it in her mind. "It was just a photo of my dad and his buddies back when he was in the army. You know, a bunch of young guys looking all cocky and tough."

Her mouth kicked up in a small grin. "It's the only picture I've ever seen of Dad with a big, grungy beard. I wouldn't have even recognized him if Mom hadn't pointed him out to me."

Then she used her hands to give Gage a rough idea of the size of the frame and the picture itself. "It was about this big with a plain brown frame. The mat was cream colored with a small decorative pattern around the edge. One of the guys from his unit had the color enlargement made and surprised my father with it as a Christmas present. Dad had it matted and framed for the office. I can't imagine why anybody would take it."

Abby didn't get it either. Why steal someone else's photograph? Trying to give Jada a little hope, she asked, "Maybe the guy who gave it to your father could make another copy of the picture for you."

Sighing, Jada said, "That would be nice, but Jack passed away a couple of years ago. Cancer, I think. Dad took it hard."

Gage joined the discussion. "Was your father in contact with any of the other guys? Maybe they have a copy and could have it duplicated for you."

Jada's immediate reaction was to slowly shake her head in denial, but then she stopped. "Maybe I could ask my godfather. He wasn't always in the same unit as my dad, but they served in a lot of the same places. It's a longshot, but I can ask him next time I hear from him."

Not for the first time Abby was tempted to hug Jada, but she wasn't sure the gesture would be welcome right now. "I hope he can help you. For now, though, why don't you pack whatever else you'll need to stay at my place for a few days? Then we'll go have lunch."

Gage opened the front door. "We'll be outside, Miss Davidson."

Abby waited until they were in the driveway to speak. "You know, now that she mentioned him, I actually met Jada's godfather the day I stopped to look in the insurance office window. His name is Will . . . something."

She paused, hoping his last name would come to her. "Darn, I've forgotten his last name. You can always get it from Jada, though, if it's important. Anyway, he stopped to check the place out, too."

Gage made another quick note. "I won't bug her about it today. She's been through enough. But I've got to ask, does it seem weird to you that Jada didn't call him instead of you?"

Come to think of it, that did seem odd. "Maybe the two of them aren't particularly close or something."

She hated to bring up Owen Quinn, but her mother had to be going crazy worrying about him. "Gage, I hate to ask, but about Owen . . . How long are you going to have to keep him locked up? I mean, now that you know he was probably covering for Jada's absence from the food truck."

He muttered something under his breath. The words were unintelligible, but there was no mistaking the cold frustration in each syllable. "Abby, you know I can't share the details of an ongoing investigation, but this much is obvious—if Owen was Jada's alibi, she was also his. Now, thanks to her confession and the eyewitness statements, I know precisely where she was during the time of the murder."

Which left Owen with no witness to his whereabouts during the crucial time frame. If Gage had found anyone who had seen him elsewhere, he would've said so. Add in the fact the murder weapon had belonged to Owen, and Gage might have no choice but to charge him with killing

Mitch Anders, even if any possible motive remained unknown. She wondered whose fingerprints, if any, they'd found on the knife. Not that she was foolish enough to ask.

"I won't bother to ask if Mom can visit him again."

"That would be best, although she won't think so."

Then, in that calm cop way of his, Gage stuck his notebook in his pocket as he took a slow look around their surroundings. "Listen, I don't have to tell you to be careful, Abby. There's something about this whole mess that doesn't make sense. Keep a low profile and encourage Jada to do the same. For sure, I'm glad she's staying with you while we figure out what's really going on. Hopefully, the guy got what he came for and won't come back, but . . ."

His thoughts on the matter drifted to a stop, or at least his willingness to share them had. She considered pressing him to continue, when he gave his head a little shake and then stepped back. "I need to get going. Remind Jada she can call me or the department if she needs anything at all. Even just to talk. Meanwhile, my deputies will keep a close eye on her place while they're out on patrol."

"I'll tell her."

He headed for his cruiser as Abby sat down on the porch steps to wait for Jada. There was still no sign of her by the time Gage's cruiser had disappeared down the road. But rather than rush her, she'd give Jada another few minutes before tracking her down.

Besides, it was nice to sit right where she was and soak up some rays. Quiet moments like this one had been rare lately. The murder and the break-in had created havoc in her life. Then there was the escalating tension between her and her mother. At least the two of them had established a bit of a truce before she'd left the house with Jada.

If she could avoid updating her mother on Owen's precarious status, maybe the peace would extend at least through lunch. It would be a crime to let a family squabble ruin the beauty of a piece of Frannie's pie. She might even step out of her comfort zone and try the strawberry rhubarb.

She checked the time again. Her mother had to be wondering where they were. To head that concern off at the pass, she sent a quick text saying they should be headed her way soon. It was time to see what was keeping Jada. The door opened just as she was about to step up on the porch. Jada peeked out and frowned at the empty driveway. "Chief Logan already left?"

Abby couldn't quite tell if Jada was disappointed or relieved by his absence. "Yeah, he had to go."

Jada opened the door wider and set a small suitcase out on the porch before disappearing back into the house. She returned seconds later with her backpack slung over one shoulder and an oversized red binder in her hand. After locking the door, she picked up the suitcase. As she waited, Abby got a better look at the notebook, and she realized the word "scrapbook" was written in gold in the center of the cover. It seemed like an odd thing to be bringing with her, but she decided not to ask. After everything Jada had been through lately, she was entitled to bring along whatever she wanted.

She must have noticed Abby staring at the scrapbook, because she offered her a closer look. "I have something to show you, but it can wait until we get back from lunch. We've kept your mom waiting long enough, and I bet she's getting hungry. I know I am."

Trying to keep things light, Abby teased, "For something healthy like a salad . . . or a giant piece of pie?"

Jada laughed. "Definitely the pie."

Lunch went smoothly, which was a huge relief. Their food arrived in record time, pie included. By unspoken agreement, they kept the conversation light, with topics ranging from Jada's classes at the college to what movie to watch after dinner. Her mother had insisted lunch was her treat, including the extra piece of pie Abby had ordered to take home to Tripp.

On the way home, they stopped at Jada's house so she could pick up her car and follow Abby back to the house. As they walked toward the back door, a soft woof coming from inside had her smiling. "I'm going to take Zeke for a long walk if either of you would like to come."

"Not me. I'm going to take a nap." Her mother walked up onto the porch and stood off to one side to give Abby easy access to unlock the door. She was also smart enough to stay out of the way in case Zeke came zooming by to do a quick circuit of the yard.

Jada jumped back to give the dog room to get past. She smiled as she watched him trot across the grass toward the trees along the back of the yard. "I would love to tag along with you and Zeke, but I really need to hit the books."

Abby hadn't even thought about Jada having to miss class to deal with the break-in. "Do you have everything you need?"

"Yeah, I brought my laptop and textbooks from home. I'll work at the dining room table, if that's okay. I also might need to print a few things later, if you don't mind me logging into your network."

Abby followed her mother into the kitchen with Jada right behind her. "The dining room is fine. Feel free to make coffee or tea if you'd like. Otherwise, there's pop and iced tea in the fridge. Remind me when I get home, and I'll dig out the password for the network for you."

"If I haven't said it enough, Abby, I really appreciate everything you and your mom have done for me. I'm not sure how I would've gotten through all of this without you."

This time Abby did hug her. "You would've managed, but we're glad you reached out to us."

Jada headed for the hall that led toward the dining room, but then she stopped to look back at Abby. "I'll explain about the scrapbook later when you get back."

As she disappeared from sight, Abby took Zeke's leash off the hook by the back door, and grabbed the small pack she carried on their walks. She'd hoped to make good on her escape before her mother could corner her, but no such luck. She'd made it as far as the steps before the hammer fell.

Her mom stepped out onto the porch with her arms crossed over her chest and a big frown firmly in place. "You haven't told me what Chief Logan had to say about Owen."

Abby clipped the leash onto Zeke's collar. "It's safe to assume there's a good reason for that."

"Don't play games. You at least asked about him. I also understand why you wanted to keep the conversation light during lunch, but don't filter information just because I won't like it."

Deliberately turning her back, Abby leaned down to give Zeke a thorough scratching. He gave her cheek a huge slurp of a lick in appreciation, making her smile. Finally, she turned back to her mother. "I asked if you could visit Owen again. He said it wouldn't be a good idea right now."

"But—"

She held up her hand to halt her mother's instant protest. "He didn't say if that was his opinion or Owen's. I didn't ask, after he reminded me he can't reveal details of an ongoing investigation. He did mention that Jada's explanation of where she was the night of the murder had been corroborated by multiple sources."

The look of confusion on her mother's face made it clear that she wasn't yet connecting the dots. "What does that have to do with Owen?"

"Mom, we've assumed all along he was protecting someone, most likely Jada. I'm guessing he knew she went missing from the food truck but not why, and he was covering for her. She doesn't need him as an alibi now."

"That's good, isn't it?"

"Not if she was his alibi, too. That leaves his absence unexplained."

Her mother's eyes flashed wide in surprise and then just as quickly narrowed in anger. "You don't think Owen killed that poor man."

"It doesn't matter what I think, Mom, but the facts do. Owen has no alibi and the weapon belonged to him. I'm sorry, but just how do you think that adds up in the eyes of the law?"

"He's not a killer, Abby. I couldn't be that wrong about him."

"How much do you know about his past? You have to know he hasn't been a barbecue king his whole life. Where was he and what did he do before moving to Snowberry Creek?"

When her mom didn't answer, Abby sighed. "That's what I thought."

By this point, Zeke had abandoned Abby to stand next to her mother, not that the woman noticed. She was too caught up in the need to defend the man currently sitting in the Snowberry Creek jail. Finally, she did an about-face and stalked back into the house. Abby considered going after her, but there was nothing she could say that would change the situation, and plenty that could only make it worse.

She tugged on Zeke's leash. "Come on, boy, let's go. I need this walk more than you do."

Her furry friend gave the back door one last worried look before giving himself a quick shake as if that would throw off the cloud of tension that had engulfed the three of them. Having left all thoughts of gloom and doom behind, he trotted off across the yard, ready to enjoy a leisurely stroll.

If only it were that easy for her to do the same.

CHAPTER 19

The walk smoothed the sharp edges of Abby's mood. She'd tried without success to come up with a plan that would help her mother deal with the fact that her boyfriend might be facing murder charges. At least when she and Zeke returned, her mother was still upstairs in her room, so bonus points for that.

Meanwhile, she made good on her promise to help Jada log into her network and connect wirelessly to the printer. With that done, she left the younger woman to continue working in peace. Still feeling out of sorts, she thought maybe her mood would improve if she restocked the cookie supply in the freezer. Besides, Zeke always appreciated her keeping his treat jar full.

Deciding on a double batch of gingersnaps and some of Zeke's favorite pumpkin blueberry cookies, she lost herself in the soothing rhythm of baking. As usual, Zeke curled up in the corner to watch. He liked to be close at hand in case she wanted his opinion on how something had turned out. Sugary treats weren't good for him—or her, for that matter—but he was always willing to clean up the mess if anything dropped on the floor. Zeke was a dog who liked to earn his keep. She liked that about him.

Just as the first tray of gingersnaps was ready to come out of the oven, a familiar face appeared at the back door. She motioned for Tripp to let himself in while she set the hot cookies on a rack to cool. After putting the next batch in the oven and setting the timer, she turned to greet her guest. "I swear you and Zeke have a secret signal that lets you know when I have cookies in the oven."

Neither male denied the truth of that statement. In fact, Tripp grabbed a paw-print cookie out of the treat jar and tossed it to Zeke like a cop paying off an informer. Having settled his debt, he helped himself to a glass of ice water and settled in at the table. Abby didn't buy his innocent act for a second. He was just waiting for the cookies to cool enough to avoid being burned when he started sneaking them off the wire rack.

"Where are your mother and Jada?"

As Abby finished filling a third tray, she smacked Tripp's fingers with her cookie scoop when he tried to snatch a glob of the raw dough. "Jada is in the dining room listening to music with her headphones on while she gets caught up on her classwork. As for Mom, I assume she's still sulking up in her room."

Was it rude to hope she stayed there for as long as possible? Yeah, probably.

Using his Special Forces ninja skills, Tripp succeeded on his second attempt to abscond with two balls of cookie dough. Looking all smug and proud of his evil deeds, he asked, "Since you're baking, I'm guessing today hasn't been a bed of roses. How did it go with Gage?"

Abby quickly gave him a summary of everything that had happened up through since she'd last seen him, before going into more detail of what they'd learned while at Jada's house. "As far as she could tell, the only thing that was missing was a photograph of her father's unit when he was in the army. It used to hang in his office, and she has no idea why anyone would steal it. It was a gift from a member of his unit from back in the day. Since the guy died a while ago, there's no way for her to get another copy. The sad thing is that she'd just gotten it back the night of the murder, when she snuck back into Mitch Anders's office during the movie."

"That's too bad." Tripp frowned as he nibbled on a cookie. "I can see why the photo mattered to her father and Jada, but who else would care about it? Heck, I have pictures of my buddies that mean a lot to me, but I can't imagine anyone else being interested in them."

After filling the last tray, she put it on the counter to await its turn in the oven. Meanwhile, she started mixing up Zeke's portion of the day's efforts. Tripp quietly watched her with those eyes that always saw too much. Finally, he said, "And how did lunch at the diner go?"

"Great, especially the ginormous piece of strawberry rhubarb pie I had. I've never had it before and felt daring."

Tripp perked up. "How was it?"

"Fabulous. Sweet and tart at the same time, and the crust was so flaky. I wish I had Frannie's recipe, but I know better than to ask her for it."

Rumor had it that the last person who asked Frannie

for one of her recipes had been banned from the diner for a month. Meanwhile, Tripp slumped back in his chair. "Sorry I missed out on it."

It was tempting to let him suffer a bit longer as punishment for stealing cookie dough, but she didn't have the heart. She retrieved the container from the refrigerator, got a fork out of the drawer, and set them both on the table in front of Tripp.

"I knew you wouldn't fail me." Tripp's greedy grin as he dug right in went a long way toward improving her mood. At least she'd made one person happy today.

"Mom is upset that Gage said it wouldn't be a good idea to let her visit Owen again." She went back to mixing up Zeke's treats. As she rolled out the dough, she caught Tripp up on the rest of that story.

He ate another huge bite of his pie before responding, probably buying himself time to consider what he wanted to say. There was a growl of temper in his voice when he finally spoke. "I can see why she's upset, but I don't understand why she thinks that any of that translates into being your fault."

She finished rolling out the dough and set her rolling pin aside. "To be honest, I have no idea. It's not like I volunteered the two of us to stumble over another dead body. I'm also not responsible for Owen's unexplained disappearance at the movie, nor did I plant one of his knives near the victim. For sure, I didn't break in to Jada's house."

Lost in the whirlwind of her thoughts, she stared down in confusion at the dough. She needed to be doing something, but right then she couldn't think what that might be. A second later, a big hand waved back and forth right in front of her face. She blinked and focused on Tripp. "What?"

"You really zoned out there for a minute. Not sure where you went, but it didn't look like it was anywhere happy."

Rather than continue to complain about her mother, she lied. "I was thinking about dinner. I just realized I didn't put anything out to thaw. After I finish these cookies, I guess I'll have to make a quick run to the store."

Which meant she needed to start cutting out the cookies. As she began arranging the bone-shaped cookies on the baking sheets, she noticed Tripp had gone quiet. His dark eyes twinkled with devilment, which made her hesitate to ask, "What are you thinking about so hard, or do I really want to know?"

"I'm debating whether or not I should offer to provide dinner tonight."

That usually meant he'd show up at the door with a couple of pizza boxes and a six-pack of his favorite beer. Sometimes he surprised her by actually cooking, usually a huge pot of chili. Either option sounded good to her. But on second thought, she wondered why he would debate the issue at all. Unless . . . Oh, no, he wouldn't. From the way he was grinning, yeah, he would.

She pointed her spatula at him. "Tripp Blackston, by any chance did Jean stop by today while we were gone?"

"Yep, she did."

"And did she just happen to bring you another tuna casserole?"

"Yep, and there's plenty to go around. For what it's worth, this one seems to be a pretty traditional version. You'll love it. Everyone will."

When she snickered at that bald-faced lie, his laughter rang out across the room. "Well, maybe that is a bit of an exaggeration. However, the offer stands."

She'd deal with her guilty conscience later, but for now she didn't even hesitate. "I'll make a salad."

"It's a deal."

If Jada didn't like the prospect of tuna casserole, she was polite enough not to say so. In contrast, Abby's mother looked slightly horrified and muttered something under her breath that sounded like she was grateful she'd eaten a big lunch at the diner. Personally, Abby was just glad not to have to make much effort to put a meal on the table. Regardless, she made an extra-large salad complete with lots of cheese, chickpeas, and several hardboiled eggs to ensure anyone who didn't eat a lot of the casserole could still get enough protein.

Her mother put out placemats and then the plates and flatware. "So you're saying Tripp just happened to have this casserole lying around when you realized you hadn't planned anything for dinner tonight."

"Yep, that's right. I told you about Jean from the quilting guild. She worries that he doesn't get enough home-cooked meals, so she brings Tripp tuna casseroles. He politely thanks her for thinking of him, and he would never hurt her feelings by admitting he's not all that fond of canned tuna."

"Seriously?" Her mom sounded incredulous.

"Tripp eats them, too. Every bite." Abby put the final flourish on the salad before turning to face her mother directly. "Even when she uses one of her secret ingredients, which have included anchovies and barbecued potato chips. However, he assured me this one looks pretty traditional."

Her mom picked up the salad and set it in the middle of the table. "Well, all I can say is that man deserves a medal."

"He does indeed."

Studying the table, Abby considered what else they would need. "Tripp will most likely drink iced tea with dinner. Can you ask Jada what she wants? And what would you like?"

"Tea is fine for me."

Just as her mother headed for the dining room to check in with Jada, Tripp kicked the back door and held up the casserole in one hand and a six-pack in the other. Guess she'd been wrong about the iced tea with dinner, which was fine with her. She wiped her hands on a dish towel before opening the door to let him in. He set the casserole on the counter. "I usually stick these in the oven for twenty minutes to heat through."

"I turned it on about ten minutes ago, so it should be up to temperature."

Tripp stripped the foil off the casserole and then slipped the dish into the oven. After setting the timer, he looked around the kitchen. "So what's for dessert?"

Abby fought back a smile. "We've already had dessert today, or did you forget that huge piece of pie I lugged home for you?".

The man had a serious sweet tooth and made no bones about it. "Yeah, I remember. It was delicious, but that was lunch. I'm talking about dinner dessert."

It was tempting to keep teasing the man, but she couldn't

resist those puppy-dog eyes. "Check the cabinet over the microwave."

He practically leapt across the room to yank the door open. His face lit up as soon as he spotted the blackberry coffee cake she'd made. For a big man, Tripp could really move. In one continuous motion, he let out a loud whoop as he slammed the door closed before grabbing Abby around the waist and spun the two of them around in circles. Before finally setting her back down, he planted a big kiss on her mouth, leaving her laughing and blushing. Then the humor in his eyes warmed into something else, something more, as he stared down at her. "Woman, you never cease to amaze me."

"Ahem."

Abby choked back a groan. Nothing like a mother's presence to throw a pall on one of the few enjoyable moments she'd had all day. "Tripp was just letting me know that he likes blackberry coffee cake."

"Is that what that was?"

At least her mother sounded more amused than disapproving. Jada followed her into the kitchen. "Is there anything I can do to help?"

Tripp had remained beside Abby, his arm looped around her shoulder. "We're waiting on the casserole to finish warming in the oven. It should be ready in a few more minutes."

Jada looked a bit disappointed, as if she needed to earn her keep. Abby pointed toward the container in the corner. "Could you give Zeke two scoops of his food and some fresh water?"

Abby had guessed right, judging from the way Jada hurried to accomplish her assigned tasks. Zeke showed his appreciation by hoovering up his kibble in record time and then washing it down with half the water in his bowl. By that point, Tripp had taken his seat at the table. The dog immediately plopped his big head on Tripp's jean-clad leg.

"Darn it, dog, how many times have I told you not to use my pants for a towel?"

It was hard not to laugh. Thanks to Zeke's mastiff ancestors, he had an amazing gift for storing extra water in his jowls. The unwary were always fair game for ending up with a huge wet circle wherever Zeke laid his head in the hopes of getting petted. "He'd probably listen better if you didn't scratch his ears the whole time you're cataloging his evil deeds."

Tripp just shrugged and kept right on with what he was doing. They all three knew he complained out of habit rather than any real desire for the dog to share his drool with anyone else. Jada joined him at the table while Abby and her parental unit continued to hover around the edges of the kitchen.

The timer on the stove went off just as the front doorbell rang, leaving Abby torn between which summons to respond to first. Finally, she delegated dinner to her mother's capable hands.

"Mom, if you'll get the casserole out of the oven, I'll see who's at the door."

Tripp immediately pushed Zeke's head off his lap. "Were you expecting anyone?"

When she shook her head, he stalked down the hall ahead of her with Zeke right beside him. She hadn't been particularly worried about who might have come calling, but Tripp clearly wasn't taking any chances. The man took his protection duty seriously.

He paused long enough to peek out the window and then jerked the door open before Abby even had time to get there. She couldn't see past Tripp, but his body language changed drastically as he leaned into the door frame with his arms crossed over his chest.

"Well, well. Owen Quinn, we didn't expect to see you tonight. Did you dig your way out of jail with a spoon, or did Gage kick you to the curb?"

CHAPTER 20

Her mother must have developed ears like a bat, because she came charging in from the kitchen and shoved her way past Abby and then Tripp. "Owen! You're really here."

Two seconds later, Owen had her wrapped in his arms, holding her close. It was tempting to flash the porch light in retaliation for the other night, but Abby squelched the urge—if only barely. Tripp knew it, too. He must have been wanting a little revenge himself. He gave her a wicked grin and reached toward the light switch. She slapped his hand away right before he would've flipped it.

Regretfully, someone had to be the adult in the room.

"Mom, why don't you invite Owen to come inside and join us for dinner? I'll go set another place at the table."

Without waiting for an answer, she grabbed Tripp's hand and hauled him back to the kitchen. At least he came willingly. They both knew she couldn't have budged him if he had thought Owen presented danger to anyone.

Jada was waiting in the kitchen. She looked past Abby toward Tripp. "Did I hear Mr. Quinn at the door?"

Tripp resumed his spot at the table. "Yeah, it's him, but he hasn't had a chance to explain what he's doing here."

Abby added a fifth place-setting on the table and popped the top on another beer, figuring Owen would appreciate a cold one after spending the past few days in jail. With everything ready, all they could do was wait for Owen and her mother to join them. Jada took a seat next to Tripp, maybe so the two of them could share Zeke's attentions, while Abby sat next to Tripp on the other side. It was another couple of minutes before the older couple finally made their way to the kitchen.

Owen studied the table and then offered Abby a hesitant smile. "I don't mean to impose, Abby. I just wanted to let your mom know I was out, so she could stop worrying so much about me."

Even Abby had to admit that was good news. "I'm glad you did. We're not having anything fancy, but you're more than welcome to join us."

Her mother pulled out a chair for him and waited until he sat down before finally taking the last spot at the table. To get things going, Abby passed the salad to Jada. "Please, everyone, dig in."

Tripp scooped a huge portion of the casserole onto his plate. "This stuff is really hot. If you'll pass your plates, I can serve."

As soon as she handed over hers, everyone else followed suit. The shuffling of the plates didn't take long. Owen caught her eye. "This all looks delicious, Abby."

"Thanks, but I didn't make the casserole." She shot

Tripp a teasing smile before adding, "Tripp's special lady friend did."

Owen's eyebrows shot up as his gaze bounced between Tripp and Abby. "Really? But I thought you two were—"

Her mother cut him off before he could finish. "It's not what you think. Tripp's friend is in her eighties. Evidently, Jean doesn't think he eats right. Although from what I've seen, he eats a lot of his meals right here."

Abby gritted her teeth to keep from lashing out in anger. She was rather proud of herself for how calm she sounded when she said, "Lately, Mom, you realize that I could say the same thing about you."

When Tripp choked on the bite he'd just swallowed, she reached over and pounded on his back. It was time to turn the conversation back to a safer topic. "How's the casserole?"

Tripp didn't answer until after he took a quick swig of his beer. "Good. Actually, really good. It's different from her usual ones."

Then he lifted another big bite of it up with his fork to study it. "I think that's fresh dill I'm seeing, and this time she used albacore tuna."

Owen joined in the analysis. "I'm thinking the cheese might just be a nice Gruyère. Phoebe, what do you think?"

After taking a cautious taste, her mom's expression immediately brightened. "Yes, I think it is. And those are fresh mushrooms, not canned. I also like the crunch of the water chestnuts."

She took another bite and smiled. "I can't believe I'm

saying this, but I might just have to ask Jean for her recipe. This is delicious."

Tripp was already serving himself a second helping. "I'll be sure to tell her. That will please her to no end."

After that, everyone concentrated on finishing their meal. As usual, Tripp took charge of the cleanup, this time with Jada's help. Meanwhile, her mother put on a pot of coffee and served their dessert. Once the chores were done, they all gathered around the table again.

It was time to find out why Owen was now a free man, especially considering he lacked an alibi for the chunk of time he'd left her mother sitting alone at the movie. The problem was how to question him without making it sound like an inquisition. The wrong tone would set her mother off again, and right now Abby was in no mood for another confrontation.

Fortunately, the man took charge of the conversation himself. Owen added cream and sugar to his coffee and then cleared his throat. He smiled across the table at Jada. "I'm glad you and Gage were able to clear the air over what happened the night of the movie. He didn't share the details with me, only that he'd confirmed where you'd been."

Jada's face flushed a bit pink as she explained her escapade the night of the movie. "I know I should've told you and Chief Logan sooner, Mr. Quinn. It was irresponsible to leave the food truck unattended like that. I didn't mean to cause you any problems. I'll understand if you want me to resign."

Abby held her breath as they waited for Owen to respond. Jada really needed that job. Luckily, he didn't keep Jada in suspense. "Your job is safe, Jada, but next time lock the door if you have to step out. We'll talk more later about when the restaurant will reopen. Unfortunately, my own situation remains a bit precarious, so I won't hold it against you if you decide to start putting out feelers to find another position. I'd be glad to give you references."

As soon as he referred to his continuing problem with Gage's investigation, Abby checked to see how her mother had reacted to that little bombshell. She'd immediately grasped Owen's hand, her worry for him etched in the lines bracketing her mouth and eyes. "What did Gage have to say about your situation?"

He mustered up a small smile that didn't quite reach his eyes. "I'm not all that familiar with the ins and outs of this kind of situation. Having said that, I think he ran out of time where he could hold me without pressing charges, but I'm definitely not in the clear. Apparently, no one can remember seeing me when I went to the food truck. Jada was gone, too, so I have no alibi. I waited around for a few minutes and then left."

"So you think Gage considers you the primary suspect?"

Abby was relieved that Tripp was the one to pose the question instead of her, but it was one that needed to be asked. She avoided meeting her mother's gaze as they waited for Owen to answer.

Finally, he shrugged. "As much as I'd like to say that wasn't the case, I can't. He has to follow where the facts lead, and I was missing in action around the time of the murder. The fact that the knife was definitely one of mine doesn't help."

Predictably, her mother leapt to his defense. "That's

ridiculous. They can't know that for sure. Anyone can order chef knives off the internet or buy them in a restaurant supply store."

If Owen's smile was meant to reassure anyone, it didn't work. "The brand is readily available, but I always burn my initials in the wooden handles on my knives. This one had my mark on it. I own a dozen of them, or at least I did. The police could only come up with eleven when they went through the restaurant, the truck, my car, and my house."

"Is there any way to tell which location the knife was taken from?"

Owen gave her mother's hand a quick squeeze before responding to Abby's question. For the first time she could see the toll all of this was taking on him. Exhaustion showed itself in the dark circles under his eyes and the gray scruff along his jawline. Even his voice had a ragged note that she'd never heard before.

"No, not for sure. The two I keep at the house were both accounted for, but I use the others in both my food truck and the restaurant. So at any given time, I couldn't tell you how many are in each place. They're checking for fingerprints, but it won't be a surprise if they only find mine and maybe Jada's."

She spoke up again. "But doesn't there need to be a motive? If you didn't actually know Mitch Anders, it seems strange that you would even be considered a suspect at all."

Oddly, rather than immediately addressing that issue, Owen glanced over at the counter. "Is there any chance I could have a little more of the coffee cake? It's fabulous."

Figuring he just needed a moment to collect his thoughts, Abby was up and moving as soon as he spoke. She carried the baking dish over to the table to serve him and Tripp each a second piece. Then she waved the dish in her mother's direction. "How about you, Mom?"

When she shook her head, Abby offered it to Jada. She also refused. "No, thanks. I'm good."

The two men dug right in while Abby refreshed everyone's coffee. Had anyone else noticed Owen hadn't responded to Jada's comment about him not knowing Mitch Anders? Call her suspicious, but that seemed significant. She glanced toward Tripp to see if she could discern his thoughts on the matter. He looked at her over the rim of his coffee cup, his eyebrows riding down low in a slight frown. When she gave him a questioning look, he shook his head just enough to let her know that he wasn't going to say anything else on the subject.

When both men finished off their dessert, Jada stood up. "I've got a little more reading I need to finish. I'll be in the dining room if anyone needs me."

As they heard the dining room door close, Owen asked, "How is she really doing? I heard there was a burglary, but not much in the way of details."

Abby thought it was really Jada's tale to tell, but evidently her mother felt differently. "As well as can be expected. The poor girl was home alone when someone kicked in her front door. He messed up her living room a little, but the only thing that was stolen was a picture that used to hang in the insurance office."

Her mom's voice dropped to a low whisper as she caught him up on everything that had happened. Pausing to catch her breath, she continued. "Anyway, the picture was one of the things she took home the night of the movie. She'd seen Mitch Anders at the park and thought it was her best chance to retrieve her father's personal belongings. Mr. Anders had refused to give them back to her and wouldn't take her calls."

There was a flash of anger in Owen's expression. "I wish she'd told me she was having problems with him. I would've helped her get the stuff back. I hope Gage is able to recover the picture for her."

At that point, he let out a long, slow breath. "Thank you for dinner, Abby, and I apologize again for dropping by with no warning. It's been a long few days, so I should be going."

Then he frowned. "Am I correct in assuming that Jada is staying here tonight?"

Tripp nodded. "Yeah, and probably tomorrow night as well. I'm crashing on the couch in the living room. Gage didn't seem to think the perp would come after her again since he seemingly got what he came for. Regardless, Abby thought Jada would sleep better if I kept an eye on things here."

Owen looked marginally happier. "Do you need me to stay and help keep watch?"

"No, Zeke and I have it covered. No one will get past us, will they, boy?"

The dog woofed his agreement, making all the humans in the room smile. Owen stood up. "Well, now that I know Jada's safety is in good hands—and paws—I'll be going."

Abby remained seated but offered up a smile to her departing guest. "We're glad you're out, Owen."

"Me too, even if it's only temporary."

It was no surprise that her mother followed him down the hall, and Abby didn't expect her back anytime soon. She had her own dark memories of when Tripp had finally gotten released from jail. It had been all she could do not to check on him a dozen times a day to make sure he was okay. Her mom no doubt felt the same way about Owen.

What an odd thing to have in common with a parent. She couldn't help but chuckle a little as she imagined what that particular bonding moment would look like. Tripp cleared his throat to get her attention. "Care to share the joke?"

Whoops, she'd almost forgotten that she wasn't alone at the table. Grimacing, she debated the wisdom of answering that question honestly, but figured what the heck. He'd either find it funny or he wouldn't. "Mom and I have had our differences lately. Seems like any little thing can set us off."

"You mean stuff like flashing porch lights and canoodling at the park?"

She punched him on the arm, a half-hearted attempt at best. "Very funny, but yeah. Anyway, I've been trying to figure out what to do about it. You know, to find some kind of common ground. We used to get along better than this, and I miss it. I just realized that she and I now have something new we both share."

By this point, he was looking pretty suspicious. "Do I even want to ask?"

"Probably not, but I'll tell you anyway. We can bond over the fact that the men in our lives are both jailbirds. Hey, maybe we could even finesse a reality show deal out of it. You know, mothers and daughters whose men are behind bars. I can see us standing outside a jail cell with a platter of cookies and serving coffee to all the guards and prisoners. What do you think?"

Tripp crossed his arms over his chest and tried really hard to look crabby about the whole idea, but it was clearly a struggle. In the end his sense of humor overruled all common sense, and his laughter came bubbling out. Maybe it was the stress of the past few days or just the chance to enjoy a few minutes alone with Tripp and Zeke. Regardless of the reason, their shared laughter helped purge a lot of the frustration she'd been dealing with since her mom had moved in.

As they slowly regained control, Tripp reached over to cup her cheek with his hand. She leaned into its warmth as he said, "Want to walk me home? There are a few things I'll need, to spend the night over here."

Abby's pulse kicked it up a notch. "What's in it for me?"

"Well, for one thing, I can pretty much guarantee my mom's not there to flash any lights at us."

Then he arched an eyebrow in what he probably thought was a sexy come-hither look. All he succeeded in doing was setting off another fit of the giggles. She finally managed to choke out, "I'd love to provide escort. I wouldn't want you to get lost between my house and yours."

Abby patted her furry friend on the head. "Zeke, you wait here and keep an eye on things for us."

Tripp grabbed her hand and tugged her toward the door. "Quick, I think I hear your mother headed this way."

In a flash, they were out the door and dashing toward the deep shadows that even the porch light wouldn't touch. Tripp led her farther into the trees at the back of the yard. No doubt they were both too old to be acting like a pair of teenagers trying to escape parental scrutiny long enough to enjoy a few minutes of privacy. Too bad.

When they were tucked behind the trunk of an enormous cedar tree, Tripp wrapped her in his arms and rested his forehead against hers. For the longest time, the only things she could hear were the sounds of both of them breathing and the noisy frogs in the nearby wetlands. She could've stayed there for hours, soaking up the peace offered by the cool night air.

Finally, Tripp moved back just far enough to give himself room to use the crook of his finger to tip her face up toward his. "Want to mess around?"

She couldn't resist teasing him a little. "Well, I don't know. I'll probably get grounded when Mom realizes what we were up to."

He glanced in the direction of the house. "Probably."

This time, she was the one who reached out to cup his cheek with her hand. "Will it be worth it?"

Soldier that he was, he accepted the challenge. "I'll make sure of it."

And he did.

Her head was still swimming when the sound of the back door opening and closing was followed by the sound of one large mastiff bounding across the yard in search of his people. When he found them, he jumped up on each of them in turn, clearly happy to have won the short game of hide-and-seek.

Accepting their defeat, they each patted Zeke on the head. Tripp took charge of the situation. "Good boy, you won fair and square. Let's head for my place, and I'll reward your impressive cleverness with a couple of those treats your mom doesn't know I have."

With that, Zeke was off and running. He circled back a couple of times to herd them along faster. The brief respite had been great, even if the real world couldn't be ignored for long. Not when Owen was on the verge of being charged with murder, a killer was still on the loose, and Jada might still be in danger.

With those happy thoughts, she followed Tripp into his house.

CHAPTER 21

By the time Abby dragged herself downstairs the next morning, Tripp was already gone, his blanket and pillow neatly folded on the end of the couch. She was disappointed, but he probably had an early class. When she reached the kitchen, there was a note propped against the coffeemaker from her mom saying she was meeting Owen for breakfast at the diner and would be back later.

She was already sitting down and eating her oatmeal before Jada wandered in with her scrapbook. Darn, she'd forgotten Jada had wanted to show her something yesterday. She hadn't said what it was, but Abby suspected she might want her opinion on whether it was something she should share with Gage.

After setting the book down on the table, Jada asked, "Have you got a minute?"

"Sure." Abby ate another bite of her oatmeal. "Why

don't you grab a cup of coffee and then show me what you wanted me to look at?"

A few seconds later, Jada sat down at the table, sipping her coffee and silently thumbing through the pages while Abby finished her breakfast. After refreshing her own cup of coffee, she waited patiently for Jada to start talking.

It didn't take long. "My mom was always cutting out newspaper articles and printing things from websites to put in scrapbooks. You know, pictures from when I played soccer as a little kid and stuff like that. When she died, Dad took over where she left off. I think it was a way of keeping her in our lives."

Where was she going with this? It seemed highly unlikely that Jada's childhood achievements had anything to do with the current situation. Rather than hurry her, though, Abby gave her all the time she needed. With her father's recent death, everything in that scrapbook no doubt stirred up a lot of memories that were good but might still hurt.

Jada turned several pages before stopping. "Anyway, Mom also collected stuff about my dad. Maybe it's a small town thing, but the local newspaper makes a big deal of it if someone opens a new business or gets an award of some kind. Dad used to get customer service awards every year from his company, and *The Clarion* always sent a reporter to photograph him holding up his latest plaque. Mom was really proud of his accomplishments. So was I."

She stared down at the page and traced her father's smile with a shaky fingertip. "I always thought those plaques would someday have both of our names on them."

The pain of lost dreams was clear in Jada's voice, and

Abby hated that for her. "I'm sure your parents would've loved that."

Jada slowly slid the scrapbook over in front of Abby, who wasn't sure what she was supposed to say. "Your father was a nice-looking man, Jada. You have his eyes."

"And Mom's coloring, but that's not what I wanted to show you." She pointed not at her father but at the wall behind him. "That's the picture that was stolen."

Then she flipped a few more pages. "On Veterans Day one year, the newspaper did a feature article about various people in town who'd served in the military. The reporter took this shot of Dad holding the picture. This copy is too small to pick out many details. I was thinking if that reporter still has the JPEG in his files, maybe we could get an enlargement made. You know, to help Chief Logan figure out why someone would want to steal it."

And with luck, maybe it would be clear enough that Jada would have a readable copy of the original. "That's great thinking, Jada. Do you want to contact Gage, or would you like me to call him for you?"

It was no surprise when Jada immediately said, "If you wouldn't mind . . ."

"Not a problem."

As she dialed Gage's number, someone knocked at the front door. *Who could that be?* She went days without anyone stopping by, especially unannounced. Zeke sounded the alarm, barking as he charged down the hall toward the door. Abby followed in his wake, leaving a message for Gage when the call finally went to his voice mail.

Erring on the side of caution, she peeked out the side window. As soon as she recognized the man on her porch, she called back down the hall, "Jada, I think this is for you."

She opened the door to greet their unexpected—not to mention uninvited—guest. Before she could say anything, he shifted to look past her shoulder. "Is Jada here?"

Well, that was rather abrupt. No greeting, no explanation of why he was there or how he knew he'd find her at Abby's in the first place. "Will, isn't it?"

He frowned and nodded. "Yeah, Will Swahn, Ms. Mc-Cree. As I told you, I'm Jada's godfather. I've been worried about her."

"I'm sorry about that. Did you try calling her? I'm sure she's had her phone turned on."

"I left messages on the landline. She might not have gotten them if she hasn't been home, and I didn't have her cell number."

That was logical, and she couldn't remember if Jada had checked for messages while they'd been at her house yesterday. Still, something about his excuse bothered her. By that point, Jada had joined her at the door. She looked more curious than welcoming. "Uncle Will, how did you find me?"

Good question. Abby couldn't wait to hear his answer. He looked calmer now that he'd seen Jada for himself. Maybe his nervous tension really did stem from his concern for his goddaughter. Looking all kinds of earnest, he hastened to explain, "I stopped by the house yesterday afternoon to check on you. The woman across the street told me about the burglary, but she didn't know where you'd gone. When I went back to your house again just now, a different neighbor wanted to know what I was doing looking in the windows. When I explained who I was and why I was there, he said you were with Ms. Mc-Cree and gave me this address."

Maybe that was all true, but it seemed pretty convenient. "Which neighbor was that? I didn't realize I knew anyone who lived in that neighborhood other than Jada."

Will frowned. "To be honest, I didn't quite catch his name, but he said he knew who you were from some committee you'd been on here in town. Something to do with the veterans, I think."

Again, possible, but still too vague for Abby's comfort. Finally, rather than continue the conversation in the doorway, she stepped back. "Why don't you come in, Mr. Swahn? I'm sure you two have a lot to talk about."

Then she smiled at Jada. "I'll fetch us all some coffee and cookies. Would you be more comfortable in the dining room or the living room?"

"The dining room would be great."

On her way back with the promised refreshments, Abby could hear the murmur of Mr. Swahn talking, but he abruptly went silent when she walked into the room. She had no idea what their conversation had been about, but Jada didn't look happy. After setting the tray on the table, she asked, "Is everything okay?"

Before Jada could answer, Abby's phone rang. She checked the screen. "Sorry, I have to take this. It's the police chief. Go ahead and serve yourselves."

She stepped out into the hall to answer the call. "Hi, Gage. Thanks for calling me back so quickly. Jada found a picture of the picture that was taken."

Realizing how confusing that sounded, she backed up and explained about the scrapbook. "Anyway, we weren't sure if it would help, but we can drop it by if you want to take a look."

She waited while he checked his schedule for the day. "Okay, I can be there within the hour, but I don't know about Jada. Let me check with her so I can let you know one way or the other."

Ducking her head back into the dining room, she smiled at both Jada and her godfather. "Sorry to interrupt, but Chief Logan would like to see us right away. Will that interfere with your plans?"

Jada nodded. "Yeah, I have a class."

Back out in the hall, Abby relayed the information to Gage. "I'll bring the scrapbook myself. And I can't believe I'm about to say this, we may need to call in Reilly Molitor."

Gage was well aware that she and the reporter from *The Clarion* had a pretty rocky relationship. They'd gotten off to a bad start back when he'd showed up on her doorstep asking questions shortly after she and Tripp had discovered a dead body buried in the backyard. The man had only been doing his job, but since then her automatic response whenever she saw him was to duck and cover.

On the other hand, she'd rather deal with Reilly herself than throw Jada in his path. "Gage Logan, laughing at me might just cost you the cookies I was going to bring down to the station. I'll let you explain to your people why they're not going to enjoy some fresh gingersnaps with their coffee."

He immediately apologized, but she wasn't buying it. "Nice try, mister. On that note, I'm going to hang up and let you ponder the error of your ways."

The fact that he was still chuckling as he hung up actually left her smiling. He knew full well she'd never punish his deputies for his bad behavior. Stepping back into the dining room, she found Jada and Will sitting in silence. Maybe she was misreading their body language, but it seemed clear to her that Jada wasn't particularly comfortable around the man.

"Gage said it's okay if I come by myself. If he needs any additional information from you, I'll let you know."

Jada fidgeted in her seat. "I really appreciate that, Abby. Are you sure that it's not too much of an imposition?"

"I actually have books to drop off at the library, which is right next to the police station. I also need to stop by the mayor's office. Her assistant wants to talk to me about continuing the movie-in-the-park program next year."

Not that Abby was interested in heading up another committee for the city, which is why she suspected Connie wanted her to stop by in person. The woman had a talent for getting people to volunteer, and Abby wasn't the only one who had fallen prey to the woman's crafty ways. No matter how many times she had walked into the mayor's office chanting "Just say no!" under her breath, she walked back out newly appointed to yet another committee and feeling grateful for the honor that Connie had bestowed upon her.

It was only later, after she got home and the glow wore off, that she realized she'd been had—again. But that was a problem for later. Right now she had more pressing matters. Her temporary roommate was staring at her with more than a hint of panic in her eyes. Jada clearly wanted help in getting rid of their guest.

"I'm sorry, Mr. Swahn, but Jada and I both have places we need to be this morning. At least you know she's fine, and we're watching out for her."

Rather than do the reasonable thing and accept that his

presence was no longer required, he remained seated and gave Jada a curious look. "So what's in the scrapbook that the police need to see?"

Abby wasn't sure they should tell him, but Jada took the decision out of her hands. "There was a picture stolen from the house the night of the break-in, and Chief Logan wanted to know what it looked like. You've seen it, I'm sure. It hung on the wall at the insurance office—the one of Dad and the guys he served with."

Her face brightened up. "In fact, I was going ask if you happened to have a copy of it so I could have a duplicate made."

His reaction to the loss of the picture was just like everyone else's. "That's what was stolen? Why would anyone want that?"

Then, without giving Jada a chance to respond, he answered her question. "I'm sorry, but I never had a copy of the picture."

Jada's hopeful expression faded just as quickly as it had appeared. "That's all right. I knew it was a long shot."

After a quick look at the clock, she reached for her laptop and closed it in preparation for making her escape. "Oops, gotta go or I'll be late. It was nice seeing you."

Abby hoped the man would take the hint, but he remained firmly seated. He kept his gaze on Jada as if that alone would stop her from leaving, as he said, "I'm sorry, Ms. McCree, I don't mean to be rude, but I would appreciate a moment alone with Jada before I leave. I have some questions for her on matters that are, to be blunt about it, none of your business. I'm sure you'll understand that she would appreciate the opportunity to answer them in private."

Zeke, who had been quietly sitting beside Jada, his head in her lap, abandoned his post to stand at attention next to Abby. He studied Will Swahn with none of his usual warmth. She rested her hand on his shoulders, ready to grab his collar if necessary.

The object of his interest swallowed hard. "That's some dog you have there, Ms. McCree. I might be wrong, but he's not looking very friendly."

What could she say to that? Normally Zeke was a teddy bear, but he wasn't acting that way right now. Will Swahn hadn't made any aggressive moves that warranted the dog's odd behavior, but she trusted him more than she did a man she barely knew. Regardless, she wrapped her fingers around Zeke's collar.

"He hasn't had his walk today, and that makes him antsy. Since Jada needs to leave for class, and the chief of police is expecting me, I'm afraid I'll have to see you out now, Mr. Swahn."

Jada quickly gathered up the books she'd left on the table while doing her homework and stuffed them into her backpack. Realizing his chance to talk to her privately had just slipped out of his hands, Will reluctantly picked up his keys off the table and stood. "Jada, we still need to talk. Call me so we can set up a time to meet."

Jada unplugged her laptop and jammed it into the outside pocket on her pack. "Sorry you were worried about me, Uncle Will. I've really gotta get going if I don't want to be late."

As soon as the words were out of her mouth, Jada bolted from the room. Abby was pretty sure she wasn't the only one who noticed Jada hadn't promised to make that call. She half expected the man to go after her, but after glancing at Zeke, Will seemed to think better of the idea. That didn't mean he'd let the matter drop anytime soon.

Abby led him the short distance to the front door, still keeping her hand on Zeke. "Thank you for . . ."

She didn't get a chance to finish because Will was already out the door and down the steps. It was just as well. There was no real reason for her to thank the man. She closed the door and locked it. Even then, she waited and watched out the window until she saw him drive away.

"Is he gone?"

"Yep, he left." Abby walked down the hall to where Jada stood in the kitchen door. "I'm guessing you aren't particularly close to your godfather."

"He was my dad's friend, but they didn't spend a lot of time together the past few years. I'm not sure why they grew apart. He came to Dad's memorial service, but I didn't talk to him very long. I did my best to speak to everyone who came, but I was barely holding it together. Most of that day was a blur to me, and this is the first time I've heard from him since then."

Abby was probably wrong, but there'd been something off about him showing up so unexpectedly. As he'd pointed out, whatever he wanted to talk to Jada about wasn't really Abby's business. Regardless, she couldn't help but wonder what was going on. "He seemed pretty determined to find you. Was he just worried about you or did he want something in particular?"

"He asked about a book he said Dad borrowed and

never returned. If he did, Dad never mentioned it. Uncle Will wants to come over and look for it himself."

Considering how intense he'd acted, that book must have special meaning to him. She couldn't point fingers, though. She had an entire bookcase full of books she'd owned since grade school. "Does he live close by?"

Jada frowned. "I'm not sure. Dad mentioned that Uncle Will and his wife had separated. I'm not sure which one of them moved out of their house."

"Well, you'd better get to class, and I'll let you know how my meeting with Gage turns out."

Jada adjusted the strap of her backpack on her shoulder. "Would you like me to order something in for dinner tonight? My treat."

Abby wasn't sure if Jada could really afford to do that, but she understood the girl's need to pull her own weight. "That sounds good. Right now I'm not sure who all will be here, so we can figure out what to order later."

"It's a deal. See you then."

Once she was gone, Abby packed up the scrapbook, a container of cookies, and everything Zeke would need for his walk and took it all out to the car in two trips. She didn't think Gage would mind the dog coming in with her since their meeting shouldn't last all that long. His presence would also give her a perfect excuse to keep the time she spent with Connie short, and she could leave her library books in the drop box in the lobby.

Zeke waited patiently for her to let him into the back seat and then stretched out on his blanket with his tongue lolling out in a doggy grin. At least one of them was happy to be heading out on an adventure. For her part, she couldn't shake off her worries about Jada, her mother, and even Owen.

Right now it didn't seem like she could do much to help any of them. Talking about her problems with somebody would help, even if the only one who was handy couldn't actually offer her any advice. As always, Zeke was a great listener. That thought had her smiling a little as she glanced at him in the rearview mirror. "You know, Will Swahn could be a great guy who only just now realized that he needs to step up to bat and help his old friend's daughter. But I've got to admit I'm thinking you were right on the money about keeping a close eye on him."

Zeke briefly met her gaze before sticking his head out the window into the breeze. His joy in the simple pleasure brightened her own mood. "Yeah, you're right. If there's nothing I can do about him right now, I should just let it all go for the time being."

Which was easier said than done, but she'd try.

Unfortunately, the most direct route to city hall took her right past Owen's restaurant. The parking lot was empty, and the CLOSED sign was posted in the window. She wasn't surprised that the place wasn't open for business, but wasn't he in there working on getting back things back to normal? She'd never been impressed with his work ethic, but that was his problem.

She was more worried about where her mother was right now and what she was doing. "Zeke, I really wish Mom would back off on her involvement with Owen until he's officially cleared of being a murder suspect."

This time her companion abandoned the window long enough to poke his head in between the front seats. When she reached up to pat his jowls, he rewarded her with a snort aimed right at her face in a show of mastiff love and sympathy. His job done, it was back to sniffing the wind and drooling on the side of her car.

Rather than commiserate anymore, she wiped her face with her sleeve and pulled into the parking lot behind city hall. "Come on, Zeke. Maybe Gage will prove to be more useful in solving my problems than you've been."

But somehow she doubted it.

CHAPTER 22

Gage didn't seem to mind Abby hovering over his shoulder while he studied several of the newspaper clippings in Jada's scrapbook. The magnifying glass he'd scrounged from the back of his desk drawer hadn't proved to be very helpful. The pictures were too faded for either of them to pick out many useful details.

He glanced up at her and tapped his finger on the framed picture Jada's father held in his hands. "All I can say is that this looks like any number of pictures I've seen over the years. In fact, I have an album at home with similar photos of the guys I served with back when I was in the army."

Well, rats. She'd been hoping Gage would pull off a Sherlock Holmes moment by pointing at the picture while shouting, "Gadzooks! Our culprit is the third man from the right, the one with the shifty look about his eyes."

While disappointing, his comment about his own collection of pictures did leave her feeling curious. "Is Tripp in any of those shots in your albums? I'd love to see how he looked back in the day."

"Maybe, but I'm not sure he'd appreciate me sharing them with you."

She retreated to sit in one of the chairs arranged in front of Gage's desk. "Come on, why not? It's no secret you two served together."

Gage set down the magnifying glass and leaned back in his chair. "That may be true, but you may have noticed that Tripp is pretty closemouthed about his life in general and especially when it comes to his time in the service. Besides, you saw him in uniform back when he was sneaking supplies to Sergeant Kevin out in the woods. Tripp didn't look all that different when he was younger. Use your imagination."

Kevin was one of the former soldiers that the veterans group Tripp belonged to had been trying to help. Whenever Tripp had met with him out in the national forest, he'd worn his uniform because it helped keep the homeless vet calm. She'd also seen him in a vintage uniform at the USO-style dance she'd helped organize to raise money for the various outreach programs run by his veterans group. That night was definitely at the top of her Top Ten list of best dates ever.

But back to the matter at hand. "So, do you think it's worth asking Reilly if he has the original JPEG of that shot so we can enlarge it? Jada wouldn't care if it wasn't as clear as the original. She'd just like to have a copy for her scrapbook."

"It's a long shot, but I'll give him a call. Considering we know the date the picture was printed in the paper, he should be able to check pretty quickly."

Zeke appeared in the doorway of Gage's office. Earlier, he'd grown bored watching the two of them studying the scrapbook and wandered out to the bullpen to visit the deputies working at their desks. That he didn't come any closer was his way of hinting that it was time for them to leave. She'd promised him a walk along the river, and he was more than ready for her to get with the program.

Surrendering to the inevitable, she joined Zeke at the door. "Well, I guess I have my marching orders."

Gage stood up, too. "Rather than me hanging on to Jada's scrapbook, I'll make a photocopy of the page to show Reilly."

She followed him around the corner to the copy machine. As they waited, she found herself asking, "Do you think this picture has anything to do with the murder?"

As soon as the question popped out of her mouth, she cringed and waited for yet another lecture on staying out of Gage's business. This time, though, he surprised her. "It's too soon to tell, but I have to think there's at least a chance it does. I've said before I'm not a fan of coincidences, especially when it comes to murder cases. Mitch Anders hadn't been here long enough for him to have built many personal connections here in town. From what I can tell, he'd barely started reaching out to his clients."

Abby cringed. "The new job didn't exactly work out for him, did it?"

"Not so much." Gage pulled the photocopy out of the machine and studied it. He hit the button that would darken the next print and tried again. "Anyway, as I was saying, Jada was one of the few people we know Anders talked to several times. I only have her side of those conversations, of course, but I tend to believe her."

That was a relief, but it still left the question unanswered if the thief had gotten what he wanted or if Jada might still be in danger. "She's planning on staying at my house again tonight. Do you think I should encourage her to stay longer?"

He paused to study the print the machine had just coughed out. He seemed a little happier with the second copy. "I wish I could give you a definitive answer. Without knowing for sure if there's actually a link between the break-in and Anders's death, it's hard to know what's going on."

There was one more person who had definite ties to the murder, at least on the surface. "Do you know if there's a prior connection between Anders and Owen Quinn?"

"I'm still trying to find out if they—"

Gage abruptly stopped midsentence to glare down at her. "Darn it, Abby, I'm not sure how you always manage to get me to tell you things that I shouldn't be discussing with a civilian."

He shoved the scrapbook into her hands. "To answer your original question, see if you can get Jada to stay another couple of days, if it's not too inconvenient. I keep thinking about the scratches on the filing cabinet. If they mean the culprit didn't get everything he wanted that night, there's a good chance he might try again. As long as that's a possibility, I'd rather Jada not be there, even if my people are still keeping a close watch on her house."

"I'll tell her. As guests go, she's not the one who's a problem, and I've got the room."

That comment earned her a smile. "You and your mom still having issues?"

When she frowned, he added, "Tripp might've mentioned something about flashing porch lights."

Her face flushed hot. "I can't believe he told you about that."

"Oh, come on, Abby. He thought it was funny."

Evidently so did Gage, which just made her crabby. "Well, I didn't. It's like she's regressed to when I was teenager or something. Mom is upset that Owen is caught up in this mess, but that's no excuse for how she's acting."

And Gage had more important things to do than worry about Abby's issues with her mom. "I'd better get a move on. I need to talk to Connie Pohler while I'm here. She wants my final report about how well things went on the movie night. Well, other than the murder."

Not wanting to get back onto that track, she offered Gage a wobbly smile. "Wish me luck. I suspect she's going to try to rope me into heading up the program next summer. If not that, then one of the other committees, boards, and who knows what else she has on her agenda. I've been practicing saying no over and over again in front of the mirror, but it probably won't stand up to that smile she breaks out on special occasions. You know, the one that makes you feel as if she's doing *you* a favor by letting you take on an enormous project that you never wanted to do in the first place."

By that point, Gage was laughing hard. Still, he patted her on the shoulder and even sounded sympathetic when he said, "Good luck with that, Abby. I should warn you that I've heard rumors that the city council wants to do a big art festival next summer."

Abby shuddered. That was the last thing she needed to get roped into handling. Besides, the timing seemed a little fishy. "Or maybe Connie started that rumor so taking on the movie program wouldn't sound so bad—you know, the lesser of two evils."

"Could be. She's crafty that way. Let me know how it turns out."

She gave Zeke's leash a tug and headed out to the lobby shared by the Snowberry Creek police department, the library, and the mayor's office. It was so tempting to make a break for it and hightail it down the street to the park. It might be cowardly, but she could live with that.

Unfortunately, the woman she most wanted to avoid chose that moment to walk in the front door of the building. Connie grinned and headed straight for her. "Hi, Abby! And is this handsome fellow Zeke? I've heard so much about him."

Her traitor of a dog ate up Connie's praise like it was his favorite dessert. With a wag of his tail and a minimum of drool, he positively preened as he encouraged Connie to give him a thorough scratching. "What a charmer! Can we step into my office long enough for me to give him one of the treats we keep on hand for special visitors?"

She immediately set off toward the door that led to the mayor's office. Zeke had picked up on the all-important word "treat" and lunged forward to follow close on her heels. Abby surrendered to the inevitable and let him drag her along behind.

Abby handed in her report that contained all the pertinent information about the movie night. As soon as Connie skimmed over it, she immediately pulled out her tablet and started studying a list. Abby knew—just *knew*—what was coming next. Connie would start by offering up sincere flattery about what a terrific job Abby had done taking over when circumstances forced the original co-chairs to step down. From there, she would move on to pointing out all the other wonderful opportunities that would showcase Abby's dazzling organizational skills. To ward off the power of Connie's magic, Abby mentally stuck her fingers in her ears and did the "just say no" chant she'd been practicing at home.

Maybe it worked, because Connie hadn't yet launched into her spiel when the mayor, Rosalyn McKay, stepped out of her office and headed straight for them. Her eyes flared wide when she spotted Zeke. "Wow, Abby. I've seen you out walking your friend there, but I never realized how big he is."

Abby was only too glad to have everyone's attention focused on Zeke rather than herself as Rosalyn slipped him another treat. "Sorry to interrupt, Abby, but I really need Connie's help with a report that's due to the council by this afternoon."

It was the perfect opportunity for a quick exit. "No problem. We were pretty much done. I promised Zeke a walk in the park, and we need to get home before my houseguest gets back from class."

Both women froze. It was the mayor who spoke next. "I heard that Jada Davidson is staying with you for a few days. That's really nice of you to open your home to her until Chief Logan can figure out what's going on."

Connie joined in. "Let me know if there's anything we can do to help. She's been through so much already with the recent loss of her father."

"Things are tough for her right now, but she's doing better. I'll let her know you were both asking about her."

Then she made good on her escape. "Come on, Zeke. Let's hit the park."

Whether it was the bright sunshine outside or the fact that Abby wasn't the proud owner of a brand-new committee chairmanship, her mood had taken a definite upswing. Zeke was also happy to wander along the river that wound through the park. He especially enjoyed the trail that made a long loop through the national forest that bordered the town on one side. There, the towering firs and cedars crowded close to the path and filled the air with their fresh scent. Drawing a deep breath, Abby let the tension she'd been living with for the past few days fade away a little more.

However, it was hard not to think about the murder when it had happened a short distance from where she and Zeke were now walking. She tried to avert her eyes as they passed by the hillside where everyone had spread out their blankets and lawn chairs to watch the movie, but her resolve lasted all of thirty seconds. She had no business wandering around the murder scene, but she couldn't resist the temptation to check it out in the daylight.

Skirting the front edge of the trees, she and Zeke walked nearly halfway around the curve of the slope when she spotted a piece of yellow crime-scene tape stuck to a tree trunk. It was only a few inches long, no doubt accidentally left behind by whoever had cleaned up after Gage and his deputies had finished their investigation.

She coasted to a stop a few feet away from the tape.

"Zeke, I don't even know why I'm here or what I'm looking for."

He put his nose to the ground and sniffed his way toward the trees. There was no telling what he found so fascinating, but he was relentless as his big head swung from side to side as he kept moving in the general direction of the spot marked by the tape. She gave in to her own curiosity and trailed along behind him. When he finally stopped, he looked back over his shoulder and grumbled.

Maybe he was picking up the scent of old blood. If so, she didn't blame him for being creeped out. She patted his head and offered what comfort she could. "It's all right, boy. Let's forget we ever stopped here and head back toward the trail."

She walked about twenty feet past the tape and then cut through the trees. As they made their way back toward the trail, she studied the ground. From the wear pattern in the grass, it was clear that she and Zeke weren't the only ones who had taken that particular shortcut. All things considered, she figured that it was likely Mitch Anders had done the same thing in reverse the night of the movie, most likely so he could sneak in alcohol without getting caught.

It also seemed logical the murderer had come through there. Using the trees as cover would certainly explain why the attack had gone unnoticed by anyone in the vicinity. The idea of a killer stalking his victim so close to where families were watching a movie gave her the shivers. Would Mitch Anders have realized his peril if he hadn't been sucking down all those cans of beer? Or had he already passed out by that point?

One part of her really hoped so, that he'd died without feeling the pain and terror of being stabbed to death. It was the only thing that made sense to her. Otherwise, why hadn't he fought his attacker, or at least screamed for help? It wasn't as if he'd been alone in the darkness. There'd been dozens of people within shouting distance. Or had he been expecting his attacker and had no reason to suspect he was in danger?

All good questions, but ones she had no answers for. Regardless, she was convinced that this hadn't been a random attack. Had the killer come prepared to execute his victim or merely to confront him only to have the situation turn deadly? If so, did that mean stealing one of Owen's knives had been a spur of the moment decision, one that would deflect suspicion in his direction? Regardless, the execution had been carried off without a hitch, and it took someone with stone-cold resolve to commit murder when the risk of discovery was so high.

Even though the sky above was a vivid blue without a cloud in sight, the day had taken a dark turn. Abby tugged on Zeke's leash. "Come on, boy, it's time to go home."

Where they'd have a solid wood door with a stout lock between them and the rest of the world.

CHAPTER 23

There was one major glitch in Abby's plan. When she and Zeke returned to the parking lot behind city hall, her keys were nowhere to be found. After patting down her pockets, she dumped her pack out on the hood of the car. No luck there, either. Darn it, when was the last time she'd seen them? In her mind's eye, she clearly pictured them in her hand as she and Zeke walked away from the car in the parking lot.

Now the question was, had she still been holding them when she entered Gage's office? No, she didn't think so, which meant she must have set them down in the police department shortly before she'd met with Gage. Maybe when she'd stopped to open the cookie container.

"Sorry, Zeke, but we've got to go back inside."

The door on the near side of the building required the use of a passcode to get in, which meant they would have to ask the sergeant at the front desk to let them back into the bullpen area. Luckily, Sergeant Jones liked Zeke and offered to keep an eye on him while he buzzed her in. Abby hustled down the hall to where she'd left the treats for Gage's deputies. Sure enough, her keys were there, hidden behind the cookies and a stack of napkins.

After sticking them in her pocket for safekeeping, she was about to head back toward the lobby when she heard a familiar voice coming from Gage's office. He wasn't the one currently speaking, although he was definitely part of the conversation. She strained to listen closely, trying to decide if it really was Owen Quinn in there. Luckily, the bullpen was currently empty. There was no telling how long that would last, and she couldn't risk getting caught eavesdropping.

Trying to look as if she had a reason to be there, she helped herself to a cup of coffee in a disposable cup. While she stirred in cream and sugar, she struggled to make sense of the conversation between the two men, but their frustration and anger definitely came through loud and clear.

At the moment, Owen was the one talking. ". . . and I didn't lie, Gage. When you asked at the scene if anyone recognized him, I told you the man's name. I admit I didn't say I'd known him under a different identity. I had no way of knowing if that information might impact your investigation. For the record, his former identity, just like mine, remains classified. I can't talk about them, especially in front of civilians. You know that."

Gage snarled right back. "Yeah, I get why you didn't say anything at the park, but you could've at least told me that much when we talked here at the station. I've kept

my mouth shut about your past, haven't I? I get that you
don't know my people and that you most likely haven't
even told Phoebe McCree about your past exploits.
That's fine, but you knew full well you could trust me. I
was part of that life, too, even if I never got as deep into
the woods as you did. Regardless, I've got a murder investigation on my hands, one I can't solve if jerks like
you hide vital information from me. You know, like there
was some kind of connection between you, the victim,
and the man whose job he'd taken over. Not to mention a
burglary that may or may not be part of the whole package."

It sounded as if Gage had thrown something down on
the desk. "Imagine how I felt when Abby brought in
Jada's scrapbook this morning, and the first thing I see is
a picture of you and Mitch Anders standing right behind
Jada's father. I knew you'd served more than one tour in
Afghanistan besides the one where we crossed paths in
2005, but not that you'd known both Anders and Davidson. Was this taken before or after that?"

There was a brief lull before Owen answered. "It was a
few years later. I didn't actually know Davidson, but Anders was in and out of that area several times from what I
heard."

Gage didn't sound much happier. "I'm pretty sure
Abby didn't recognize you, but then she's never seen you
with dark hair and sporting that stupid beard you were so
proud of. I don't think for one minute you killed Anders,
but only because you aren't stupid enough to paint a target on your own back. But get this through your thick
skull—I can't protect you if you insist on keeping me in
the dark. I'm getting major pushback from the prosecut-

ing attorney's office because I haven't charged you with the murder. In case you've forgotten, you have no alibi and it was your knife."

Abby shivered. If Gage ever talked to her with that much cold fury in his voice, she would duck for cover. Owen was made of sterner stuff. "Yes, you've protected my secrets, and I thank you for that. And I swear, if there's any indication Anders's death is due to something from his time in the service, I will do everything I can to get you the information you need."

"You'd better, or I'll throw you right back in that cell until you rot. Understand?"

"Yeah."

Gage's chair creaked like it did when he leaned back. "I talked to Reilly Molitor earlier, and he promised to hunt down the JPEG for this picture for me. When that happens, I'm going to want you back in here to see if there's anything more you can tell me about it."

"Just give me a call."

When she heard the scrape of a chair, she realized Owen was about to leave. Time to disappear before the two men figured out that they'd had an audience. There wasn't much Owen could do about her newfound knowledge, but it might give Gage an excuse to make good on his continuing threat to let her experience life in one of his cells firsthand.

It was tempting to run for the exit, but that would look really suspicious if she crossed paths with one of Gage's deputies. On the way, she stopped to use the restroom to buy herself a little time to calm down before she reclaimed Zeke. Sergeant Jones was a nice man, but he was very much a cop. If she returned breathing hard and looking guilty, it would be sure to trigger his spidey senses.

While waiting for her pulse to slow down to something close to normal, she dumped the unwanted coffee down the sink and tossed the cup in the trash.

She peeked out the restroom door to make sure she wasn't going to walk right into Owen on his way out. The coast was clear, and she made it to the lobby without incident. After retrieving Zeke, they hustled out the door and around the corner to the parking lot.

Naturally her luck didn't hold out. While she and Zeke had to go the long way around, Owen had taken the shorter route to the parking lot through the back door. He was already out of the building and heading for his car as she and Zeke rounded the corner. Maybe if they remained right where they were he wouldn't notice them. She hauled back on Zeke's leash to slow him down. Sadly, Owen possessed the same uncanny sense of his surroundings as Tripp and Gage, no doubt honed by that mysterious past that Gage had alluded to.

He'd had his back to her, but he paused midstride to turn back around. His first reaction was to smile, but that quickly morphed into a frown when she kept her distance. "Abby, what's wrong?"

The parking lot probably wasn't the best place for this confrontation, but it was time she got some answers of her own. She didn't bother faking a smile as she marched toward the man. Like Gage, she wasn't particularly happy with Owen Quinn right now. The chief of police might have a murder case to solve, but Abby had her mother to protect.

When she got close enough, she finally answered his question. "Yes, Owen Quinn, or whatever your real name is, something is wrong. You've been lying to all of us, including my mother, about who you are."

Another two steps put her within arm's reach of her target. She poked him in the chest with her forefinger to show him she meant business. "I don't much care why you moved to Snowberry Creek. That's your business—or it was right up until you decided to involve my mother in whatever games you're playing."

At that point, Zeke shoved himself between the two of them to join the conversation with a low growl. That's when she realized that Owen no longer looked all that friendly. There was a sharp edge to his expression she'd never seen before, giving her a glimpse of the dangerous man underneath the friendly veneer he routinely showed the world.

She backpedaled a step and let her hand drop back down to her side. Maybe it was time to ramp down the anger. "I accidentally overheard you and Gage talking. I get that it was all meant to be hush-hush, but I don't intend to go blabbing it all over town. I even believe you had nothing to do with Mitch Anders's death. I just don't want to see my mom hurt."

For a long few seconds he stared at her as he weighed his options. Finally, he took a deep breath and let it out, his tension quickly dissipating. Even Zeke slowly wagged his tail to acknowledge the dangerous moment had passed. Owen petted the dog and offered Abby a rueful smile. "I knew both Tripp and Gage worry about your ability to attract trouble, but I didn't understand until now what they were talking about. You have a definite knack for being at the wrong place at the wrong time."

Her cheeks flushed hot, but she wasn't sure if it was because his observation was infuriating or embarrassing. It didn't really matter, and now wasn't the time to pour gas on the situation. She'd already told the man what she wanted to know, so she crossed her arms over her chest and waited him out.

Finally, he let out one more slow breath as he glanced around the parking lot. "Fine, Abby, I'll explain what I can, but I'm counting on your promise that this conversation goes no further. If you have any questions about me or my past, you come to me or even Gage. He won't be able to give you much in the way of details, but then neither can I. Agreed?"

She nodded. After all, what choice did she have?

"I was in the military when I was recruited to work for another agency. Understandably, most of what I did was classified. I almost died on my last assignment, and that's when I walked away from that life. I changed my identity and chose a new career where I figured the worst thing that could happen would be a flat tire on my food truck."

He allowed himself a small smile. "As to why I picked Snowberry Creek, it's close to all kinds of fishing, and there wasn't a decent barbecue restaurant within forty miles."

Despite the lack of specific details in his explanation, she found herself believing him. Her mother would probably have a hissy fit if she found out Abby had had the audacity to ask Owen what his intentions were, but that didn't stop her. "And how does my mom fit into this new life of yours?"

"That's up to Phoebe. She's waiting for me at my house, and I already planned to tell her the same things that I just told you." He ran his fingers through his hair, looking frustrated. "Look, I swear that if I thought for one minute the things I did in the past would put your mom in danger, I would break things off with her immediately. Having said that, she means a lot to me, Abby. She's an amazing woman, and I treasure the time we spend together. I hope you'll give me a chance to prove that I'll treat her right."

What could she say to that? She didn't know him well enough to know how trustworthy he was, but Gage seemed to think a lot of the man. All things considered, she gave him the only answer she could. "Fine, but just know I'll be watching you like a hawk. Hurt her, and I'll be coming after you with everything I've got."

Rather take offense at her threat, Owen grinned and stuck out his hand. "It's a deal."

After they shook, she started toward her car when Owen spoke one more time. "You can tell Tripp, too, if you want. Gage says he knows how to keep his mouth shut. Besides, the man shouldn't be kept in the dark, especially since he seems pretty determined to stand guard over both you and Jada."

As peace offerings went, that was a dandy. "Thanks, Owen. I know Tripp will appreciate your faith in him. So do I. Good luck with Mom, by the way. You may need it."

He just laughed as he walked away.

Four hours later, Abby glanced at the clock and grumbled, "What's keeping Mom, Zeke?"

It wasn't that she expected the dog to answer, but she needed to talk to somebody as she paced the length of the hall and back again. She'd had the house all to herself when they'd gotten home, and it had been tempting to fix a huge mug of Darjeeling tea and lose herself in a good book. Instead, she'd taken advantage of the opportunity to catch up on few chores.

With the vacuuming and laundry done, she'd tried to

work on her quilting but gave up after a short time. She'd been too restless to focus, and now found herself dithering about nothing. The problem was that she hadn't heard from her mother since long before her confrontation with Owen in the parking lot. The logical part of her brain insisted the woman was an adult and could take care of herself. They often went a week or more without speaking, so it wasn't as if she always knew how her mom spent every minute of her time. She only hoped Owen had made good on his promise to fill her mother in on his background.

Abby would've given anything to listen in while he explained his mysterious past. Considering how few details he could actually share, the talk shouldn't have taken all that long, and she'd expected her mom to check in afterward. At least Abby's mind instantly threw up roadblocks whenever she started thinking too hard about how else her mom and Owen Quinn could've spent the afternoon besides just talking.

No way she wanted to go there. Nope, not at all.

On the other hand, the emotional side of her mind couldn't help but worry. The longer her mother's absence continued, the crazier the possibilities became. Her latest was that Owen and her mother were now on the run, out of fear that he'd be charged with murder and end up back in jail. The hamster wheel of worries spinning in her head made Abby furious. If she ever stayed missing in action like this, she'd never hear the end of it.

As she made the turn at the end of the hall to head back to the kitchen, someone pulled into the driveway, hopefully her mother. Instead, she watched Tripp park his truck and then waited to see if he went straight to his place or if he would head her way. Once again the man sensed her watching him. He paused on his porch long enough to wave before disappearing into his house. She tried to tell herself that she wasn't disappointed, but no doubt he had homework and chores of his own to take care of.

She was about to return to her pacing when she caught a movement out of the corner of her eye. Yay! Tripp was headed her way, beer in hand. She opened the back door and let Zeke brush past her to charge across the yard to greet his best friend. Deciding a cold drink sounded good, she grabbed a can of pop from the fridge and followed Zeke outside. After tossing a stick a few times for Zeke, Tripp joined her on the porch, sighing as he sank down onto one of the Adirondack chairs.

As he stretched his legs out, he said, "Boy, this feels good. It's been a long one."

"Yeah, it has." She studied her companion, noticing the fine lines around his eyes looked deeper than usual. "Tough day at school?"

He held the cold beer against his forehead as if fighting a headache. "No more than usual. Sometimes just being around all the youthful enthusiasm of my fellow students makes me tired."

She snorted. "Yeah, you're such an old man."

He looked even more grim. "By their standards, I am. I've got a solid twenty years on some of them. Seen things, done things they can't even imagine. The difference that makes in our world views is mind-boggling at times."

He stared off into the trees. "It's like we're not even speaking the same language."

Not for the first time she wondered what he was seeing in his mind when he got that distant expression in his eyes. Before she could ask, he shook his head and then glanced at her. "How did your day go?"

Where to begin?

"For starters, Will Swahn, Jada's godfather, showed up at the door uninvited, and I'm guessing mostly unwelcome. He claimed to have found out where she was staying from one of Jada's neighbors." She frowned. "I'm not sure why, but I have serious doubts that's what happened."

"Are you going to let Gage know about him showing up like that?"

"I already did."

She paused to take a drink before launching right back into her diatribe. "Mom left before I got up, and I haven't seen her all day. She hasn't called, either."

Tripp shot her sideways glance. "You do know phones work in both directions. If you're that worried, you could call her or even send a text if you don't actually want to talk to her."

Although he didn't exactly smile, she had a sneaking suspicion he was laughing at her. "Yeah, I thought about that, but it felt too much like flashing a porch light. You know, because she's with Owen."

Then she gave him a narrow-eyed look. "Speaking of which, thanks for sharing that little tidbit about the porch light with Gage. He thought it was hilarious."

The man wisely looked apologetic. "Sorry, it sort of slipped out. I didn't mean to embarrass you."

She conceded the point. "No, that was my mom's intent, not yours."

Tripp steered their conversation back to safer territory. "So what did this Swahn guy want?"

"Allegedly to check on Jada and make sure she was

okay. She hadn't heard from him since her dad's funeral, but then he tracked her down here to bug her about some book her father had borrowed. Maybe he waited this long out of consideration, but I don't buy it.

"When Jada said she needed to leave for class, he acted pretty weird and asked me to step away so they could discuss something in private. She clearly wasn't too keen on that idea, so Zeke and I saw him out. I have a feeling he'll be back at some point, though. Either that or he'll wait until Jada returns home and corner her there. I could be misreading the situation, but I don't think so."

She gave Tripp a frustrated look. "But who knows? It's not like he knows me at all. Maybe he wasn't sure how much he should say in front of a relative stranger."

"Could be, but your instincts when it comes to reading people are usually right on target." Tripp propped his feet up on the porch railing as if settling in for the duration. "To switch topics, what's for dinner tonight? Sorry to say, I'm fresh out of tuna casserole."

She stuck her tongue out him. "Don't be a jerk. Actually, Jada plans to order in when she gets back from class, her treat. I'm guessing she feels like she needs to contribute something toward meals while she's living here."

"Can't blame her for that. She might seem like a kid to us, but she's had to do a lot of growing up these past few weeks. You'd want to pay your own way if you were her."

It would be hard to be totally dependent on people who had been total strangers to Jada only days before. "True enough. It's been a while since we've had Chinese, so I thought I'd suggest that. It's cheap, and we both like it."

"Sounds good."

She was in no hurry to end the comfortable silence that

settled between them, but she had yet to tell him about her meeting with Gage. Then there was her discussion with Owen that had followed. There was no real urgency, but she'd rather fill Tripp in on everything while the two of them were alone. She started off with the easy part first. "I took Jada's scrapbook to Gage today. We looked through the pictures of Mr. Davidson's office, but it was hard to pick out any important details even with a magnifying glass. He planned to call Reilly Molitor to see if he could track down the JPEG of the one that had the best shot of the stolen picture."

Tripp set his beer on the porch railing. "Well, learning anything significant from a bunch of old newspaper clippings was a longshot."

"I'm mostly hoping he can make a clear print of Mr. Davidson's army unit for Jada."

"Who knows, Reilly might come through for her." Tripp shot her a wicked grin. "Maybe he'll make more of an effort if I promise not to toss him out in the street to see how high he bounces the next time he gets all in your face about something."

"I'm sure that threat could spur him onto greater heights."

Tripp groaned. "Tell me that isn't your idea of funny, because it seriously wasn't."

She pretended a hurt she didn't really feel. "Fine, be that way. But while we're talking about non-funny things, I had an interesting conversation with Owen earlier this afternoon."

It was hard to tell if it was the subject matter or her grim tone that had Tripp sitting up straighter. There was no question about his heightened interest in what she was about to say. "Do tell."

She hated keeping secrets from Tripp and was glad she didn't have to this time. On the other hand, he wasn't going to like the fact she'd listened in on Owen's conversation with Gage. Deciding confession was good for the soul, she started by explaining why she'd ended up back in the police station.

"So, while I was getting my keys, I accidently overheard Gage and Owen having words."

Just that quickly Tripp had the same tough-guy expression on his face that had scared her a bit when she'd seen it on Owen's. Her reaction was far different this time, though. While Tripp might get mad, he never scared her, not even at his angriest.

"And you didn't stop to think their conversation wasn't meant for your ears?"

She prayed for patience. "Like I said, I was there to retrieve my keys, not to spy on Gage. Besides, they should've closed the door if they wanted to keep the discussion private. Anybody in the general area would've heard them. From what Gage said, he wasn't planning on sharing what Owen told him with his own deputies."

Now her handsome tenant looked nothing but disgusted. "You say that like it excuses you for hanging around long enough to get an earful."

Her conscience tried to stir to life, but she quickly squelched it. Going on the offensive, she snapped, "All right, Mr. High-and-Mighty, what would you have done?"

"I would've let Gage know I was there in case he needed to do damage control. Now you possess information regarding the case that he considers confidential. You need to tell him."

"I already let Owen know, which is what I was going to tell you before you so rudely interrupted."

"And what did he have to say about that little bomb-shell?"

She did a little glaring of her own. "He told me that both you and Gage have warned him that I have a pen-chant for getting into trouble. For the record, I didn't ap-preciate that one bit."

He angled himself to look more directly at her. "What can I say? We call them as we see them."

Considering how many times Tripp had had to come to her rescue, there was no way she was going to win that particular argument. Time to move on. "Owen gave me specific permission to let you know what we talked about, so don't think I'm telling tales out of school. I've suspected all along that Owen had been in the military. What I didn't know is that at some point he got recruited to work for some government agency. He didn't say which one, and I didn't ask."

She paused in case Tripp wanted to praise her for her forbearance. When he didn't, she picked up where she'd left off. "In short, he retired after his last mission went badly, Owen Quinn isn't his original name, and his old identity remains classified. If that wasn't interesting enough, it turns out the same could be said of the murder victim, Mitch Anders. The two of them knew each other back then, and they're both in that photo of Mr. David-son's unit, the one that was stolen. Gage wasn't happy to find out about that little fact from the scrapbook instead of from Owen himself."

An odd question popped into her head, one that would never have occurred to her to ask before today. "Say, is Tripp Blackston your real name? You can tell me if it isn't. I promise to protect your identity."

He'd just taken another drink of beer, which he promptly

spewed right back out in a burst of laughter. Luckily, the spray missed her, but Zeke gave Tripp a puzzled look as it landed on his fur. "That's some imagination you have, lady. But yes, it's the name I was born with. I was Special Forces, not a spy with a decoder ring."

"Good to know." Although for some strange reason, she was a bit disappointed. She kind of liked the idea of having an ex-spy for a tenant. "Anyway, back to Owen. After we parted ways, he was going to tell my mother the basic facts. He also swore that he'd break things off with her if his past ever presented any kind of threat to her."

Tripp gave her a doubtful look. "And so now that you know he has a secret past, you're okay with them being together?"

Actually, she'd been mulling over that exact question all afternoon. "Gage trusts him, which says a lot. Owen also seemed sincere about caring about Mom and wants to make her happy. It also helps that I know why he plays his cards close to his chest. He deserves a chance to prove himself to not just me, but her as well."

"That's good. Maybe if you quit questioning her life choices, she'll quit questioning yours." Having dropped that little bombshell, he drained his beer and stood up. "I'm going to grab another cold one from your fridge. Want anything while I'm inside?"

Before she could respond, Tripp disappeared into the house, leaving her staring at his back as he shut the door hard enough to rattle the windows. Okay, then. Clearly she wasn't the only one having issues with her mother.

CHAPTER 24

Abby had no idea what her mother had said to Tripp that indicated she didn't approve of his relationship with her daughter. When he came back outside, he handed her a beer even though she hadn't asked for one. She couldn't fault his instincts, though. A little alcohol would go a long way toward blunting the edges of her temper right now.

Once he was settled back in his chair, she leaned toward him. "Tripp, if my mother said anything that made you feel less than welcome in my life, she and I will be having words on the subject."

He reached across the short distance between them to take her hand in his. "Don't sweat it, Abby. She's understandably not happy that you keep getting drawn into murder cases since moving to Snowberry Creek and wants you to return to the safety of your old life. She knows the friends and connections you've made here make that un-likely. I can handle whatever she dishes out, except when she rips into you. That makes me furious."

Abby, too, which meant it needed to stop. "Maybe I should've pushed back harder the other day when I parked the car and walked away. At the time, I was too angry and hurt to have anything close to a rational conversation. But as I told her, I love the life I'm building here in Snow-berry Creek, and you're a big part of the reason why. If she won't accept that, it's her problem, not ours."

He tugged on her hand. "Come here."

Abby didn't hesitate. As soon as she stood in front of him, he tumbled her into his lap. Her arms found their way around his neck almost of their own accord as his wicked smile signaled his intentions. That was okay, con-sidering she suspected her own smile mirrored his. She was leaning in for the kiss they both wanted when the sound of a car pulling into the driveway had Zeke sound-ing the alarm.

Chances were either Jada or her mother would be putting in an appearance any second. Too bad. Abby was going to kiss Tripp while the chance presented itself. They kept it short, but the sense of urgency packed a hefty dose of *wow* into the brief encounter. She was about to clamber back up to her feet when Jada came around the end of the house.

As soon as she saw them, she grinned and backed up a step. "Maybe I should leave and come back again, say in an hour or so."

Tripp lit up as if he was considering taking her up on the offer, but Abby dropped back into her own seat. "Ig-nore him. Come on up and have a seat."

Jada accepted the invitation, sounding relieved when

she dropped her backpack down onto the porch and stretched her legs out in front of her. "Boy, this feels good."

She smiled when Zeke nudged her hand and hinted for her to pet him. As she stroked his fur, she glanced at Abby. "Did you guys decide what you wanted for dinner tonight?"

"We were thinking Chinese sounded good, if that's all right with you. I like broccoli beef, and Tripp will eat whatever you put in front of him."

Instead of acting insulted, Tripp just laughed. "She's not wrong, especially when I don't have to cook."

Jada pulled out her phone. "Great, I'll place the order and tell them to aim for delivering dinner in about an hour."

After Jada disappeared into the house, Tripp went back home to take care of a couple of chores. Zeke opted to go with him, probably hoping for a few extra treats while he hung out on Tripp's couch. Meanwhile, Abby set the table and then read in the living room while she waited for dinner to arrive.

When a car pulled up out front, she set the book aside and quickly texted Tripp to let him know dinner had arrived. Rather than wait for the driver to carry the bags of food all the way to the house, Abby walked out to meet him halfway. Jada had probably added a tip to the bill, but Abby slipped him an extra five anyway. "Here you go, Cody."

He pocketed the money and grinned at her. "Thanks, Abby. Enjoy your dinner."

She suspected she was one of Cody's most frequent customers. His grandmother was a member of the quilting guild, and she'd shared that he was putting himself through college delivering meals for several of the local restaurants. "Let me know if you add any new names to the list of places you deliver for. I'm always up for trying out different menus."

"Will do. I was supposed to start delivering for Mr. Quinn's barbecue joint, but it's been closed for the past few days. I'll let you know when I get everything set up with him."

Rather than explain why that might take a while, she said, "Well, I'd better get this inside. Tell your grandmother hi for me."

As Cody drove away, she noticed a car parked a short distance down the street. It seemed vaguely familiar, but it took her a few seconds to place it. Unless she was mistaken, it looked like the dark blue SUV that had cruised by Jada's house the day Abby and her mother had stopped by to check on her. Could it also be the same one that Jada had mentioned to Gage? If someone really was spying on Jada, it probably wasn't a coincidence that same SUV would suddenly appear on Abby's street.

She set the food bags down on the porch and then pulled her phone out of her pocket. If she could get a clear shot of the car's license plate, Gage could run it to find out who owned the car. Of course, it could simply belong to somebody visiting one of her neighbors. If that was the case, she would apologize for any inconvenience she caused the owner.

Rather than sticking to the sidewalk that led directly to the street, she cut across the grass to use the cluster of rhododendrons in the front corner of her yard as cover. If there was someone in the car watching the house, it would be best to avoid drawing any attention to herself for as long as possible. Unfortunately, the reflection of the early evening sun off the windshield made it impossible to tell for sure if the car was occupied.

Her plan worked fine right up until she realized she was too far away and at the wrong angle to get a straight-on shot of the SUV's license plate. Leaving the deep cover of the bushes, she edged forward to the point there was only one large rhody left between her and the road.

From where she now stood, there still was no detectable movement in the car. Maybe luck was with her, and it was unoccupied. Deciding to go big or go home, she boldly walked out into the road as if crossing to the other side. At the last second, she spun to snap a picture. She was about to take a second one when the car surged forward. The sudden movement startled her into nearly dropping her phone. Then there was a loud roar just before something plowed into her, carrying her the rest of the way across the street to tumble to the ground in her neighbor's yard. The impact knocked the breath out of her, but she still managed to screech in protest.

Before she could holler for help a second time, a big hand clamped down on her mouth. "Abby, shut up. It's me."

Her frazzled brain finally managed to recognize the voice. "Tripp?"

He glared down at her. "Yeah."

She gave him a hard shove, which had no impact on him at all. "Why did you tackle me?"

He kept her anchored right there on the grass long enough to snarl, "Oh, I don't know. Maybe I thought you'd prefer that to being flattened by that SUV barreling right towards you."

Then, without giving her a chance to respond, he rolled to his feet and pulled her back up to her feet with one powerful tug on her hand. As he marched back toward her house, dragging her behind him, he growled, "We'll continue this discussion behind closed doors."

Contrary to what he'd just said, he started railing at her again as soon as they crossed the boundary back into her yard. "What the heck were you thinking? I swear I've never known anyone so determined to get herself killed."

That was outrageous. How could he even think that? She planted her feet, refusing to go another step. "I was not trying to get myself killed!"

He wheeled around to stare down at her, crowding close as an unspoken reminder of how much bigger he was. "Really? Were you out there playing in traffic for no particular reason at all?"

"Don't be ridiculous. I had a reason." She held up her phone after checking to see it had survived their fall. "I think that SUV was the same one that drove by when Mom and I stopped at Jada's house. She also told Gage she'd noticed a dark blue SUV in her neighborhood on day of the break-in. I wanted to get a picture of the vehicle's license plate, so Gage can check out who it belongs to and find out why they're hanging around our neighborhood. Besides, I thought the car was empty."

"Well, it wasn't, was it? I suppose it didn't occur to you to simply call the police to come investigate." He clenched his fists at his side. "No, of course not. Why contact trained professionals when you have Abby McCree, amateur sleuth, on the job?"

Well, if he was going to look at the situation that way, she guessed it did sound bad. "Why don't we go inside and eat? The food is getting cold."

He went completely still and then shook his head. "You know what, I'm going to give dinner a pass. I've got better things to do with my time right now than to try and talk sense to a total nitwit."

That last part really hurt, but she didn't want to let him walk away mad at her. "Come on, Tripp. There was no harm done. Come inside."

He no longer looked angry. Instead, his expression was incredibly sad. "Sorry, Abby. I can't do this. I told you once before that I've already lost too many friends in this life. I don't want to hang around until you finally do something that gets you killed."

Her heart broke as he walked away.

Miserably unhappy, Abby retrieved the bags that she'd left on the porch. Tripp wasn't the only one whose appetite had disappeared, but it wouldn't be fair to Jada to let their dinner go to waste. She carried it into the kitchen and unloaded the boxes of food on the table. She was just putting Tripp's plate back in the cupboard when Jada walked in. "Isn't Tripp eating?"

Abby blinked hard trying to stave off the tears threatening to spill down her cheeks. "No, he went home."

Jada inched closer, moving slowly as if not sure if her presence would be welcome. "Did you two have a fight?"

"Yeah, sort of, anyway. I made a decision he didn't like, and he's mad." Trying to pretend that was no big deal, she sat down at the table and started opening the containers. "We'd better eat before everything gets cold."

Jada joined her at the table. "Is there anything I can do?"

"No, it'll be fine." Okay, that might not be true, but she really hoped it would be. "I'll give him a chance to cool off and then go talk to him. I can always use taking him dinner as an excuse."

Jada spooned rice onto her plate and then added some sweet-and-sour pork over the top. "I don't mean to be nosy, but I'm a good listener if you want to talk about what happened."

There was no reason not to share. Jada would find out what happened as soon as Abby gave Gage a call. With her luck, he'd probably yell at her, too. To buy herself a bit of time, she took a bite of the broccoli beef. If it had any flavor, she couldn't taste it. Setting her fork down, she leaned back in her chair.

"I walked out front to meet Cody, the driver who delivered the food. When I spotted a dark blue SUV parked a short distance down the street, I decided to take a picture of the license plate for Gage. I was hoping he could track down the owner." She lifted her gaze to meet Jada's. "You know, to see if it was someone who might be tied to either the murder or the break-in."

Rather than being grateful, Jada looked horrified. "Abby! What were you thinking? If that was the killer or even the burglar, who's to say they wouldn't have tried to stop you? Or that they won't come back?"

Okay, maybe taking that picture wasn't the brightest thing she'd ever done. It had seemed reasonable at the time, but clearly she was in the minority on that. "It's too late now, but at least I did get the picture. I'll call Gage as soon as we're done eating."

She rustled up a small smile. "I should be safe, though. If he reacts like both you and Tripp did, he'll toss me in a cell for my own protection."

Jada looked at her as if she'd totally lost it. "That's not funny, Abby. No wonder Tripp's upset."

Abby studied the array of food on the table. "I'm sorry I'm not doing justice to the meal you paid for, but we can always have it for lunch tomorrow. Right now, though, I'd better go call Gage."

Jada started to say something, but then her eyes widened in surprise. "I don't think you're going to have to call him after all, Abby."

"Why not?"

"Because he's standing on the back porch."

Bracing herself for another confrontation with an overprotective male, Abby got up to let him in. When she stood facing him through the window that formed the top half of the door, he gave her his angry-cop look and held up pair of handcuffs.

Abby grimaced and then glanced back at Jada before opening the door. "So tell me, how do you think I'm going to look in one of the Snowberry Creek Jail orange jumpsuits?"

CHAPTER 25

A braver person might've been able to stand her ground and face down the irate lawman on her back porch. But at that moment, that wasn't Abby. In fact, she wasn't sure how much longer her legs were going to support her. Worried she'd collapse in a hot mess on the floor, she motioned for Gage to come inside and quickly retreated to her seat at the table.

As he closed the door, she pointed toward his usual chair. "Would you like to join us for dinner?"

He remained standing, towering over her. "Playing the gracious hostess card won't cut it this time, Abby. You'd do better trying to convince me not to slap these cuffs on your wrists and haul you off to that cell I've been warning you about."

She'd been staring down at the table, but now she dragged her gaze up to meet Gage's. "I know an apology isn't much, but it's all I have to offer. I really wasn't try-ing to interfere with your case. I wanted to help."

To substantiate that claim, she slid her cell phone across the table in his direction. "I saw what might be the same vehicle parked out on my street that Jada and I both saw in her neighborhood, and decided to snap a picture of it. I thought if you could read the license plate, you might be able to track down the owner to see why someone is following Jada around."

When Gage made no effort to reach for the phone, she sighed. "And yes, I realize now that I should've called nine-one-one and asked for a deputy to swing by to check it out. I was just afraid the vehicle would be gone before anyone could get here."

Okay, that idea hadn't even occurred to her, but it was important to convince Gage she hadn't acted completely on impulse. It probably wasn't smart to lie to him about anything, but it didn't matter. It was all too clear her ploy hadn't worked, considering his expression hadn't soft-ened at all. Either he didn't believe her or else he didn't care what she'd been thinking at the time.

"I'm guessing Tripp called you."

"He did."

Those two sharp-edged words clarified what really had Gage so upset. Her rash actions had not only endan-gered herself, but they'd hurt Tripp as well. Once again, her eyes burned with the sting of tears, but she didn't de-serve the release they would offer her. She swiped at her face with a paper napkin, wincing at the feel of the rough paper against her skin.

"I've already apologized to him, but I know it's not enough."

"No, it's not."

His words were still chilly, but at least Gage finally sat down. When he was settled, he tossed the handcuffs on the table between them, a harsh reminder that she still wasn't in the clear on this. "Show me the vehicle."

Her hands were shaking so hard that it took her several attempts to find the picture on her phone. With everything that had happened, she hadn't had a chance to look at it herself. Thank goodness both the make of the SUV and the license plate were crystal clear.

When she passed it over to Gage, he studied it for a few seconds before handing it to Jada. "What do you think? Could this be the same one you spotted outside of your place?"

It worried Abby when Jada didn't immediately answer. It was bad enough that she might've permanently damaged her relationship with both Tripp and Gage. It would be so much worse if she'd done so for no gain. Jada finally nodded and handed the phone back to Gage. "I can't say for sure, but it could be. The overall shape and color look right."

He set the phone down on the table and got out his own. Abby didn't know who he called, but he asked the person on the other end of the line to run the plate for him. While he waited, he yanked his spiral notebook and pen out of his pocket. She had no experience with how long such things took, but it was only a matter of seconds before Gage started writing something down. When he was finished, he said thanks and disconnected the call.

He leaned back in his chair, his eyebrows riding low as he frowned. "Well, that's certainly interesting."

It was tempting to ask questions, but right now the less she said the better. Jada looked curious as well as they both waited for Gage to decide he was ready to share. "What can either of you tell me about Eve Swahn?"

At first the name didn't mean anything to Abby, but Jada looked more surprised than confused. "Will Swahn is my godfather. Eve is his wife . . . or possibly his ex-wife now. I'm not really sure. Before he stopped by here, I hadn't actually seen Will in ages other than at my father's funeral. Dad and Will used to be pretty close, but not so much for the last few years. I can't say I really know Eve at all."

"Any idea why she'd be lurking around wherever you happen to be?"

Jada only looked more puzzled. "No. Even when Dad and Will used to hang out together, it was usually just the two of them. Eve never came with her husband at all after Mom died, so I have no idea why she'd suddenly take an interest in me."

Thanks to her own rather contentious divorce, Abby actually had a thought about why Eve Swahn might be lurking around. The trouble was, she wasn't sure if anyone—especially Gage—would want to hear it. Finally, she raised her hand while feeling a bit foolish for doing so. Gage pinched the bridge of his nose and sighed. "This isn't elementary school, Abby. You don't have to wait to be called on."

Well, fine. It wasn't as if he always welcomed her input. She dropped her hand back down to her lap. "Maybe she's hoping to cross paths with Will. Jada mentioned earlier she didn't know where he was staying these days, and maybe his wife is having the same problem. Even if neither of them is contesting the divorce, that doesn't mean they've come to an agreement on dividing up their assets or even the value of those assets."

Jada frowned, as if not quite following, so Abby did her best to explain. "It's like this, Jada. My ex-husband and I owned a business that we started together. After we separated, he'd agreed to buy me out but then decided to be a jerk about it. He lied to the court and said that I was little better than a file clerk and deserved a small severance package rather than half the actual value of the company. Fortunately for me, our records clearly proved that I was both co-owner and chief financial officer. It all worked out in the end, but it wasn't fun."

Gage looked sympathetic for the first time since he'd walked through the door. "Unfortunately, that sort of stuff is more common than most people know. Maybe something like that is going on between Mr. and Mrs. Swahn."

He picked up his notebook and pen and stuck them back in his pocket. "Looks like I need to have a talk with the lady. I'll call if I have any further questions for either of you."

As he stood up, he also pocketed the handcuffs but then leaned down to look Abby right in the face. She instinctively tried to put a little extra distance between her and the anger in his eyes. "I'm going leave you on your own recognizance—for now. Don't make me regret it. In fact, consider yourself under house arrest until tomorrow. If you can't stay out of trouble for that long, we'll revisit the matter."

He stopped to toss Zeke a cookie from the treat jar on his way out. "Keep an eye on her, dog. You've got your work cut out for you."

Zeke gulped down the treat and then woofed his acceptance of his orders. Gage was chuckling as he headed out the door. Jada picked up her plate and stuck it in the microwave. "Do you want me to reheat your dinner, too?"

Abby carried her plate over to the counter and stared out toward Tripp's house for several seconds. "Thanks, but I think I'd better try to mend a few fences."

Her decision made, she took several plastic containers out of the cabinet and dished up a generous amount of food for Tripp. After debating whether or not to heat it up for him, she decided against it. If the man was hungry— and when wasn't he?—he could nuke it himself. Too bad she didn't have a fresh-baked pie to go along with her makeshift peace offering. It was probably too much to hope that he'd forgiven her rash actions, but she had to at least try to make up for the pain she'd caused him.

Zeke whined as she gathered everything up and started for the door. Should she take him with her? No, it wasn't fair to the dog to have to deal with the emotional tug-of-war if his two favorite people couldn't be civil to each other. "I know you have your orders from Gage, Zeke, but you should stay with Jada. I probably won't be gone long."

And if that didn't sound pathetic, she didn't know what did.

Jada gave her a quick hug. "Good luck, Abby. Tripp is only mad because he cares. I'm betting he's cooled off by now."

"Maybe."

With considerable effort, she managed to slip past Zeke's determined efforts to come with her. Her journey across the yard took both too long and not nearly long enough. All too soon she stood on Tripp's porch, where it took every bit of courage she had to knock. Seconds passed in silence, and she'd almost given up when she finally heard footsteps approaching from the other side of the door. Her breath caught in her throat as she waited to see what, if anything, Tripp would say to her.

When the door swung open, Tripp planted himself in the middle of the doorway, clearly in no hurry to welcome her inside. Disappointing, but not surprising. He also didn't say a word, which left it up to her to break the impasse.

"I know you're angry, and you have every right to be. No matter how good my intentions were, it was impulsive and stupid on my part, so I'll say it again. I'm really sorry, and I hope you'll forgive me."

Then she held out the bag full of food. "I don't want you to go hungry because of my mistake."

When he didn't immediately accept the offering, she set it down on the porch and turned to walk away. Before she'd gone more than four steps, a big hand came down on her shoulder and spun her back around. Her first instinct was to fight her way loose and run for the privacy of her room, but Tripp wasn't having it. He pulled her close and wrapped his arms around her. "Don't cry, Abby. You know I hate that."

She sniffled against his T-shirt. "I can't help it. I hurt you, which hurts me, too."

He sighed. "Yeah, about that. I admit you scared the heck out of me. But looking back, I probably overreacted. I'm pretty sure that car swerved to the other side of the road long before it passed by, so the driver wasn't really aiming at you. I was just putting on my shoes to head your way when you stepped up on the porch."

She looked up to see if he meant that. "Really?"

He grinned just a little. "Look for yourself. I only managed to put on one before you knocked."

She glanced down to see he was sporting a single un-tied shoe while his other foot was clad in a sock. Consid-ering how damp the grass was, that couldn't be comfortable. "So I see. Why don't we take this conversa-tion inside?"

At least he kept his arm around her shoulders as they walked back toward his porch, stopping only long enough to retrieve the bag she'd left for him. That went a long way toward convincing her that their friendship hadn't been totally destroyed. It was amazing how much that lit-tle bit of knowledge improved her outlook on life. When they were safely inside with the door locked, she pointed at the bag he'd set on the counter in his tiny kitchen. "I brought enough for both of us on the off chance that you didn't hate me anymore."

Tripp didn't comment, but at least he handed her dishes to set the table for two while he warmed up their dinner. To break the silence, she said, "So, Gage ran the plates on that SUV. Turns out it belongs to Eve Swahn, Jada's godfather's ex-wife."

"I assume Gage will track her down."

"Yep, although there's no guarantee he'll tell us what he finds out." Which was frustrating, but there wasn't much she could do about it. Not with the memory of those handcuffs still dancing in her head.

Tripp passed her a beer. "Tell me you're not thinking about asking him to keep you in the loop."

It was more of an order than a question, but she an-swered anyway. "Nope, I know better."

She risked a small grin as she shared a little more about what had happened during Gage's visit. "Espe-cially considering he showed up at my back door waving a pair of handcuffs in my face. He also put me on house arrest until tomorrow. He even assigned Zeke guard duty, bribing him with a dog treat I baked for the furry traitor."

Tripp didn't look amused. "And yet here you are at my house, not yours."

She arched an eyebrow. "True, but I'm still within the boundaries of my property lines. He didn't say I couldn't go outside at all."

His answering snort made his thoughts on that all too clear. That was okay, though. All that mattered was the two of them were back on speaking terms. For now, she'd enjoy their time together. Tomorrow could take care of itself.

They were just finishing up the few dishes when Abby's phone pinged. She set the dish towel aside to check her messages. Her mother had finally made it home, thankfully alone this time. "Mom's back. I'm surprised Owen isn't with her."

"Those two are really joined at the hip these days, aren't they?"

"Yeah, although I was wondering if that would still be true after he explained his past to her."

Tripp walked over to the front window to stare out into the darkness. "I wonder how much he actually told her. More importantly, how much did she actually understand? Her life experience wouldn't give her any frame of reference for the kinds of things he likely did."

Abby suspected Tripp wasn't only talking about Owen. "Mom would've listened anyway, especially if she thought it would help him in some way. Contrary to the past few days, she's normally a nice person with lots of empathy."

Tripp glanced back at her, his mouth quirked up in a hint of a smile. "So, like mother like daughter?"

Abby joined him at the window, slipping her arm around his waist. "Maybe we do have a few things in common."

She waited to see what he'd say next. It was a few seconds before he finally spoke. "One of the reasons I moved out here was to get away from my mom. It wasn't just that she kept trying to fix me up with every single woman in town. She doesn't understand why I'm so different from the boy she knew before I enlisted, and I can't explain."

"Because you don't want to burden her—or me—with your memories." Even though her heart hurt for Tripp, she retreated a step to avoid crowding him too much. "I'd better head back in case Mom needs me for some reason."

Tripp grabbed his keys off the counter and headed toward the door. "I'll walk you home."

Abby blocked his path and pointed to his feet. "Fine, but you might want to put on your other shoe first. Well, unless you plan to hop all the way there."

Then she grinned up at him. "I bet you could do it, what with all your Special Forces ninja skills. But why waste the energy?"

He just grinned and slipped on his missing shoe and tied the laces.

CHAPTER 26

The next day started off blissfully peaceful. Both Jada and Tripp had early classes at school. Owen had an appointment with his attorney to deal with the fact the prosecutor was still pressing Gage to file charges, and her mother had gone along for moral support. The only thing that took a bit of the shine off her good mood was a disappointing call from Gage saying his attempt to track down Eve Swahn had been unsuccessful. As it turned out, both she and Will had moved out of the house they'd been renting. He'd promised the search would continue, and he'd keep them posted.

She texted back to let him know she'd gotten the message, and added she'd let him know if she heard from either of the Swahns. "Well, Zeke, that's disappointing, but Gage will figured it out."

Meanwhile, the dog parked himself by the door to

wait. Evidently she wasn't the only one who needed to work off some nervous energy. After filling a to-go cup with coffee, she grabbed Zeke's leash and her keys. "Come on, big guy. We're off to the park."

An hour later, the two of them made the final turn leading back toward the parking lot. She paused briefly, debating whether to take another lap along the trail. She rejected the idea, considering how hard Zeke was panting as he flopped down on the grass. After giving them both a chance to catch their breath, it took two tugs on Zeke's leash to get the big dog up and moving again. "Come on, you can take a nap while I do chores."

He looked pretty disgruntled, but one of them had to be the adult in the room. She glanced in the rearview mirror to tell him exactly that, when the car behind hers caught her attention. Granted, SUVs were a dime a dozen these days, but this one was following a little too close and looked all too familiar. She punched the accelerator to put a little more room between them to get a quick peek at the license plate number.

Darn, this was one time she was sorry to be right. After her last conversation with her friendly neighborhood chief of police, there was no way she would deal with the situation without calling Gage. If she got his voice mail, she would head for city hall and call nine-one-one for assistance.

"Abby, what's up?"

The familiar sound of Gage's deep voice allowed her to breathe again. "Zeke and I just left the park, and I'm pretty sure Eve Swahn is following me. I'm afraid to go home, where I'd be alone except for Zeke."

"I'm only about a block from your place, Abby. I'll pull around back, so my cruiser won't be visible from the front. I'll also have one of my deputies head that way."

"And if it's just a coincidence that she's going the same direction?"

"I still need to talk to her. At least I can give my deputies her last known location. I need to alert them, so I'm hanging up now. Do you want me to call you back?"

It was tempting to cling to the lifeline he offered her, but she was only a couple of blocks from home. "Thanks, but I'll be fine."

She hung a right onto the side street that led to her house. When the SUV followed suit, she didn't know whether to be alarmed or relieved. Regardless, for Jada's sake, they needed to find out what was going on with the woman.

In her hurry, she cut the corner into the driveway too short and went bouncing up over the curb, hoping she didn't damage anything other than her dignity, since Gage was standing right there watching. At least he looked far calmer than she felt, which helped soothe her frazzled nerves. "Don't worry, Abby. Take Zeke inside while I see what the lady is up to. I'd rather not spook her into making a run for it, if possible."

"Will do."

Then he walked toward the street, presumably to flag down Eve Swahn. After parking, Abby clipped on Zeke's leash before letting him out of the back seat, and then hustled over to open the back door. The dog would've preferred to hang out with Gage, but she didn't give him that choice. "Get inside right now, mister. There'll be plenty of time later for you to mooch treats from him."

Once inside, she decided to wait out of sight in the

hallway. Zeke seemed confused when she used his leash to keep him tethered to her side. He kept tugging on it, trying to head for his favorite sunbeam in the living room. "Wait here, boy. It shouldn't be long."

He gave up and dropped down on the floor with a disappointed sigh. She knelt to stroke his fur to reassure him all was well. A short time later, Gage knocked at the front door and called her name. She hustled to the entryway and took a quick peek out the window. He was standing next to a clearly unhappy woman. Abby could only assume she was looking at Eve Swahn in person, but there was only one way to find out.

She flipped the dead bolt and opened the door. As she did, she grabbed Zeke's collar before he could shove past her to check out their guests. He was clearly happy to see Gage again but a great deal more cautious when it came to Eve Swahn. The dog's sudden appearance had the woman backpedaling a few steps. "Whoa, he's huge."

Abby tightened her hold on Zeke. "Don't worry. He's actually very sweet."

Well, most of the time, anyway. He would defend Abby from an overt attack, but it seemed unlikely she was in any danger, not with the chief of police standing right there. Then there was the second cruiser pulling up in front of the house.

Gage performed introductions. "Abby, this is Eve Swahn. She's going to explain why she's been lurking in your neighborhood and why she followed you home."

"Please come in."

She led them into the living room, keeping Zeke close at her side. As always, she had to fight the urge to rush to the kitchen to make coffee and gather up a heaping pile of cookies to offer her guests. *Sorry, Aunt Sybil, but not this time.* Whatever excuse Eve Swahn had for her actions, Abby didn't feel all that welcoming right now.

She waved her hand toward the available seat choices in the room before taking her personal favorite in front of the bay window. "Please make yourselves comfortable."

Eve chose the wingback chair on the other side of the room while Gage parked himself on the sofa. While everyone got settled, Abby released her hold on Zeke, who immediately stretched out at her feet in the sunbeam where he liked to doze most afternoons. Having no experience in interrogating a stalker, Abby opted to let Gage take charge of the discussion. He didn't fail her.

"So, Mrs. Swahn, tell me what's going on here."

His words sounded polite, but there was a definite edge in his voice that had the woman sitting up taller and glancing at the door as if considering a run for it. Evidently she didn't think much of her chances for a successful escape, because a second later she slumped back in the chair. "I do apologize, Ms. McCree, if my actions frightened you or Jada, especially when you took a picture of my car."

If Tripp had forgiven Abby's rash actions, the least she could do was pay it forward. "While I don't appreciate being spied on, Ms. Swahn, I know you swerved wide to drive around me."

Well, actually, it was Tripp who had come to that conclusion. If Gage was surprised by that bit of information, he hid it well as he pressed Eve to answer his original question. "Now that we have that out of the way, I still want to know what's going on."

Eve glanced at him and then Abby before finally focusing her gaze at some point outside of the bay window. After a deep breath, she took a firm grip on the arms of her chair and started talking. "My husband and I are going through a rather contentious divorce."

Abby suspected what was coming next. No matter how good their intentions had been at the outset, they were bound to have run into some hiccups along the way.

"We were renting, so breaking the lease wasn't a problem. We also divided up our belongings without much trouble. The problems began when we started dealing with our finances. Some of it was cut and dried, but I have good reason to suspect he's hidden some assets. A few months ago I overheard him talking to Don Davidson about some kind of investment they had from the war, but I haven't been able to locate any record of it. With Don's death, I don't have anyone else I can ask, and Will acted evasive when my lawyer pushed him for more information. Will had moved into a small apartment that rented by the week, but suddenly our letters to him started coming back undeliverable. I have no idea where he's staying now."

She blinked several times and then turned her gaze back to Gage. "My attorney suggested we hire a private investigator to hunt for Will, but I can't afford that."

Gage looked up from the notes he'd been taking. "So you decided to do a little sleuthing on your own."

"Yeah. It was stupid, I know, but I'm desperate. I'm sure he's hiding money. After we finally split, I learned he'd been out looking at new boats and cars. But if he had the cash to pay for anything like that, there's no record of it. I just want my fair share. He owes me that much."

"Did that sleuthing involve breaking into Jada Davidson's home?"

"Certainly not. I'm not a thief."

If Eve was faking her shock at that suggestion, Abby

thought she deserved an Oscar for her performance. That didn't stop Gage from asking one more tough question. "Were you at the park the night of the murder?"

The woman's face, already pale, took on a gray pallor as she gripped the arms of the chair hard enough that her knuckles were white. "I was out of town that day. My mother lives up near Bellingham, and she wasn't feeling well. I went up to help her with a few things."

"I'll need her name and number to verify that."

After she rattled off the information, Gage changed directions again. "So tell me more about what's going on with your husband."

"Will has really changed since we separated. At first, we could carry on a rational conversation. But once we started questioning him about the money, he became volatile to the point that my attorney suggested I should consider a restraining order. I decided against it, though."

Gage clearly didn't like the sound of that. "Why, especially if you were worried about your safety?"

Her eyes bleak, she sighed. "Because if he was really intent on hurting me, a court order wouldn't stop him." She drew a shaky breath. "Besides, I'd prefer to keep things as cordial as possible until we get this money thing straightened out."

Although Abby never had reason to fear her ex-husband, she understood all too well what Eve was going through. The money was important, but it was also probably a matter of pride. It was hard enough to fall out of love with the man she'd pledged to spend her life with, but having him disrespect her enough to steal from her was especially hurtful.

"You hoped to catch him visiting Jada because she's his goddaughter."

Eve nodded. "I didn't hear about her father's death until after the funeral was already over, but I figured Will might show up on her doorstep at some point. I drove by her house a few times a week, hoping to catch him. I've also kept an eye on a couple of bars where he likes to go. I planned to follow him to wherever he's been hiding out, so my attorney could serve legal papers."

"How did you find out that Jada was staying here with Abby?"

Good question. Abby had been wondering that herself. Eve shot her another nervous look before turning back to Gage. "I followed her here. I happened to drive by Jada's house when I saw your police cruiser parked out front. I circled around the neighborhood to see what was going on. After you left, Jada came out of the house with a suitcase and got in the car with Ms. McCree. I hung back and followed them here. I had no intentions of approaching either of them directly. I was just hoping Will would put in an appearance."

"That stops now, Ms. Swahn. You will not come near Jada or Abby again. I sympathize with your problems, but that does not justify your actions. I will do what I can to help you track down your husband. I have some questions for him, too."

He stared at Eve until she slowly nodded. Satisfied that she understood that she was on shaky ground when it came to her actions, Gage turned to Abby. "Do you have any questions for her?"

All kinds, but none that Gage would appreciate her asking. "Nope, I'm good."

Gage flipped his small notebook to a new page and passed it, along with his pen, to Eve. "Write down your contact information, your attorney's name and number, and your place of employment."

Eve quit writing long enough to protest that last bit. "My boss won't like it if the police come around during work hours."

"I won't contact you there if I can avoid it, but no guarantees. If your boss has a problem with it, I'll deal with him."

Abby hoped Eve trusted that Gage would do what he could to protect her from any negative consequences. The man in question pocketed his notebook when Eve handed it back. "I'll walk you out, Mrs. Swahn. I trust we won't have to have this discussion again anytime soon."

Abby followed them outside and couldn't help but notice Eve looked exhausted by the encounter. "I'm recently divorced myself, Ms. Swahn. It's not easy, but life does get better once the dust settles."

Eve mustered up a small smile. "I hope so, Ms. McCree. Sometimes it seems like I'll never get free of all this tangled-up mess."

Gage hung back until Eve drove away.

"Think you'll be able to hunt down Will Swahn for her?"

"I'll try, but it sounds like he's doing a pretty good job of flying under the radar. If Will shows up here again, call nine-one-one. Don't let him back into the house even if Tripp is here. The guy is probably harmless, but anyone's behavior can become unpredictable if they're feeling cornered. Jada should also avoid him if at all possible."

"I will." Abby rubbed her arms, feeling chilled despite the warm sun and blue skies overhead. "Thanks for coming so fast today, Gage. Maybe I overreacted, but being followed weirded me out a bit."

"You had good reason to be concerned by her actions. I get she's desperate to find where Will is hiding out, but there's no excuse for her stalking innocent people."

He started to walk away but then turned back. "By the way, Reilly Molitor finally came through on the picture of Jada's dad. He's supposed to drop by this afternoon with a flash drive as well as prints of the picture. I'd like to see you, Jada, your mom, and Owen around four o'clock at my office to look at it. Might as well make a party of it, so tell Tripp he can tag along, too."

"I'll let him know, although I don't know how much help we'll be."

"I think Jada will appreciate having you there."

It was just like Gage to care about making the young woman as comfortable as possible. "When life gets back to normal—meaning when my mother goes home—maybe you'd like to go out for burgers and a friendly game of pool at the bar with Tripp and me."

The laugh lines around his eyes deepened. "Maybe, but only if you promise to spot me a few points. Tripp already warned me about your wicked skills with a pool cue."

She snickered. "He's such a sore loser."

Gage was still grinning when he backed out of the driveway.

"Have you tried calling Jada? She should be here by now."

Abby prayed for patience. "Yes, Mother, I did. I've also texted her, but she hasn't responded."

Gage had asked them to wait in a small conference room until everyone arrived. Tripp and Owen had just wandered down the hall to help themselves to some coffee. They'd promised to bring some back for her, but her mother had declined their offer. Thank goodness, because the last thing that woman needed was caffeine. She hadn't taken her eyes off the big clock on the wall, her tension increasing with each minute that ticked by.

"What could be taking her so long?"

Before Abby could come up with an answer that wasn't snarky, Gage poked his head in the door. "Jada has arrived. Sergeant Jones is escorting her back."

Yay, Abby's sanity was safe for another few minutes. Jada walked in looking a bit frazzled but otherwise all right. She set her backpack down in the corner before sitting down. Gage rejoined them, with the other two men right behind him. He waited until everyone was settled before speaking.

"Thank you all for coming. I have enough copies for each of you to have your own." He paused to pass them around. "I don't expect everyone to be able to offer up any great insights, but you never know. Take a second to study them, and then we'll talk."

Reilly had made prints of the original photo of Jada's father holding the framed picture, but he'd also managed to make a reasonably clear enlargement of the original picture. At least Jada would have a copy of her father's unit for her scrapbook.

Gage tossed his copies down on the table and pointed at one man in the first row and two in the second. "Unless I'm mistaken, the guy in front is Jada's father. The two right behind him are Owen and Mitch Anders."

"Yeah, that's my dad." Then Jada held the picture closer to her face and then glanced at Owen. "Wow, I wouldn't have recognized you, Mr. Quinn."

Her mother studied him for several seconds and then smiled. "I've never much liked a lot of facial hair, but that beard looked good on you."

He laughed and winked at her. "Maybe I should grow one again, but it might not be as impressive in shades of gray."

Abby refrained from commenting, focusing instead on the picture. Everyone in it looked so young. It was all too easy to imagine Tripp as part of the group. She glanced in his direction only to find him frowning big-time as he slowly rotated the picture three-hundred-sixty degrees.

"Do the faces look clearer upside down?"

Okay, that wasn't the best joke she'd ever made, but she didn't expect Tripp's expression to turn quite so grim. "Gage, I need that magnifying glass Abby mentioned the other day. And bring a pad of paper and something to write with while you're at it."

What was he seeing that she couldn't? It was disappointing Gage didn't bother asking for an explanation for Tripp's demands before leaving the room. On the other hand, Owen must have figured it out, because he started twirling his picture, too.

When Gage came back, he handed the magnifier to Tripp and set a tablet and mechanical pencil within easy reach. Using the magnifying glass, Tripp started at the top right corner and moved left from there, stopping every so often to make notes. It took him about five minutes to complete the full circuit. When he was done, he pushed the tablet across to Owen and said, "My Arabic is a bit rusty. See if I missed anything."

It wasn't until then that she realized Tripp was studying the pattern on the mat that surrounded the photo, which had looked purely decorative to her. Evidently it was far more than that. Someone, presumably Jada's father or one of his friends, had written a message in Arabic. Had Tripp actually known Owen could read that language, or had he just been guessing? Not that it was important right now.

It didn't take Owen long to finish his assessment, probably because Tripp had already done most of the work. After making a couple of small corrections, he handed the pad of paper to Gage. In the meantime, Jada was getting fidgety, not that Abby blamed her. It had to be disconcerting to find out that there was hidden meaning in the picture she'd been looking at for years.

Gage studied Tripp's notes for several seconds before glancing at the other two men. He turned the paper facedown on the table, preventing the women from seeing it at all. "Well, that's interesting. I'm going to need to make some phone calls."

Jada finally spoke up. "Why? What does it say?"

When Gage finally responded, he was definitely sporting his best grim cop expression. "I'm going to ask all of you to keep this to yourselves." He waited until everyone nodded before continuing. "Without going into detail, Jada, it's a message from your father to his friends, one he knew they'd be able to read. I'm guessing Anders could, too, which undoubtedly threw a wrench in the works."

By that point, Abby's mother was frowning. "Chief Logan, I swear I'm not trying to cause problems here, but I feel as if I must speak up. Since whatever Tripp and Owen just wrote down has all of you looking pretty darn serious, I have to ask if Jada should have an attorney present before you continue."

Abby hoped like heck he'd say that wasn't necessary.

Unless she was mistaken, there was a flash of sympathy in Gage's expression when he turned his attention to Jada. "You know, that's probably a good idea."

Then he held out his hand. "Pass me the pictures."

The room went silent except for the shuffling of papers and the pounding of Abby's heart. She could only imagine how much worse it was for Jada. After gathering everything up, Gage stood up. "I'll lock all of this up until we meet again. Ms. Davidson, if you need the name of a good attorney, let me know. Once you have someone lined up, we'll set a time to meet again."

He started for the door but then turned back. "By the way, you haven't done anything wrong. I just want to make sure someone is looking out for your best interests."

If he was trying to reassure Jada, Abby wasn't sure how successful he'd been. It was time to head home to regroup. Tripp signaled he'd be along in a second, so she wrapped her arm around Jada's shoulders and led her back to the lobby. "I plan on making a double batch of Tripp's special brandy tea for all of us. It might not solve any problems, but we won't care."

Jada's laugh was definitely shaky. "Sounds good. Today already pretty much sucked, and finding out Dad's picture contains some super-secret message doesn't help."

Abby stopped just shy of the lobby to wait for Tripp. "Did you have a problem with one of your classes?"

"No, afterward." Jada leaned against the wall, clearly running short on energy. "Someone vandalized five cars in the back parking lot, mine included. They knocked out windows and popped the trunks. The campus cops had already responded by the time I got out of class. They figured someone was looking to grab any valuables out of the cars. They hadn't located any witnesses, so all security could do was write up a report in case any of us need one for our insurance companies. They'll also report it to the county sheriff's office, since the school is in their jurisdiction."

"Was anything taken from your car?"

"No, I don't keep much in it—a flashlight, jumper cables, and stuff like that. Luckily, I had my books and laptop in my backpack."

Maybe it was another coincidence that Jada's car was involved, especially considering it was just one of several. But what if the other cars were camouflage to obscure the perpetrator's real intentions? Abby gently grabbed Jada's arm and spun her back in the direction of Gage's office. "We need to tell Gage about this."

Jada fell into step beside her, but she didn't look too happy about it. "Why? The college isn't even in his jurisdiction."

Even if that was true, past experience had taught her that he wouldn't appreciate being kept out of the loop. "He'll still want to know, even if it turns out to be pure happenstance that your car was targeted today. I'm sure he'll check with campus security to see if this has been happening a lot or is a one-off."

They were about halfway down the hall when they ran into Tripp, who looked apologetic. "I didn't mean to keep you waiting so long. Your mom went out the other door with Owen, since he'd parked behind the building."

"That's fine." Great in fact. "We have something to tell Gage, but it shouldn't take long."

She didn't give him a chance to ask why, for fear Jada might change her mind about involving Gage with this latest incident. It didn't come as a surprise that Tripp decided to tag along.

It was relief to find Gage alone. He was just sitting down when she all but dragged Jada into his office. "Sorry to bother you again, but Jada has something to tell you. It might be nothing, but I think it could be something."

He leaned back in his chair, crossing his arms over his chest. "Okay, I'm listening."

CHAPTER 27

Early the next morning, Tripp wandered over to where Abby was trimming back the roses along the side of the yard. "Where's Jada?"

Abby took off her gardening gloves and tossed them along with her pruning shears into the wheelbarrow. "She had an appointment to get her car window fixed."

He frowned. "I don't like the idea of her going anywhere on her own right now."

Did he think Abby liked it any better? "She turned down my offer to go with her. Besides, the glass shop is in a strip mall right on Main Street. She should be safe enough there."

She hoped so, anyway, but she couldn't help but worry. Although she'd insisted Jada tell Gage about her car being vandalized, she'd secretly hoped he would blow the incident off as just bad luck. Unfortunately, he hadn't. In fact, he'd immediately checked in with the head of campus security, who said it had been the only such incident in recent history. They'd finally tracked down one witness, a student who'd spotted someone bashing out a car window with a crowbar.

The culprit had run off into the trees as soon as he realized he'd been seen. The witness thought it was a man, but the baggy sweatpants and an oversized hooded sweatshirt made it impossible to know for sure. Sadly, the campus police had no real leads to follow in determining who had been behind the attack or what they'd been after.

"Is Jada going straight to school after the window is repaired?"

"No, her afternoon class was canceled for some reason, so she planned to stop by a body shop to see how much it would cost to fix her trunk, before coming back here. She wants to get it repaired as soon as possible."

Tripp grinned. "Don't tell me she didn't like the look of the camo duct tape I used to fasten down the trunk lid."

"Okay, I won't tell you."

"Can't please some people."

"So true."

When she pushed the wheelbarrow full of clippings over toward the garage, Tripp followed along in her footsteps. "How long do you think she's going to stay here with you?"

"Not much longer, I'm afraid. While she appreciates that I've let her stay here, she doesn't like leaving her own home unattended. I'm guessing she'll be moving back there tomorrow at the latest."

"Did she have any luck finding an attorney?"

"Yeah, she called a local guy who'd done business with her father in the past, and they have an appointment to meet with Gage in the morning. He's going listen to what Gage has to say. If it turns out she needs more specialized advice, he'll help her find someone suitable." She let some of her frustration show. "It's hard to know what's going on, with you men being so closemouthed about what was written on the picture."

She held up her hand when Tripp started to protest. "I know it's not your fault, but it's why things are a bit up in the air for her right now."

He shoved his hands in his hip pockets. "I'm sure Gage will fill Jada in on everything and help her figure out where to go from there."

"I hope so. She's already been through a lot."

When they reached the side of the garage, Tripp handed her the shears and her gloves before emptying the clippings into the yard waste container. As he put everything back in the toolshed for her, she pondered how to break another piece of news to him.

Tripp took one look at her face and said, "Out with it, Abby."

Had the man developed some sort of secret sonar that picked up on her thoughts somehow? It wouldn't surprise her. She tried to buy herself a little time by asking, "Out with what?"

He rolled his eyes. "With whatever has you all tied up in knots right now. You know you'll tell me eventually, so why not just get it over with?"

It was always better to play it straight with Tripp. Besides, Jada hadn't said that Abby couldn't tell him. She bit her lower lip as she pondered what to do. Finally, she caved just like he'd said she would. "Jada asked me to go with her and the attorney to meet with Gage. I told her I would."

For once, Tripp didn't look all that concerned by her decision. "If Gage doesn't think you should be there, he won't hesitate to say so. The same goes for the attorney. Having said that, they'll probably be glad that Jada has someone with her whom she trusts. It doesn't sound as if she knows the attorney all that well, and she'll appreciate your input on what she should do about what Gage has to tell her."

"That's what I'm hoping. I know he worries about me getting drawn into his investigations, but apparently Jada doesn't have anybody else she can turn to for advice or even emotional support. She hasn't mentioned any extended family, her friends are away at college, and she doesn't trust her godfather."

Tripp was about to say something when Abby's phone rang. She pulled it out of her pocket and checked the caller ID. "Speak of the devil."

After swiping the screen, she said, "Hey, Jada, how did it go with the window?"

"Abby, I don't know what to do. Will Swahn just called and said we need to meet at my house this afternoon. He won't take no for an answer, even though I said I had another appointment this afternoon and that you were expecting me back for dinner. I told him I had another call I had to take and hung up."

Jada wasn't the only one freaking out right now, but Abby did her best to sound calm. "Don't meet with him alone, Jada, especially since his ex-wife says he's gotten volatile. Come directly here. Tripp and I will be out front watching for you."

There was a long silence on the phone, to the point Abby thought for a second that the call had been disconnected. She was about to hang up and dial Jada back when the girl finally spoke again.

"Abby, he's here. How did he track me down?"

Abby's heart did a slow roll in her chest. "Where's here exactly?"

"The glass shop parking lot. They finished replacing my broken window, and I was about to leave. He just pulled into the parking lot and stopped right behind my car. I'm freaking out here. What should I do?"

"Can you lock yourself in the car?"

Jada's breath was coming in ragged bursts, a clear sign of how scared she was. "I'll have to as long as he's blocking me in. There's no way I can get back inside the glass shop without him catching me."

The younger woman wasn't the only one on the verge of a full-on panic attack. "Don't hang up, Jada, but don't let him know I'm listening in."

"He's getting out of the car and coming toward me. I think he wants me to roll down my window."

Abby heard the faint sound of someone knocking, evidently Will Swahn's way of telling Jada she needed to lower the window so they could talk. "Uncle Will, I'm sorry, but I'm in a bit of a hurry."

"That's what you told me at that McCree woman's house. Like I said on the phone, we need to talk. Now. Today." His frustration came through all too clear. "It won't take long. I'll follow you back to your house."

Abby crossed her fingers that Jada wouldn't cave in and agree to do that. There was no way to know how he would react if he realized someone was listening in on his conversation, so she remained silent. Finally, Will spoke again. "Come on, Jada. I'm your godfather, and your father was my best friend. Surely you can make room in your schedule to talk to me for a few minutes. If you don't want to go to your house, is there someplace else that would work?"

Jada's heavy sigh sounded like surrender. "I can give you a couple of minutes right now, Uncle Will, but that's all. I have an appointment I can't miss."

After a brief pause, he said, "It's not ideal, but it's better than nothing. Let me be clear about one thing—this stays between the two of us. What I'm about to tell you has to do with your father and me back in the day. He wouldn't want you to go blabbing all about it to your new friends."

"Okay, I won't tell them."

Smart girl, she wasn't even lying about that. After all, he'd told Abby himself even if he probably wouldn't appreciate the distinction.

He was talking again. "Things have already taken a real bad turn, and we don't want the situation to get any worse. You've got to believe me about that, Jada."

"Okay." Jada might've been shaky on the inside, but she managed to sound pretty calm, especially considering that last comment he'd made. Was he talking about the theft of the picture, or something else? There was no way to know.

"You see, your dad, our friend Jack, and I, brought some money back from when we served together. Let's call it bonus pay from our time in combat. I know it sounds bad, but you have no idea how screwed up things were over there. We figured we'd be lucky to come home alive, much less in one piece. Nobody came looking for the money, and we figured we'd earned it."

Jada's response was almost a whisper. "I can understand that, Uncle Will. Dad always said those were scary times."

"Yeah, they were. But the point is, your dad always had a good head for numbers, so Jack and I let him invest it for all of us. The plan was to let the money sit and accrue interest until we retired, unless something unexpected came up. You know, like when Jack got hit with that cancer diagnosis. He needed his third of the money to help pay off his medical bills. I didn't know until recently, but your dad also was using his third to pay for your college."

Will was almost breathless by that point, clearly trying to lay it all out for Jada in the short time she'd allotted him. Abby could hear him drawing in several deep breaths before he launched back into his tale. "I've got no problem with that, but now I want my part of the pie. You've got to give it to me."

"But I don't have it, Uncle Will. There's no record of any large sums of money in Dad's files. He left some insurance, a little in the checking account, and a few thousand in the savings account. He had a 401(k) through his employer, but that money came from his paychecks, not from any kind of outside investment account."

A loud bang was followed by Jada gasping. "Hey, why did you kick my car?"

"Because you're not taking this seriously, Jada. Do you think it's a coincidence that Mitch Anders came looking for me right after he moved into your dad's office? I'm guessing all it took was one look at that picture on the wall for him to notice the pattern on the mat was a message written in Arabic. He could read it just like your dad and I could. That's how he figured out what was going on, even if he couldn't get his hands on the money with that alone. It was just the key needed to interpret the records your father kept of all the transactions. Imagine if Mitch had also gotten his hands on that information. Everything your father, Jack, and I worked for would've been gone."

"Do you think that's why he was killed?"

Abby could barely breathe. Had Jada just accused him of murdering Mitch Anders? If so, it would be a miracle if her godfather didn't go on the attack. To her surprise, Will calmly said, "I have no idea. Considering some of the messed-up stuff he was involved in back in the war and afterward, there's probably a whole lot of people who wouldn't have minded seeing him dead."

Thankfully, Jada changed the subject. "I really need to leave, Uncle Will, or I'm going to be late."

"Fine, go. But one more thing, Jada. Don't play games with me. That money is mine, and I want it. I know for a fact your dad had the ledger. Hand it over and soon, or I'll come looking for it myself. You won't like it if that happens."

"But I have no idea what I'm looking for, Uncle Will. Is it an actual book or an electronic file?"

"It's a ledger book, the kind you can buy at any office supply store. If I remember right, it's blue."

"I'll try to find it."

"You'll have to do better than just try, Jada. I wasn't going to touch the money until after my divorce was finalized. But now my soon-to-be-ex is hot on my trail, and I need to disappear before she manages to get her hands on any more of my money. She's already burned up twenty-five years of my life. I'll be darned if I'll let her ruin my future as well."

After a few seconds of silence, Jada whispered, "He's leaving, Abby."

"Tripp and I will meet you at your house if you want our help looking for the ledger."

But Jada had other ideas on the subject. "No, I think I'd better come to you, but it will take me a little while to get there. I have a couple of stops to make on the way. Besides, if Uncle Will is still watching me, I don't want to lead him straight to your house. When I get there, I'll pack up my stuff and move back home. That way maybe he'll believe you don't know anything about what he just told me."

It was tempting to pitch a fit and demand that Jada abandon her plans and drive straight to Abby's house, but she suspected it wouldn't do any good. She settled for asking, "Is there anything I can do to help?"

After a brief hesitation, "Yes, you can call Mr. Quinn and ask him to come over if he can. This concerns him, too."

"How about calling Gage Logan, too?"

"Maybe after we talk."

Calling him right then would be the smart thing to do, but the line went dead before Abby could ask any questions or get reasonable answers for the ones she knew Tripp was about to ask. Rather than call Owen, though, she rang her mother's number. "Mom, can you two come over to the house? There's something going on with Jada, and she asked if Owen could be here. I don't know any more than that, but I'm worried. Really, really worried."

CHAPTER 28

Abby glanced outside for the fifth time in the past half hour. No sign of either her mother or Jada. Turning away from the window, she paced the short distance across the living room and back again. Tripp sat sprawled on the sofa, watching her with a slight smile on his face. "They'll get here, Abby. Sit down before you wear a hole through the rug."

She shot him an angry look, but she gave up and did as he suggested. "Why are you so relaxed? You're usually the one who goes all protective and prowly when something is going on."

Now he looked mildly insulted. "First of all, I'm pretty sure 'prowly' isn't even a word. But to answer your question, after twenty years in the army, I learned to appreciate the calm before the storm. There'll be plenty of time to rev up the engines once we know what's going on."

Then he closed his eyes as if preparing to take a nap. It was tempting to toss a handy book at his head, but she aborted the mission at the sound of a car pulling into the driveway. A second one followed almost immediately afterward.

"They're here, Tripp."

Just that quickly, he was on his feet, alert and ready for action. "Where do you want to hold this briefing? Here or the kitchen?"

Either would work. "Let's use the kitchen. Right now, I want to be as close to the coffeepot as possible."

Not to mention the cookies. It wasn't smart to binge on sugar in times of stress, but desperate times called for desperate measures. Earlier, before she and Tripp had adjourned to the living room, she'd put together a tray of cheese, crackers, and fresh fruit. She'd left it up to Tripp to decide which kinds of cookies to dump on a second one. His efforts weren't exactly artistic, but no one would go hungry.

She led the charge down the hall to the kitchen just as her mom and Owen filed in the back door a few seconds ahead of Jada. When no one said anything, Abby automatically went into hostess mode. "Have a seat and help yourself to a snack if you're hungry. There's fresh coffee, pop, iced tea, and wine to drink."

She offered up a small smile. "Depending on how this impromptu meeting goes, I can also break out the hard stuff if it would help."

No one laughed, but at least everyone took a seat and helped themselves to the goodies. As she passed a plate of lemon bars to her mother, she kept a worried eye on Jada, who looked pretty shaky. That was understandable after dealing with her godfather. What was of more concern was the way she avoided making eye contact with anyone at the table. Maybe all she needed was a little time to come to terms with the knowledge her father had been involved in something shady that was possibly— even likely—criminal.

When it appeared everyone had what they needed, Abby jumpstarted the conversation. "Jada, would you like to tell Owen and Mom about your encounter with Will Swahn today, or should I do the honors?"

Jada had been staring down at her plate as if a few pieces of cheese and fruit were the most fascinating things in the world. She slowly looked around the table as she drew a deep breath. "I took my car in this morning to get the window replaced. It was broken out in the university parking lot yesterday." She paused to look at Owen. "The campus police don't know who vandalized five different cars. I can't say for sure if my car was the real target, but I suspect it was. My godfather is desperate to find a ledger he claims my father used to keep track of some money. Uncle Will called it 'combat pay,' but we all know that's not what it was."

Once again, Phoebe showed her capacity for empathy. "Jada, don't let what your father did or didn't do during the war affect how you feel about him. He was your father, and judging by how you've turned out, a good one. Remember that about him and let the rest go."

Abby smiled at her mother. "Well said, Mom."

Jada managed a slight nod as she filled everyone in on the conversation she'd had with Will in the glass shop parking lot. "While he denied murdering Mitch Anders, I'm real sure he threatened me if I don't find the ledger and turn it over to him."

Tripp spoke up for the first time. "I have a question,

Jada. Why aren't we involving Gage in this conversation?"

Good question, but Abby suspected the answer was that bringing the police into the conversation would make Don Davidson's shady dealings all too real. His daughter was torn between the need to protect his reputation and the threat presented by Will Swahn. Before Jada responded, Owen joined in the conversation. "What can you tell us about this ledger or where your father might've kept it? That is, if it even exists."

"Oh, it exists all right." Jada reached for her backpack and pulled out a manila envelope. "I got this out of Dad's safety deposit box today. I originally ran across it when I went through the box a few days after he died, when I was looking for his will. He'd taped a note to the front cover that said if something ever happened to him, I should ask Uncle Will to explain it. At that time, I was barely functioning, so I just put it back to deal with later. I'd almost forgotten about it until Uncle Will told me what I should be looking for."

She pulled a faded blue book out of the envelope. It was less than half an inch thick and had the word "ledger" embossed on the cover. "I didn't ask you to call Chief Logan because I was considering giving this to my attorney and letting him decide the best way to proceed. There's no way to prove that Mitch Anders ever realized what was written on my dad's picture, so we don't know if his death was connected to the ledger or the money that both Uncle Will and his wife have been talking about."

All of that made sense, at least on the surface. Abby suspected that everyone sitting at the table wanted to get a glimpse at what was written inside the ledger, but Jada held it in a death grip. The ensuing silence grew more awkward by the second. Finally, Owen spoke again. "I'd like to tell you those things aren't related, but they almost have to be."

She finally passed the book over to Owen. "I haven't had much time to study its contents, but none of it makes sense. We need to use the key from the message on the picture to figure out the code Dad was using."

Owen flipped through several pages, stopping every so often to study the neat rows of numbers on the pages. "I could probably crack the code if we had more time. But with Will pushing so hard to get his hands on this, that's not going to happen."

He handed it over to Tripp, who gave it a cursory look before passing it to Abby. They were right. Without the key, the mix of numbers and symbols was pretty much gibberish. She returned it to Jada. "So, what do we do now? Your godfather presents a real threat to you. All things considered, I think he most likely stole the picture from your house and probably broke into your car as well. He clearly considered Mitch Anders a real threat to his plans to make a run for it. He's desperate and getting more so by the moment."

Jada studied the cover of the book. "If we give this to Uncle Will, maybe he'll disappear for good, and my life can go back to normal."

That was possible, but Abby had her doubts. Besides, Gage already knew about the money. If Will managed to abscond with the rest of the cash, would that leave Jada on the hook for all of it? She had no idea what the legal ramifications were. As important as that might be, right now ensuring Jada's safety had to take precedence. It was time for some hard truths.

"Maybe there's a chance it would play out that way,

Jada, but there's no way to know for sure. I understand that you want to protect your father's reputation, but you need to think beyond that. If Will really is behind the break-in at your house, not to mention your car, that makes him a criminal. He needs to face justice for what he's done."

Tripp went one step further than Abby had. "Jada, what if he did murder Mitch Anders? If he manages to leave the country, that could leave Owen here on the hook for a crime he didn't commit. Even if you could live with that, don't believe any promises Swahn made about taking the money and disappearing. You're the one person who knows for sure he was involved in all of this. Will you ever feel safe knowing he's still out there?"

There was nothing but silence for a full minute before Jada finally responded. "I really want this to be over with."

"We all do, Jada." After a brief pause, Abby's mother had more to say. "I can't sleep nights for worrying about what's going to happen to Owen. I hate that my daughter and her friend are both caught up in another murder case. None of this is easy for any of us, and it's worse for you. Having said that, you're the only one who can help Chief Logan put an end to the threat your godfather presents to all of us. I won't lie and say it will be easy, but you won't be alone. We're here to help."

Jada winced at the stark picture Phoebe had painted, looking even younger than she really was. But she drew back her shoulders and sat up straighter as she laid the ledger down in the middle of the table. "So, what's the plan? Do we call Chief Logan to come here or do I need to go to his office?"

Owen picked up the ledger. "We go to him."

* * *

After some discussion, only three people made the trip down to the police station. Owen drove with Abby in the front seat and Jada in the back while Tripp and her mother stayed at the house. Gage wasn't going to be happy with what they had to tell him, and there was no use in everyone getting caught in the crossfire. At least that was the excuse Abby had given her mom. The truth was she didn't trust her mother not to go ballistic if she didn't like what he had to say to either Owen or Jada. They needed to have a calm, reasonable discussion with Gage, not another major blow up.

When they'd called ahead to say they were coming, the first thing he'd asked about was Jada's attorney. Unfortunately, the man was in court and unable to come. Abby worried about Jada's decision to proceed without him, but she trusted Gage would do his best to protect the young woman's rights.

Owen dropped them at the front door of the city hall building and drove around back to park. They waited in the lobby until he joined them before making their way down the hall to Gage's office. He silently pointed at the three empty chairs he'd arranged in a semicircle. There were also three bottles of water on the front edge of his desk where they could easily reach them. Abby took the far seat, letting Jada have the one in the middle between her and Owen.

Once they were settled, Gage sat back in his chair. He looked at Owen and Jada in turn before aiming his angry gaze directly at Abby. "Tell me what I've missed out on this time. I don't need or want excuses, just the facts."

Why target her? Especially when both Owen and Jada were closer to the action than she was. On the other hand, while she might be willing to throw Owen under the bus, she couldn't bring herself to do the same to Jada. So, where to start?

"You know everything up until what happened today, so we haven't been keeping you in the dark."

For long, anyway.

Who knew an experienced cop like Gage could roll his eyes with the same disdain as a teenage girl? "Like I said, no excuses. Just tell me, Abby."

So she did, starting with Jada getting her window fixed. When she got to the part about Will Swahn confronting her in the parking lot at the glass shop, Gage held up his hand to stop her. "Okay, maybe I do need an excuse. Why didn't you call nine-one-one to tell us what was going on?"

"Because I didn't want to hang up and leave Jada completely on her own to deal with him. And I thought you might want a witness to what he had to say."

Gage closed his eyes and drew a deep breath. "And if he'd attacked her?"

As soon as he posed the question, he sighed. "Never mind. Just keep going."

So she repeated what Will had said to Jada about her father and their other friend. About the way Jack had used his third of the money, and how Don Davidson had used his to pay for Jada's schooling. That Will knew Mitch Anders had discovered the message on the picture. If he'd realized that it was only part of the puzzle, that might explain why he wouldn't return it or any of Don Davidson's other personal items to Jada when she'd asked.

"I feel like I've been babbling. Was all of that clear?"

Gage nodded. "I have a few questions, but I want to hear the rest of it first."

To Abby's surprise, Jada took over telling the story. "Uncle Will said whatever was written on Dad's picture contained the key to the code he used to track the money. He was convinced Mitch Anders had read the message on the mat and had been hunting for the ledger, too. For sure Uncle Will doesn't know where Dad kept it, because he ordered me to find it. If I don't, he plans to take over the search. He said I wouldn't like it if that happened."

She stopped talking long enough to open a bottle of water and took a long drink. Clearly confession was thirsty work. "He went on to say his wife had used up twenty-five years of his life, and he wasn't going to let her steal any more. When she told you and Abby about her suspicions that Will was hiding money from her, I don't know how much she actually knew about the situation."

When she paused this time, it was to pull the manila envelope containing the ledger out of her backpack. "I did ask him if he thought all of this was why Mitch Anders was killed, but he said he didn't know. He thought it was equally possible that someone else from Mr. Anders's past had reason to come after him. I don't know about that, but I'm sure Mr. Anders must have pressured Uncle Will to share the money."

Then she passed the envelope across the desk to Gage. "This was in my father's safety deposit box. Like I told Abby and the others, I saw it right after Dad died when I was looking for some legal papers. There was a note from Dad saying I should talk to Uncle Will about the ledger, so I left it in the box. I would've gotten around to it at some point. I just had more important things to think about at the time."

Gage pulled the book out of the envelope. "So is that everything? No more surprises for me?"

Owen spoke up. "For the record, I didn't kill Mitch, but Will's assessment of the man was right on target. Mitch would've made a deal with the devil himself if he thought he could make a quick buck. That's one reason I avoided him as much as I could. I've reached out to some . . . well, let's call them some mutual friends. If he's been causing any problems lately, they hadn't heard anything about it. As far as they could tell, he'd been keeping his head down since he started his new career. That could just mean he was doing a good job flying under the radar. He had the right training to pull it off."

Gage didn't look surprised, which made Abby wonder if he'd done a little checking of his own. He glanced through the ledger and then set it to the side, looking as if he was about to launch into a tirade. Jada derailed it when she put a small piece of paper on his desk. "Uncle Will dropped this through my car window. It's his new phone number. I'm guessing it's a burner phone."

Okay, that was new to Abby. Jada had been keeping secrets from more people than just Gage. She leaned forward, trying to see what was written on it. There were numbers scrawled across the top with a few words written below. She couldn't read them from where she was, but it was clear whatever it said had Gage seeing red.

"This is a definite threat, Jada. I don't want you going home until we have this guy in custody. In fact, I'd like to contact the county sheriff to see if they can put you up in one of their safe houses."

She was already shaking her head. "I'll stay at Abby's, but that's it. If I miss any more classes, I could lose credit for the entire quarter. I can't let that happen."

He sighed and looked up at the ceiling. "Please, someone, save me from stubborn women."

Owen started to laugh and then tried to disguise it as a cough. Gage shot him a dark look. "Okay, smartass, you try keeping people safe when they refuse to use common sense. The next thing you know, they'll be wanting me to use them as bait to draw Will out of hiding."

Holding up his hands in surrender, Owen apologized. "Sorry, Gage. But now that you mention it, the whole bait idea isn't a bad one. Only, let's use me instead of Jada or Abby."

Gage leaned forward, elbows on his desk. "What do you have in mind?"

CHAPTER 29

Abby didn't like the idea of anyone she cared about putting themselves in harm's way. It hadn't been that long ago that she would've been happy if Owen Quinn disappeared from her mother's life, but having him playing bait to trap Will Swahn wasn't what she'd had in mind. Besides, even she had to admit the man had a certain charm, and he clearly cared about her mom.

"Are you sure that Gage will keep Owen safe?"

The worry and fear in her mother's voice was understandable, but this wasn't the time for lies and platitudes. The unexpected could happen at any time. After all, criminals weren't exactly predictable. "Gage and his people will do their best to protect him. And don't forget everything Owen told you about his past. He's a trained professional with decades of experience dealing with dangerous situations."

Her mother shuddered. "You say that like it's a good thing."

"Under the circumstances, it is." Abby slipped her arm around her mother's shoulders to give her a quick hug. "Mom, retired or not, it's who he is. If you can't accept that about him, you shouldn't let this relationship continue. It wouldn't be fair to either of you."

"Like you accept Tripp's past?"

"Yes, exactly." It was hard not to get a bit defensive. "Don't forget that both Tripp and Owen sacrificed a lot for our country. It's no surprise that it left a mark on both of them. Tripp's a good man, Mom."

"I'm not saying he isn't. It's just taken a bit of an adjustment to see you with a man like him. He so different than Chad."

Abby managed a small smile. "All things considered, that's not a bad thing."

"Maybe not." Her mom turned to stare out the window. "I just wish this was all over."

"Me too."

Her mom had totally freaked out when Gage and Owen had explained the plan to lure Will Swahn out of hiding. Owen was going to call the man and tell him that Jada had found the ledger in her father's safety deposit box. She'd immediately asked Owen to act as intermediary. The only problem was coming up with a believable reason that she would do that. It was Jada herself who had provided the perfect excuse. Will had scared her badly when he'd confronted her in the parking lot, especially when he'd kicked the side of her car hard enough to leave a dent in the door.

From that point, they made quick work of putting their plan in motion. Owen placed the call, saying Jada was having a friend deliver the ledger to Owen. That part would be carried out by Tripp. He had left about fifteen minutes ago to drive over to the restaurant. He was to pull up at the front door and wait for Owen to step outside. After giving him the manila envelope, Tripp would head straight back to the house. In the meantime, Abby, her mother, and Jada were all supposed to remain inside with the doors locked with one of Gage's deputies stationed right outside of her house.

Once Owen had the ledger in his possession, he would text Will to come pick it up. Both Jada and Owen promised to keep their mouths shut, so Will would be free to get on with his plans to leave the country. Owen had added a stern warning that Will had to deal directly with him. If the man made any attempt to involve Jada, all bets were off. Additionally, if he wasn't there within the hour after receiving the message, Owen's next call would be to Will's ex-wife, who would be delighted to get her hands on the book. In the interim, Gage and his deputies had positioned themselves out of sight around the restaurant, ready to scoop up Will as soon as he showed up.

On the surface, it seemed simple. Nothing could go wrong. Right?

All they could do was wait and see what happened. Of the three of them, Jada seemed to be handling the situation the best. Right now, she was seated at the dining room table with her earbuds in, listening to music while she worked on a class assignment. Maybe keeping busy was the right idea. Time would pass more quickly if Abby could get her mom to concentrate on something besides waiting for the phone to ring.

"I could use a cup of tea, Mom. How about you?"

Without waiting for her mom to answer, Abby set the

kettle on the stove to heat. "What kind of tea would you like?"

"Decaf if you have some, otherwise anything would be—"

Before she could finish her answer, a loud crash coming from the front of the house froze both of them as they tried to figure what was going on. Seconds later, that was followed by a heavy fist pounding on the front door as a familiar voice shouted, "Jada, I know you're in there. Let me in before that cop comes to. I want that ledger. I warned you what would happen if you involved anyone else in this."

Jada poked her head out of the dining room. "What should we do?"

Abby motioned her to go back inside. "Stay out of sight, Jada. We'll deal with him."

But how? Meanwhile, her mom whispered, "What's Will doing here? He was supposed to go to the restaurant, not here."

"I don't know, Mom."

By that point, Zeke was pitching a fit. The dog would do his best to protect his people, but Abby was terrified Will had come prepared to defend himself if Zeke attacked. She looked around for a possible weapon. Her mom must have been thinking along the same lines, because she grabbed a small cast-iron skillet from the cabinet. "Why didn't the deputy stop him?"

Abby had been wondering the same thing. "Maybe Will crashed his car into the cruiser, trapping the deputy inside. Either way, we need to phone for help and do what we can to keep him from getting anywhere near Jada."

Before she could carry out their plan, Will shattered the narrow window next to the door.

Her mom tightened her grip on the skillet and started down the hall toward the door. "You make the call while I keep that man from getting inside."

Abby wanted to argue, but that would only delay help arriving. She dialed nine-one-one and waited for the dispatcher to pick up. "Hello, this is Abby McCree. Please tell Gage Logan that Will Swahn is trying to break into my home. I think he may have hurt the deputy who was parked in front of my house."

She confirmed her address and answered a few quick questions. After hanging up, she peeked down the hall to check the situation. Jada was nowhere in sight. Good. Meanwhile, her mom was hollering right back at Will, swatting at his hand with her skillet every time he tried to reach through the window to unlock the door.

Abby was about to enter the fray when it occurred to her that if Will somehow managed to get past both her mother's fry pan and Zeke, he couldn't take Jada anywhere if his car was immobilized. Surely Tripp had to be on his way by now, not to mention the cops. They just needed to hold down the fort for a little longer.

Doing an about-face, she charged back through the kitchen and straight out the back door. She made her way across the yard to the driveway and crept along the side of the house toward the front. She stopped at the front corner of the house to evaluate the situation. Good, judging by the amount of yelling going on, it sounded as if her mom was still keeping Will at bay.

As long as his attention was focused on her, maybe he wouldn't notice Abby sneaking past to disable his car. She cringed as soon as she peeked around the corner toward where the police cruiser was parked on the street.

The front end of Will's car was jammed against the driver's door. Fury washed through her veins when she realized it was Deputy Chapin slumped over the steering wheel.

How did Will plan to make his escape in a vehicle that was clearly no longer drivable? Momentarily at a loss what to do next, she stayed where she was and hoped like heck the police arrived before anything more happened.

Then she caught sight of a familiar SUV parked a short distance from the police cruiser. Could this day get any weirder? What was Eve Swahn doing there? Hadn't she heard Gage's warning to stay away from both Jada and Abby? Should she warn the woman that her ex was in the middle of a total meltdown and more police were on their way?

Crouching low, she inched forward, trying to make sure Will couldn't see her over the low wall that surrounded the porch. From there, she darted down the driveway to the cluster of tall rhododendrons near the sidewalk that ran along the edge of the yard. After another quick look at the porch, she dashed across the grass to the opposite corner of the yard to duck into the same bushes where she'd hidden the last time Eve Swahn had been scoping out the house.

By that point, she was close enough to realize the SUV's engine was running and Eve was in the passenger seat. That didn't make sense at all. Well, unless Eve and Will were working together. Why would they do that? Had they both been lying about their separation and impending divorce? She'd believed Eve's sad story about Will hiding money from her, but maybe Abby had bought into that scenario because of her own experience with

Chad. That wouldn't account for Gage's acceptance of Eve's claims, though.

None of that mattered right now. Although it had been several minutes since she'd called for help, there was still no sound of approaching sirens. It was time to make sure that neither of the culprits made an escape before Gage and company arrived.

Still crouching, she waited until Eve was looking in the opposite direction before scrambling down the sidewalk to hide behind the SUV. Her pulse was all she could hear as she crawled around to the driver's side. Well aware that if anyone was watching, she'd look like a crazy woman as she shoved her favorite chef's knife hilt-deep into the side of the back tire. Yanking it back out, she went into full retreat.

She'd almost made it back to the bushes when a car door opened. It was too much to be hoped that she'd simply missed hearing Tripp pulling into the driveway. A glance back toward the SUV verified her worst fears. Eve was out of the vehicle and heading her way, screaming, "What did you just do to my car?"

Deciding now wasn't the time for caution, Abby took off running toward the back of the house. As she passed the porch, Will yelled at her. "Hey! I need to talk to Jada. Where are you hiding her?"

Picking up speed, she prayed she had one more sprint left in her, just enough to reach the relative safety of the kitchen. In her hurry, she stepped wrong and almost hit the ground. In the time it took her to regain her balance, Eve Swahn had closed the gap between them and now stood only a few feet away. Abby knew she should keep moving, but the sight of the huge knife in Eve's hand

DEATH BY INTERMISSION 323

temporarily short-circuited her ability to move. The woman held the knife at her side as she said, "If you don't want to end up like Mitch Anders, you'll give us what we want, Abby."

Yeah, like that was going to happen. Doing her best to sound calm, she said, "I see you've tracked down your ex. Congratulations, I'm guessing you've convinced him to share the money he's been hiding. One question, though. He was supposed to pick up the ledger at Owen Quinn's restaurant. What are you doing here?"

The woman's eyes held a whole lot of crazy in them. "The jerk didn't believe Jada would be stupid enough to give the ledger to her boss. He figured she still had it with her."

"She doesn't."

Actually, the police had it. Abby kept backing toward the porch, hoping to get close enough to make one last dash to safety. "How did you convince your husband to share the money?"

Eve's smile was chilling to behold. "I pointed out what happened to Mitch Anders when he tried to play games with me about the money. That jerk swore he'd already decrypted the key on the picture and knew where the ledger was. But once he got a good look at the knife I 'borrowed' from the food truck, he admitted he lied about that last part. I wasn't happy to find out that Mitch had double-crossed me and offered a better split to Will."

She pointed the knife at Abby. "That didn't end well for Mitch, but it's amazing how much that has inspired Will to cooperate with me. He decided to quit screwing around and put pressure on Jada to turn the ledger over to us."

Realizing she was facing the real killer, Abby picked

up speed. The back steps were only a few feet away when Eve upped the ante. "Stop moving, Ms. McCree. Just tell me where the ledger is or you'll be sorry."

Pretty sure her heart just skipped a beat—or several— Abby ignored the threat and took off running. Surprisingly, she actually made it to the first step just as Eve shrieked, "Will, come help me!"

Abby risked a quick look back only to see Deputy Chapin, bruised and bleeding, wrestle the crazed woman to the ground. Will must have noticed the deputy had escaped their trap, because he was shouting a belated warning as he came tearing around the corner. Unfortunately, he was so focused on the couple grappling on the ground that he didn't notice the very real threat bearing down on him from behind.

Abby watched in equal measures of admiration and horror as her mother swung her skillet straight at Will's head. The man hit the ground hard and didn't move a muscle. Her mother stood over him, weapon in hand, snarling, "Take that, you jerk. Threaten helpless women, will you?"

Abby didn't think her mother looked all that helpless at the moment and doubted anyone else would, either. Regardless, it was hard to tell if Will was truly unconscious or just afraid a second blow would cause permanent damage. Either way, her mother's actions had taken him out of the equation. By that point, Deputy Chapin had also managed to subdue Eve Swahn. He had her arms behind her back with a zip tie on her wrists. Her knife was safely out of reach, lying on the grass several feet from where he stood.

Jada peeked out the back door. "Is everyone okay?"

Abby sank down on the steps, struggling to catch her

breath. "Yeah, but would you grab a damp cloth for Deputy Chapin? He should put something on that gash on his face until the EMTs get here."

At that point, she became aware of a whole lot of other people charging across her lawn. Most were in uniform, with Tripp and Owen being the only exceptions. Owen had the good sense to approach her mother slowly, waiting for her to recognize him before wrapping her in his arms. It took him a few seconds longer to convince her to release the skillet into the care of a nearby police officer.

At the same time, Tripp made a wide detour around the deputy and his prisoner in his determined march straight toward Abby. When he finally reached her, he scooped her up in his arms and carried her up onto the porch where he sat down in one of the Adirondack chairs and settled her on his lap. Evidently Owen thought that he had the right idea, because only seconds later he dropped into the next chair with his arms locked tight around her mother.

The four of them watched the swarm of police action taking place only a short distance away. Finally, Owen glanced at Tripp. "So this was what you were talking about when you said the McCree women were magnets for trouble."

Tripp jerked his head in a quick nod. "Yep, exactly. To tell the truth, I've lost count of how many years have been shaved off my life expectancy dealing with just this kind of situation."

There was a hint of laughter in Owen's voice when he said, "But I suspect it's been worth it."

Abby held her breath as she waited for Tripp's response. He tightened his hold on her, pressed a kiss to her temple just before he finally said, "Yeah, it has. But I've gotta say, Owen, I swear I had easier missions back when I was still on active duty."

Abby didn't know whether to hit him or hug him. She was still debating the issue when Gage stepped up on the porch, his notebook and pen in hand. "Okay, ladies, who wants to go first?"

A week later, Owen invited them to the grand reopening of his restaurant. Her mother had driven back down for the occasion. He'd reserved a table for their party in a private room near the buffet table.

Their waitress walked up to the table. "Can I take your order?"

Abby looked up from her menu and smiled at Jada on her first night back at work. "I'll have the brisket platter with slaw, and the cheesy scalloped potatoes."

Her mother said, "I'll have the same."

Jada turned her attention to Tripp, and Gage, who was sitting on Tripp's other side. "How about you two?"

Tripp collected their menus and set the stack on the corner of the table. "I don't know about Gage, but I'm having the all-you-can-eat buffet. You might want to warn Owen to brace himself. I'm feeling extra hungry tonight. I plan to consume a whole lot of ribs and a piece of that peach cobbler I saw listed on today's specials."

Gage also surrendered his menu to Tripp. "Me too. The buffet keeps me from having to choose between Owen's brisket, ribs, and the pulled pork."

As Jada jotted down their orders, the man in question appeared and took his seat next to Phoebe. "Eat all you want, you two. I knew you were coming, so I smoked twice the normal amount of meat for tonight."

Jada picked up the menus. "I'll go get your food started."

Abby waited until she'd disappeared to ask Owen, "How is Jada doing?"

"Okay, as far as I can tell. She admits the first night back at her house on her own was a bit rough, but it helped to know the man who broke into her house is safely behind bars. I've also been giving her a hand, helping her figure out her finances. She's in better shape than she thought and will be able to pay her remaining tuition with no problem. Once she graduates and gets a real job, she should do just fine."

Her mother joined the discussion. "The prosecuting attorney verified Jada's clear of any legal issues regarding the money. She had no way of knowing what her father and his buddies were up to, and he's sure the feds will agree. I was really glad to hear that." She threaded her fingers through Owen's with a bright smile on her face. "Also he admitted that Owen had nothing to do with the entire affair, as well."

Abby really would've preferred a lighter topic for their pre-dinner conversation, but she did have a couple of questions for Gage. Keeping her voice low so Owen's other customers didn't hear her, she asked, "So did the prosecutor decide which one of the Swahns killed Mitch Anders? Was it really Eve?"

Gage glanced to make sure they were alone before answering. "They're busy pointing fingers at each other, so we're still trying to sort it all out. Will admitted to breaking into Jada's house, but he says it was Eve who vandalized the cars and killed Anders. We know she lied about her whereabouts on the day of the murder. She did visit her mother that day, but she left in plenty of time to kill

Mitch Anders. We think she saw Jada leave the food truck and used that opportunity to steal one of Owen's knives. Even if she denies it, Deputy Chapin can testify that he overheard Eve telling you that she killed him. One way or the other, both Will and Eve are facing long prison terms."

At that point, Jada arrived with a big basket of corn muffins, a tub of honey butter, and three empty plates for the men. "Okay, gentlemen, here you go."

All three headed for the buffet line, the whole time giving each other a hard time about who could consume the most food. Jada watched them go with a grin on her face. "I'll go get your dinners, ladies. And for the record, tonight's on me. I can't thank you enough for everything you all did for me. And thanks to Chief Logan, I'm even going to get my dad's picture back from the police."

Abby immediately protested. "That's great, Jada, but you don't have to pay for our dinner."

Jada just grinned and walked away. "That may be true, but I want to. Enjoy your meal."

"We shouldn't let her pay for all of this, Mom. She's a college student struggling to make ends meet, but she's too stubborn listen to reason."

Her mother shrugged. "Reminds me of someone else I know. As I recall, it wasn't Jada who rushed into danger with a chef's knife and no worry for her own safety."

Abby rolled her eyes. "Says the woman who took out a bad guy with a cast-iron skillet. What can I say? We Mc-Cree women are tougher than we look."

They were both still laughing when the men returned. Owen took one look at them and asked, "What's so funny?"

Her mother smiled at her man. "Nothing. It's just a mother-daughter moment."

Owen clearly wasn't buying it. "Tripp, Gage, what do you say? Should I be worried?"

"Don't ask me. I'm off duty tonight." Then Gage picked up a rib and dug right into his dinner.

Owen turned his attention to Tripp next, who winked at Abby. "Yeah, we should both be worried. But like I said the other day, it's so worth it."

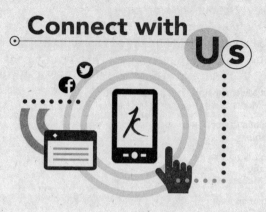